MW01274301

First Edition
July 13, 2010
Printed in the
United States of America
for
Inspired Originals Publishing House
U.S.A.

SoulNTRust@aol.com

1

THE CLADE LETTERS
In the Beginning

By

Cosette Riggs

Dedicated to
God, the Author and Finisher of Life

and to
Courtneay Guy

2

CHAPTER ONE

"Nora Lansing Coup, you have been declared by this council to be a witch. You, therefore, will be executed this very night by hanging. After which, we will burn your mortal body and your soul will go back to your father the Devil." Cleric Joshua Wells stood waving his hand in front of Nora's grief stricken face. "Do you have anything to say?"

Nora, staring down at her fingers, gripped the thick dark green chair in which she was sitting. She strained hard not to let it happen, but the inside and sides of her hands started to turn that same dark green. She quickly put her hands underneath her apron. "I am no witch" she spoke in a normal tone of voice. "I am no witch." Then she stopped speaking and dropped her eyes down looking only at the floor.

All eyes were watching as Nora was led up the steps of the gallows that had been quickly built that afternoon especially to hang her. The whole of the community was there. So was Sara Waters and her seven children; orphans she had taken in when a large wagon train had been massacred and only the babies were left. Six of them were from that train. They were standing back under the elm tree at the entrance to the town. Sara held two year old Jewel in her arms. She held back her tears and her knowledge.

Below Nora was a large pile of branches, twigs and straw. The pile reached almost up to the trap door of the hanging platform. Jeremy Towne, the blacksmith, was tonight the executioner. He put the noose over Nora's head and around her neck and pulled the loop up snug, making her head tilt to the left. Nora's eyes stayed fixed on the little girl in Sara's arms. Jeremy looked at Nora's neck that had turned the same yellowish brown as the hanging rope and watched as the color traveled both up her neck into her face and hair and then down where her exposed wrists and hands took on the same color and markings of the rope. She looked like a rope with a dress on.

3

The group close to her gasped as they witnessed this phenomenon. "Kllaaap!" the trap door swung down dropping Nora through the hole and as the rope snapped her neck, her feet bounced and sank into the pile. The Olson brothers put their torches to the pyre and the flames soon consumed Nora's lifeless body.

July 6, 2009, Bakersfield, California

The morning was hot. A utility truck, with an oil field logo on it "Oil man? Oil right!" and a picture of a he-man character standing by an oil rig, came off Oildale Drive and continued onto the inner city freeway for two off ramps. The sprinklers along the road caused a loose spray to hit the windshield of the truck. The white sides of the truck reflected the gold and orange colors of the lantana plants making the truck seem like part of the landscape.

The truck finally turned up Singing Bird Drive. The driver waved at a lady picking up the morning newspaper. She responded by waving her paper at him. The truck drove on.

The lady turned on her sprinkler and went around the house to the sliding glass doors. As she stood by the doors, she bent down and turned off the backyard sprinkler unaware that her colorful house robe was reflected in the glass doors.

Going in, she walked down the hall. She looked in an open door and saw her daughter still sound asleep in her messy room. Shaking her head, she headed for the garage.

As she passed the washer and dryer, she jammed her toe into the corner of the vacuum cleaner. "Ouch" she blurted out as she reached for the dryer to steady herself. "Who..?"

She started to ask who left the vacuum out when she saw what was happening to her arm. Her arm from fingers to elbow had turned bright white like the dryer. Quickly, she tightened up her forearm and took a few deep breaths. The white faded and her arm returned to its own color. "Darn!" she contorted her face with a downward shrug, biting her lip.

4

When the pain in her toe subsided, she continued out to the garage.

Jadin, her seventeen year old son, was standing in the middle of the garage. "What happened?" he asked. "Did you yell?" "Yes, I stubbed my toe on the vacuum cleaner. I wonder who left it out." She glared at him.

"Hey" he laughed "I'm not guilty of vacuuming. Where do you want me to put all those boxes?" he pointed up to the top of the garage.

"Well" she put her hands on her hips. "I think, if you put them down here, I'll go through them and send most of that stuff to the thrift store."

His eyes lit up. "Why don't we have a yard sale? We could make some money."

"I guess that would be alright. But, I don't want to do it. You can. Maybe Autie would like to help." "Cool." he responded as he handed down a box to her. "Ugh" The box hit her hands. Dust flew everywhere. "You know what?" she called up to him. "What?" "I'm going in. Come and get me when you have all the boxes down. Just drop them down. I don't think there is anything that will break. Stack them over against the wall and finish cleaning up. You know, put out all the trash and sweep out. Ok?"

"Ok, child slave driver" He threw down to her. Susan Tanner looked up and smiled at this beautiful child of hers with his tanned muscles, messy blond hair and that wide crooked smile that would melt your heart. "No wonder the girls are crazy about him" she thought as she left the garage.

Passing through the hallway, she called out loudly, "Get up Autumn" then proceeded into the kitchen.

Two hours later, Susan looked up at movement in the hallway. "Mom!" Autumn whined still wearing her pajama pants and a spaghetti strap top.

"It's 109 out there. Anyway, it's Jadin's turn to pick up the dog stuff."

"Jadin helped me clean out the garage this morning, while you slept in. I really don't think it will hurt you. Just do it." Susan retorted.

"It's your dog, Mom." Autie threw back over her shoulder as she slammed out through the sliding glass door into the back yard.

Susan stood looking at her daughter then picked up a chalk and wrote something on the blackboard hanging over the kitchen trash can.

Jadin and Autumn would be eighteen in three weeks. Susan had waited not wanting to enlighten her twins on the strange phenomenon that had been a trait of their family since the latter part of the Seventeen Hundreds. She wasn't sure they could handle the tough resolve that they would have to have to endure and control it.

Autumn came back in and headed for the refrigerator. "I'm dying of thirst." She hesitated than looked around at her mother, "That dog has a problem. I think you should take her to the vet. No dog should go that much."

Grabbing a water bottle from the fridge, Autumn glanced at the board. "Snotty Autie? What's that for?" she yelped. "For your rude behavior. Every time you're ugly to me, I'll write that up there for the world to see how you treat your mother."

Autumn stormed out of the room, tripped over Jadin's feet which were extended out into the walkway and literally slid head first into the arms, or should I say legs of Samantha their brindle colored boxer.

Samantha jumped up with a start at Autie's scream and impact. Jadin jumped up too and ran to Autie. "Are you ok?" he offered her his hand.

Autie, stunned for a moment, recovered herself and seeing the shock and big eyes of her observers, started giggling. "I'm ok, I think. That was fun."

She allowed Jadin to lift her up.   But her ankle gave way and she sat back down. Samantha sat down very close to her and started licking her face.

"My ankle hurts." she looked up at Jadin, but stopped as she saw the puzzled look on his face. He was looking down at her arm, the one between her and the dog. "What…?" she stopped talking in mid air as she saw what he saw.

Her arm up to her elbow was the exact color and pattern as Samantha and it was continuing on up her arm. It stopped where her arm and Samantha parted.

Jadin's and Autie's eyes connected in a shocked way and then went back to the arm.   Autie quickly pulled her arm away from the dog and watched as it slowly resumed its own color.

"What was that?" Jadin said in a low almost secretive whisper. Autie put her arm back close to Samantha and waited in silence as the color of the dog crept up her arm again. This time, Autie leaned into the dog so more of the arm could touch Sam's fur.   The color went on up and stopped near her shoulder. Slowly she pulled it away from Sam. The color faded and her own skin was there again.

She couldn't talk.   Jadin held out his hand in a halt type position. "Stay there. Don't move." He almost shouted. He turned and went into the kitchen. "Mom! You got'ta see this."

"What?" Susan started "What's wrong?" Fear jumped into her chest.   Seeing Autie sitting in the middle of the floor, Susan drew a sharp breath.   "Autie, are you alright?"   Autie just looked up at her with a silly grin and shrugged her shoulders. "I don't know Mom, I'm turning colors."   With that she put her arm next to Sam's and watched her mother's expression as Sam's colors colored her arm.

"Oh," Susan sighed with relief, "That. I thought you were hurt." Their mouths dropped open at Susan's reaction.

"What?" Jadin's voice came out an octave higher than usual. Susan looked at her children. "Ok, kids, it's time for a talk. Dad will be here soon and we will sit down and talk about this."

Autie kept putting her arm near than away from the dog "So cool. Do you think the light is doing this?" she looked around the room trying to figure where the light was coming from. "You are so lame" Jadin shouted at Autie. "This isn't just a light trick, goof, it's something inside you." Autie sat back against the wall and was silently just looking at her arm which was now the right color.

"Ok" Susan shrugged "we won't wait for Dad. Come in here with me." She went to the desk and pulled out a package.

"Here are the letters that have been passed down to me from my ancestors." Jadin and Autie didn't utter a peep. "Here is the very first letter; a copy of it really as it has been passed down quite a ways and copied for others."

She handed the first letter to Jadin. Autie scrunched in real close to him to read it with him. "I can't see, hold it up"

Susan reached for the letter. "Here, I'll read it to you, so you can hear it at the same time." Jadin handed the letter back to her. Susan slid down on the rug and leaned back on the couch.

"It is 1872. My name is Hattie Bonne. I used to be Hattie Johnston. We lived in the southwestern territory of Canada in a settlement called O'Beran's Town.

My father's name was James and my mother's name was Ruth. I don't remember my mother as she died when I was two. When I had reached my tenth year, I was taken by some Indians and sold to Mr. Etienne Bonne.

Mr. Bonne and I became husband and wife when I was sixteen, which was just seven months ago. We moved to the Morrison Settlement in Northern Colorado. Mr. Bonne taught me to read and to write. This is my Journal of my life. He said I should start it before my baby arrives. He is helping me put the correct words to this.

8

I have a twin sister, Viola, and I have been missing her for all these years. I do not know where she is or how to find her. But, I do know that we are true twins and share the same secret. This diary being private and meant for just husband and myself and our baby, I will write down my secret.

Since I was eight, sister Viola and me discovered that we were different than other people. We turn colors like the Chameleon lizards. When we are upset or scared or really happy, our skin turns the same color and pattern of whatever we are touching.

Our father was very cruel to us. When he saw how we turned colors, he would slap us in the face or hit us with his belt and tell us to hold our crying, to hold our thoughts and not to move. Sister and I tried very hard not to get sad or scared, but when it would happen we would remind each other not to give in to it. It took until we were nine to stop getting such horrible beatings. When we were nine, we could control what was happening.

Sometimes, we played games with this. We would take off our clothes and play hide and seek and turn the color of trees, grass, buildings or anything that we wanted too. Sometimes we just laid down by a stream and became like the water.

We guessed that we were witches, but Mr. Bonne, says we are not. He says it is a phenomenon and that it just must happen to some people. It is something in us as sure as our blood is in us. We don't know why, but it is there.

This Journal will be passed down to my children and they will be taught early to control this as I do not ever intend to be cruel to my children. Mr. Bonne has helped me to make a plan to instruct the children in this phenomenon. As we are one in the Lord, he has taken my woes as his woes. January 3, 1873.

"My baby is to be born in about two weeks. Mr. Bonne has arranged for Mrs. Foreman from the next settlement to come and be a nurse for me. I will name my baby James if it is a boy and Jaime if it is a girl. That would be after my father, who although I thought cruel, husband said he beat us out of love so that no one would think us a witch.

I have made all the baby clothes and Mr. Bonne has made a cradle. So now we anxiously wait for our baby. March 13, 1873."

"March 23, 1873   I, Etienne, with sad heart finish my wife Hattie's journal. Hattie died while giving birth to our daughter Jaime on March 20, 1873. The Doctor says he could not see any reason for her to die, but that her blood seemed extremely thin and he could not stop her from hemorrhaging. Jaime is hale and hearty and cries for her milk and I think her mother.

My Hattie was my heart and I intend to see to it that Jaime is treated with the love and respect that Hattie would have given her. I will make sure Jaime is prepared if she too has the same affliction as her mother. I will also see that this letter is passed down through the generations.   Signed Etienne Bonne, husband of Hattie."

Jadin and Autumn sat silently absorbing the science-fiction-like-story. Susan looked at her two children with tears starting to slide down her cheeks. "I sorry" She said shaking her head slowly. "I probably shouldn't have had children, but I wanted you so bad and I can't imagine life without you two." She knelt down in front of them "I didn't prepare you. I didn't want to hurt you or be mean to you. I should have, I know that now." Jadin reached for her hands and pulled her up and beside him. "Mom, is this really true?" "Yes" she shrugged and leaned in close to him.

After a long silence, Susan went over to the box and pulled another letter out. "Can you stand another one?" Two heads nodded as one but no one spoke.

"To my daughter Adrienne, My name is Jaime DeBurge. I live in Seattle, Washington with my husband George DeBurge. George makes maps for the government. I have inherited the ability to change colors.

My father Etienne Bonne told me about my mother and how she was mistreated by her father to keep her from letting the phenomenon happen. She learned young to control and use this thing when she played with her sister Viola.

My mother died when I was born. My father taught me to control this without hitting or hurting me. I am so grateful he did not use the methods of my Grandfather James Johnston. So far, I can change color to whatever is around me at will. I have also learned how to repress the color that happens if I am mad, or hurt or even happy.

I write this to you my darling daughter and to your children, if you have them. My mother told my father that she thought her father told her it was started with a lizard bite on one of our great great Grandmothers. I am not really sure that I remember what he said in a right way. I do know that it is passed on and I will teach you and have already started, but I want you to have this letter as a history for those coming after us. Your Mother, Jaime DeBurge, Seattle, Washington."

Susan folded the letter and put it back in the box. "I'll make a copy of these letters and give you each a box to keep for your children." Jadin and Autie nodded in unison.

"Is there more letters?" Autie asked. "Yes, three more. But then I have to write a letter too."

Susan pulled out the last two letters and laying one on the floor beside her, she opened the letter from Adrienne Douglass.

"My name is Adrienne DeBurge Douglass. I am writing this letter to Mildred, my daughter. I love you and want you to trust God with your gift. I call it a gift because it is. God did not make witches and we are not witches. We are just His people who happened to have something altered in our bodies to make us turn colors.

I wish I knew what had happened before Grandma Hattie was lost to her family. I know her sister Viola must have children and grandchildren my age. I hope that someday we will find them or you will find some of our relatives.

Be strong Mildred and use your gift to help someone, never selfishly. Read your Bible and pray every day daughter. Keep this to yourself. You father has never seen me change colors. I fear he would not understand. He is a hard working man, but has little tolerance for strange things. That is why I was so hard on you when he wasn't around. You were so compliant, he did not suspect.

Be careful of anyone who wants to know more about you in this way. I love you, Your Mother, Adrienne."

Susan picked up the next letter.

"Dearest Children and Grandchildren, as you know by now, after having read the three letters before mine, we are in a strange state of things. We are Chameleon. I pray that you all do learn to control your gift. I call it a gift. I am not a witch and neither are you. God did not let this happen to us for us to be witches or evil. We are to use our gift for good. I beg you, that you seek out a way to use your gift for the betterment of mankind and in accordance with God's will.

It is possible to bring on and calm your skin in its pigmentation changes, even to the point of looking completely like your closest surroundings. You must not let the rest of the world know about this gift. They cannot and will not understand and be tolerant. I am sure that if God allowed this to happen to us, He will help us overcome the control of it.

Be wise, dear children, you can be happy or you can be very distraught with your gift. It is your choice. It is hard, but I conquered it and I know that you can too. Be careful of all your acquaintances. I feel most will not accept this thing we have. With my love and prayers through the ages to come, Your Mother, Mildred Jones."

Susan took the last letter and began to unfold it. Autie reached over and gently took it from her "Let me, Mom" she said in a startling grown up voice. Susan relinquished the letter to her.

Autie cleared her throat and began.

"This is May 13, 1967. It seems that I have just had you, my daughter Susan, but you are fifteen now and this letter is for you and your children. You have probably read the other letters. So I start with my story.

I married your father Ralph Williamson. We met when he was visiting his Aunt in Seattle. We stayed our first year with my parents and then we moved to Colorado Springs where you were born.

Your father and I decided to wait until you were at least seventeen to tell you about your abilities, as I did not realize I had them until I was eighteen. However, you were an early bloomer and started to blend into things at eight. You do know how to control yourself and I am proud you have the inner strength to make it happen or not happen. It has helped you to excel in your studies and all the other things you have attempted to do.

I shall put down this memory, also. When you were ten, you had forgotten your homework and your teacher scolded you and sent you to the principal. While waiting in the office, you blended so well with the drapery as your blouse and pants were light green like the background of the drapes, the school called home to see if you had gone home. When I came up to the school, there you were still, standing completely camouflaged to their eyes. But I saw the whites of your eyes. I was furious that you had been sent to the principal for just forgetting your work. I presented them with your papers and when they left the room, your color resumed and you went back to class.

I don't know why this weird gene is in our make-up from a bite, but I do want to warn you to keep it a secret and as my mother said, use it for good and not evil. With my love forever, Your Mother Charlene Wills, Colorado Springs, Colorado."

"Well, there it is" Susan held up her hands in a surrender type gesture. Except tonight, I will write my letter.

Jadin and Autie looked at each other and they seemed to share a grin that reached from one side of his face to the other side of hers.

"Awesome" Jadin stood up and walked over to their drapes and put his arm on it. Nothing happened. "How do I know if I have the gene?" He frowned.

Autie walked over and put her arm next to drapes. The colors of the drape started to slowly creep up her arm. "How did you do it?" he asked. "I just tightened up the inside of my arm and thought about it really hard." Autie stepped away as soon as the color had completely covered her body.

Jadin tightened his arm until his muscles ached and gritted his teeth with a little grunt. Still nothing happened. "Jadin, relax" Susan encouraged him "It will happen and once it does it will always happen. Don't try to get it going too soon or you will have to work with it all the time." Jadin kept trying.

"Well," Susan told him rather sharply "If you are intent on doing it, here." She slapped his face hard causing him to fall back and sit on the couch. Immediately his arm then his body turned the same color of the couch he was sitting on, only his clothes showed.

Autie started laughing "That is sooo cool." Jadin was holding his cheek, "Thanks, mom" he said in a pretend irritated way. "I needed that".

"Obviously!" Susan came over and hugged him. "Now, you will have to learn to control it."

Ron Tanner opened the door of his house to find his wife waiting with a frosted glass of iced tea in her hand outstretched to him. He handed her his lunch pail and took the tea. "Is this a good sign? Or a bad one?" he looked deep into her eyes. "Good and bad, Darling." She smiled at him. "Go change, dinner will be on the table in ten minutes."

Ron passed her drinking deep of his tea and looking back over his shoulder keeping eye contact. She was grinning that grin that meant something was happening.

Ron sighed deeply as he pulled off his oily Levis. Then he showered and put on his soft walking shorts. It was good to get into something comfortable. However, he didn't have a comfortable feeling about going to the dinner table.

CHAPTER TWO

"Jewel?" Henry called from inside the covered wagon. "What is this box you've put in here? It has a lock on it. Heavy, too." Jewel peeked her head inside the cover, "It belonged to my mother. And," She grinned back at him "I absolutely will not leave without it."

Henry Johnston, twenty years older than sixteen year old Jewel, smiled at the pretty little thing, still not believing that she would actually marry an old cuss like himself, no less go off into the wilderness of Canada with him, a trapper. "Darl'in," he winked "you can take the whole house for all I care." They both laughed as he lifted her up onto the seat beside him.

He cracked the whip over the team of oxen and their journey began. She had said goodbye to Sara and accepted with surprise the box that Sara said contained her mother's property. She thought her mother and father had died in a wagon train attack and all their goods stolen.

There were only two things Sara told her. One was that she kept the box upon a promise to Jewel's mother and the other thing was that Jewel should exercise her self control as she would someday need an extremely large amount of it.

Jewel thought briefly about the things Sara put her through to "Make her tough" and grimaced. She had sometimes hated Sara, but then loved her, too, as Sara treated her with love and affection along with the spurts of exaggerated and mean-type teasing.

"To get your goat" she used to say. Once she slammed a door in Jewels face and made her stand there with her nose pressed up against it and told her she was not to move for an hour and definitely not to get mad. "Think happy thoughts" she told her. Twice, while giving her a hug, she stepped back, slapped her across the face, then demanded that Jewel not move a muscle or makes any kind of emotional response. Jewel learned quick to control her emotions.

As the wagon passed by Sara Water's house, Jewel put her hand on her chest feeling the key that was on a string hanging between her breasts. She was anxious to see what was in her mother's box, but would exercise patience so that she would be alone with the box at some point and have time to ponder over whatever was in there.

Henry reached his big hand over and squeezed her knee. Jewel held her breath. They had just got married that afternoon and she knew she would be intimate with him but didn't know what would be happening. The warmth she could feel of his hand through the layer of material in her dress frightened her.

She happened to glance down at her left hand that lay next to the plaid blanket Henry had placed beside her. Her eyes took a second glance. Her little finger and apart of the side of her hand didn't seem to be there. She squinted. They were there alright, but they were colored exactly like the blanket, yellow and tan stripes going across red.

She looked ahead watching the oxen pick up speed as they pulled the wagon up to the small hill just at the outskirts of town.

"You might want to wave at Sara" Henry pointed back down the hill at the woman standing waving at them. "Oh, sure" Jewel took her right hand and waved back at Sara.

Looking back down, Jewel thought "How can this be?" A scared feeling crept over her making her scalp feel like it was crawling. "Am I a witch?" She remembered some of the townspeople talking about the witches they had killed and especially the one that turned into colors like a lizard. The witch had turned the color of whatever was near her just like a Chameleon lizard.

Jewel scolded herself "No" she gritted her teeth "No". The colors faded and her hand again was normal. "I'll not let that happen again" she vowed to herself.

Henry laid his hand on his nineteen year old son's shoulder. "James, you need to talk to your mother, but, don't stay too long and tire her out. She is dying son. Go to her." James put his arms around his father and held on tight. The horror of the past afternoon still had a grip on his heart.

Both he and his father at the same time had seen his mother enter the front door with the deadly snake still attached to her hand. Neither could comprehend how the snake or the burlap bag that lay on the front steps could have gotten there. Jewel instantly turned blue and her breath was faltering. Henry had cut the snake in two with his large knife while it was still hanging onto Jewel. They all knew there was no cure.

James entered his parent's bedroom in the four room cabin that he grew up in. There, propped up on several pillows, lay his mother, whom he loved dearly, dying. "Mother" he came and knelt down beside her bed. "Mother, I'm here."

"James" Jewel softly said his name. "There is a box under my bed. It belonged to my mother and it has things in there from her mother and from me. Please take time to read the journals very carefully.

I know you think I have been too hard on you making you keep your emotions under control. But my dear child, I had a good reason that you have already seen. I have faith that you can have the control necessary."

She took a key on the string around her neck and put it in James' hand and closed his fingers around it. "Here". She said in shallow breaths. "Put the key around your neck and keep the contents of that box private and safe. Promise?" she looked deep into his eyes.

"Of course I will Mother," James took the key and put it around his neck. "There, see?" He smiled at his mother wishing he could hold back the hands of time and not let her go. Her hands went limp and she whispered "Get your father."

As his mother's casket was lowered into the ground, James stood by his father's side trying hard to keep control of his tears. When the minister finished talking, James picked up one of the roses to throw down onto the casket and as he did, he saw his thumb and first finger turn to the exact shade of the pink rose with white edges. Looking up he saw Rev. Cloud looking at his hands, then look away quickly. He tightened his large forearm and held it tight until the color left.

This seemed to be happening more and more to him. It started when he was seventeen.

The first time it happened, was when his mother, after hugging him before he went off hunting with his father, quickly and without any provocation, slapped him hard across the face. His hands instantly turned into a flower print of pinks and yellows, the pattern that was on his mother's apron that lay close to his hands. Fear and anger came over him as he watched the colors creep up his arms.

Jewel put her hands tenderly on his face "James. Tighten up your arms. Make your mind work strong. Tell it 'No'." He did. The colors started to fade. He weakened and the colors started to come back. He tightened up again and said "NO" out loud. The colors ceased. No words were spoken until later after he had returned.

"James" his mother whispered after her husband had gone to sleep, "It is a family ailment from my family. It has to be crushed each time. No one can know about it. No one would understand. They would say we are evil and from the Devil. You must promise me not to let it happen and not to talk about it. Promise?" "I promise" he told her.

Now, as he thought of what she had said, he was anxious to be alone with that box.

Early the next morning, James pulled out the mystery box and lifted three letters and laid them on his lap. Opening the first, he began to read.

"Diary of Elizabeth Stockton: June 18, 1770 - this is the first day that I have been able to write in my new diary. This will be my first entry.   Last Saturday, a week, I was bitten by a lizard that seems to have been a stowaway in our wagon.   The wagon master, Mr. Sholholter, said it looked like a type he had seen in his home country, called a Chameleon, one that changes colors.   Before we could see if he changed colors, he disappeared in the tall grasses and was gone.   Mrs. Norris put a comforting poultice on my arm and soon the pain disappeared, but the swelling didn't go down all the way until last night. Mrs. Norris' son William has been very helpful.   He has brought in firewood for our family and Papa has asked him to eat with us each night.   I find William very handsome.   He is seventeen and I just turned sixteen.

August 3, 1770 -   My arm is all well now.   However, William continues to bring in our firewood and Papa keeps insisting he eat with us.   Tonight, I made a special cake for his eighteenth birthday.

January 1, 1771 -   I purpose to write in my Diary at least once a week. Mother seems to think it would be a nice thing to pass down to my children someday. This day, William asked Papa if he could take me for a walk down by the river where we are camping. We are in the Colorado Territory. It is beautiful country and William told me he would like to start his farm right here near a settlement called Trinidad.

January 4, 1771 - Tonight William asked me to marry him and stay in Trinidad as the wagon train is going to leave to go further west at the end of the week.   I have agreed with the blessing of my parents.

January 5, 1771 - Tomorrow, William and I will marry. Mother has given me her wedding dress to wear and has altered it to fit me. I must admit I am scared. Today something very strange happened.   I was gathering blue field flowers for my wedding bouquet and suddenly a feeling of fear passed through me and when I looked at my hands, they were the same blue and pattern as the flowers I was holding. By the time I had found my Mother, the color was gone. She thought I made it up. Strange happening.

January 23, 1771 - My Name is Elizabeth Stockton Norris. I have been married for 17 days now and find that married life is very strange and wonderful all at the same time. Another strange happening occurred on my wedding night. Husband was totally unaware that my hands turned the same color as my wedding quilt. I told him of the happening and he told me not to worry. Probably just honeymoon jitters.

November 14, 1771 - I haven't found time to write as husband and I are working from sun up to sun down. Two weeks ago I gave birth to our baby girl Nora Marie. Husband delivered our baby and witnessed the strange happening of me turning the same color of the striped bedspread I had made for our bed. We decided that since the chameleon had bitten me that he changed the makeup of my skin. William is very sweet to me and our new baby.

October 29, 1774 - Our Nora is three today, a very active and smart child. She has found out that she too, has the strange ability as I do to change colors. She loves to play at surprising us and herself by making herself turn completely the color of whatever is surrounding her. This very morning, I was working at making a stew and all of a sudden I noticed that the curtains were moving. There she had taken off her clothes and was completely the color of the curtains, pattern and all. She laughed gleefully and ran to tell Daddy. "I turn". He scolded her for being naked, but was shaking his head and laughing as he came into the kitchen."

"September 1, 1788 - My eyes have grown dim and have decided to turn this Diary over to Nora. Nora is now a young lady and will someday marry. She has learned to control our unusual happenings. Elizabeth"

James pulled out a letter written on a coarse piece of brown paper.

"My name is Nora Marie Norris. I am known here as Nora Lansing Coup, a name I made up. This is my last will and testament.

I am going to be hanged today and they have given me time to pray and write a last statement. I will give this to Sara. I have carefully kept my mother's diary through the horrible ordeals I have endured. And will have Sara save this letter with it for my Daughter.

In Trinidad Settlement in the Colorado Territory, when I was seventeen, Martin Black and his raiders came through our settlement and shot all the men and women, my Father and Mother being among them. Mr. Black took me and made me be his wife but did not marry me. He took me and three other girls from our settlement to Ohio where the three other girls were given to some of his men. He allowed me to take some of my belongings and I hid my mother's diary from him.

One girl, Millie, took her life with the gun of the man who had her. I don't know what happened to Sally and Helena as I escaped from Mr. Black when he over drank and passed out. I hid in the willows of the river outside of Willstown. I could hear them looking for me for hours, but I was fortunate and was not found.

After two days, I was hungry enough to take a chance. I went to the outskirts of the town. There, I met Sarah who had the orphans. Being pregnant and very dirty, Sarah was sorry for me and took me in and kept me a secret until I had my baby. I became her helper and was starting to be a part of the community until Barton Wells took an interest in me and one day saw my skin turn the color of the bouquet of heather he had brought me.

I had tried to control my coloring, but it seemed to pop out at the worst times. More people saw me color and told Barton Wells' father, the minister in the town. Cleric Wells has declared me a witch. Barton has not helped as he is afraid of his father. Cleric Wells has two sons; Barton the oldest and Wilson the younger who seems very happy to watch me hang. I told them I am not a witch and tried to get someone to look at my Mothers diary and see how she was bit by a lizard. They said it doesn't matter, that I was a witch.

I know I will die and have some comfort that Sara has promised to raise Jewel as her own and to teach her to hide the curse if she has it. The town people think Jewel is a daughter of a wagon attack victim. My life has been hard and sad and I am reconciled to this end. I hope that when you read this dear Jewel, that you will understand where you came from and that you will try to hide your curse. I don't have anything to leave to you but these two letters. I love you, Your Mother Nora Marie Norris."

After reading his Grandmother Nora's letter, James pulled a light blue letter out.

"My name is Jewel Johnston. I am married to Harry Johnston. I write this letter to my son James. I am a Chameleon. I have inherited something that makes me change colors and look like whatever I am around. You have inherited it too, James and that is why I have been mean to you and that your father has been very strict. You have mastered the control quickly. Don't let anyone know you can do this. I have told you this and I am telling you again. Be careful, I know that someone wanted my mother dead because of it. I think it was a minister as she was called a witch and hanged and burned. There will be more that will want us dead. I love you son and pray that your life will be happy.

Be brave but careful. Just like your father taught you about a gun. Have it ready, treat it seriously and aim true. A gun in the hand of an enemy is dreadful. If your color changing is known by the wrong person, it will be deadly. I love you, Your Mother Jewel.

James sat back and sobbed into his arms. Why did this pass to him? He didn't want it. It was two days since he and his father dug her grave out by the roses she loved so much.

That evening, they packed and left the cabin for the deep wood and hunting.

CHAPTER THREE

Cody, Wyoming July 8, 2009

In contrast to the scene at the Tanner's house in Bakersfield, the air in the mountains of Wyoming was cold and brisk. Blane Benson sat in the log cabin on a ranch that he and his wife Connie shared with their sixteen year old daughter Brianna. Looking up at Connie, "I can't believe we have been married seventeen years and you just now tell me you're a lizard! And, that Brie could be a lizard, too. This is too crazy." He said. His head was still reeling from seeing Connie's arm turn the same exact shade and coloring of the paneling in their den.

"I'm sorry" Connie shrugged. "It has been so hard just to keep it under control. This is not something that I am proud of. You get burned as a witch for this sort of thing. I had to tell you, because I have to tell Brie. She will be seventeen soon and it might start happening to her."

Blane got up and yelled madly "Why did you even allow yourself to get pregnant?" "Oh yeah" she got right back into his face, "Like I knew that was going to happen." He blushed and put his arms around her." I'm sorry sweetheart" he squeezed her tight. "I guess we didn't think did we?" He grinned down at her. "No, there was no thinking that night, that's for sure."

He held her back away from himself. "I don't get it. How does this, I mean why does this happen? You're not an alien are you?"

Connie put the box she had brought in from her closet on the table. "Here is all the information I have. This box has come down from my ancestors. There are letters written by and about ten generations.

It all started with my very great great Grandma Elizabeth who was bitten by a Chameleon lizard and somehow it must have altered her DNA, except none of them knew about DNA.

Her daughter Nora was burned as a witch and so it goes down the line. I know I must have cousins that are in the same predicament. I don't know anything other than what is here."

Connie started to pace back and forth. "I have not been as hard on Brie as my mother was on me. Anyway, we need to read these letters to Brie and make a plan so she can live with this and not be a freak." She put her arms around her husband. "Help me with this please. She will need the both of us."

He looked at his wife who, until this moment, he thought to be a normal average person with no hang-ups or secrets. He was still angry inside that she had not told him, but he never wanted to make her mad or upset. Blane had been a veterinarian for years and this was so foreign to his thinking he couldn't process it.

Opening the box, Connie pulled out the pile of letters. She and Blane took turns reading the letters out loud to each other. First, there was the Diary of Elizabeth, then Nora's letter. After reading the one from Jewel, Blane opened the letter from James and started reading.

> "To my dear daughters Viola and Hattie: As you know, we are different. I have been hard on you, but I know I have to be. You must not let anyone know you are different. Your skin will change when you are mad or upset or even when you are neither. You can control this. You can make it come on or you can make it not come on.
>
> Your great Grandmother was burned as a witch. It was her mother that started this whole thing when bitten by a Chameleon. We have no choice in the matter. We must control it. I have learned and now you must learn. I will make you learn. It is for your own good.
>
> You will both have a copy of these letters. Read them carefully and pass them down to your children. Better yet, don't have children. It will save a lot of anguish. However, I know you probably will.

My mother was a kind soul and she tried to teach me to control my curse or is it a gift? She died of snake bite. We don't know how that the snake came to our house or how that a burlap bag just happened to be at the same spot. Maybe it was by someone who wanted her or us dead. I don't understand any of this, but I do urge you two to be especially careful and prudent with any of your actions.

I have written more for you two as I have seen how you have accepted this curse as a gift and have become quite adept at using it. Beware and careful. Use it wisely and not for fun.

Now, I mention that your Mother loved you so much. She died of diphtheria when you were two and she wanted me to teach you the way of the Lord. I have tried in my limited way. I hope I have not let you two down. She wanted me to remind you that God loves you and you are not witches. Remember that. Be good Christian women. Your loving father, James Johnston

Ps I have only one box now and that goes to you, Viola, as your sweet sister is no longer with us. Viola, use this for only good, never evil. "

Connie then read her great great great Grandmother Viola's.

"Dearest children Mary, Sarah and Victor,   I add my letter to your boxes of family history. It is so sad and so exciting. You are both blessed and cursed to have in your being the ability to change the color of your skin to that of the colors and patterns around you.

All three of you found your trait early and it was fun playing with you as small children, changing colors and playing hide and seek. However, as you already know, I have been trying to train you to be in control of

27

this gift or curse. It will be a gift if you hide it from the world and a real curse if you let others know you can do this.

As I have told you, my sister Hattie and I used to play with this gift and then my dear sister was stolen by the Indians and I never saw her again. I fear she is dead. Be very careful Children, there is an enemy that seeks us out.

My Father, James Johnston, was found hanging from a tree at the edge of our property. He had been hanged and then burned like his Grandmother Nora. You have her letter too. The last person to see my Father alive was Reverend Paul Shimmer. He came by and told my Father he wanted to have a talk with him. He told the Sheriff that he left my Father at the gate of our property early in the evening. The sheriff said they would try to find who killed him, but that there was not enough evidence to show who was with him way out there. I truly don't believe the preacher as I noticed him watching Father whenever we did go to church with a strange look about him.

My mother was a believer and I know I am and I read my Bible. After Father died, I did not go to church and made sure that the pastor never saw me.

I met your father Raul Martinez at a dance in a barn just outside of town. I loved him the minute I met him. He married me and took me to where he was stationed right outside of Santa Fe, New Mexico, then still a Mexican outpost. There I had you three and have been blessed with a quiet life with a good husband. Raul has been so kind and considerate of me and has taking my gift in stride. He actually enjoys seeing me turn colors. He has been careful to guard me and you children. You will know about this letter before you are grown and will take a copy of each of your ancestor's letters when you are grown up and leave home.

Watch people for their attention to you and for their actions. If they seem overly religious, strange or secretive, watch them. I believe that it might be a church or ministry family that seeks to kill us. Watch out for each other. Viola Martinez"

Blane was ready with the next letter.

"1904 - My name is Mary Martinez Rolfstein and I live in San Francisco with my daughter Beth. I am a widow as my husband Sidney Rolfstein, a gambler, was shot two years ago.

I have my own business here in the city. I make dresses and have my own shop on Main Street. It is a successful business. I am leaving this letter for you Beth and even though you are only four, you already know and can master our gift. How many times have you and I played amongst the bolts of materials and hid from one another just by turning the same color as the material.

I have saved my letters for you, Beth, and have kept the box they were in when I got them. My mother is still alive and I have no reason to believe she is going to be killed by anyone. I think the deaths of our ancestors were just deaths or murders, yes, but not because of this phenomenon. I hope I am not wrong, but I don't intend to be afraid everyday as my mother has been and still is. She is still living on her ranch in New Mexico and has the protection of the gauchos. Father has made sure of that.

I do think, Beth, you should be very careful who you let get intimate with you. Your father was a worldly man and he did not like to think of my gift. He told me never to use it around him. He said it made him sick. As soon as we moved to San Francisco I knew I would need a job as your father was not a very good gambler and he did seem to make enemies fast. I think you have all the information that you need in this respect as you have all the preceding letters.

I love you and pray that you will be careful with what you do and who you know. I had a sister, Sarah, but she had no children and I am sorry to say, hanged herself. Your Mother, Mary Martinez Rolfstein."

Connie had made some coffee and handed Blane a cup. He picked up another letter. "Gosh" he accepted her offering, "Your family is like a movie. It's hard to comprehend all of this."

"I know" Connie sat back down beside him with her coffee and a plate of cookies which she thought since there was such a drama going on here it would justify eating the calories. Blane smiled as he watched her enjoy a cookie. He liked her a little plump and especially liked it when she enjoyed something.

"Here we go" Blane made a big gesture of picking up the letter and then started reading:

"Mercy, it is 1932, June 13th, and you have just had your sixth birthday party. Seems like every child in San Francisco was here, riding ponies, laughing at the clowns. Your Father, Mr. Darnell, sure spoils his little princess, doesn't he?

Mercy dear, if you are reading my letter, than you have read all the others. You already know you are special and different than the other children.

Your father seems to think maybe you are an angel that God gifted with this "gift" and not a real girl. We know better, don't we? It is hard to have this gift.

You have been unhappy with me because I have been stern and made you practice controlling yourself when your Father always let's you have your way. You will thank me someday. I will continue to train you for your own protection.

It was only last Christmas that we lost both my mother and my grandmother. You won't know this until you read all the letters, but they were both killed in a bizarre accident. Grandmother Viola had come out for a visit and she and my mother were somehow locked in mother's clothing store and it was set on fire. Someone did this purposely. There was a painting of a lizard in a noose on the sidewalk in front of the store and words that said "Die Witch." And there were two initials J.W. beside it.

There is now an ice cream store where Mother's shop was. The police have no clues who did it. I think that it was murder and because they were both Chameleon. Yes, that is what we are. The only initials I know of, that are J.W. are in our great Grandmother Nora's letter. Joshua Wells was the preacher that had her hanged. I don't know how this could pertain, but I feel it does somehow.

Be on your guard Mercy. You may be a princess, but you must also be a warrior. Stay strong and of good courage. I hope I live to see your children and grandchildren, but if I don't, you must even more so try to be safe. Love, Your Mother Beth "

"I'll take this one" Connie picked up a blue letter and another cookie.

"My name is Mercy Darnell Hart and I am a Chameleon. I inherited this condition from a grandmother who was bitten by one. I am writing this statement for my two daughters Judy and Crystal.

It is now June 4, 1955. I have already told you girls about this as you are already using your power. I will call it a power as I don't think it was a disease or a gift. It was a bite. It is a powerful tool if you can control it. I have gotten out of two dangerous situations in my life time and it was because I could blend into my surroundings and hide.

When I was sixteen, a man dressed in a black suit with a high clerical collar came to our house. I had just come home from school and had come in through the back entrance as it was closest to my bedroom.

I peeked downstairs and could see my mother talking to a man who had just come up to the door. I went in my room and was just putting on some shorts and a green blouse when I heard some scuffling downstairs.

I crept down the stairs and saw only too clear, my mother being strangled. As the man started to turn around, I turned the green and white stripped color of the stairway wall and my white shorts and legs were the identical white as the floor and wainscoting. I stood drop dead still and waited. The man, in his preacher outfit, laid mother on the couch and checked to see is she was breathing.

Then he quickly left, but not before he wrote "Die Witch" on the entrance hall. He obviously did not see me. I waited until he was down the front steps then I ran to mother and then to the hall to call for help.

Mother was still alive, but barely. She died, however, a week later. My Father was never the same after her death. He traveled the world as much as he could on his vacations. He never took me after that. He said he was afraid to stay close to me and get his heart broken again. My heart was broken.

Then I met your father, Bob Hart and we have been very happy. Bob has been a good husband and father to the both of you. Stay strong daughters. Love, Mother"

Connie beat Blane as he reached for the last letter. "I'll do it. It's my Mother's." Blane sat back against the couch and gave a nod of assent.

"My name is Crystal Hart Jenkins, I am married to Marshall Jenkins, a railroad engineer and we live in Sonora, California. This story is for my Daughter Connie.

I am a Chameleon and I am not a witch, an alien or anything other than a normal woman. I will give you all the letters to read to make you understand what has happened.

No one can explain it, but we are in a line of people that turn the color of their surroundings. It can be controlled and I have started training you very early to not give in to whatever makes you turn colors.

In doing this, I have allowed you to have fun with it and have encouraged you not to have children as it might be a dangerous life for them.

It is obvious that there is a person or people that want to kill us. I have felt their presence and my ancestors have met strange and violent deaths. I know I am in danger, but choose not to live in fear. I am careful, however, and do watch what I am doing or who I am with.

These people need to be exposed and stopped. I also know there are more Chameleons as my sister is out there somewhere. We haven't spoken since we were separated at seventeen. That was when my mother died and my father left us.

My mother was shopping in a local supermarket when a car that didn't have a driver smashed through the front of the store and killed her. Pastor Jerry Barnes and his wife Cara took me into their family and my sister went with a lady from the church that was leaving for Colorado Springs. I was so distraught and caught up in the Barnes family I did not even know the lady's name and didn't ask. I deeply regret that now.

The Barnes sent me to college and after college I married Marshall Jenkins. Those were busy years. I had learned early to control my colors from changing and I hope that you will learn early too. I will try to teach you this.

Cara Barnes told me one day that a minister had been around asking about my mother and the whole family; how many kids she had and all. Cara told him that my mother had died and didn't mention me. She seemed to think, that though he had a clerical collar, he seemed evil and she didn't want him to know about me. I am thankful she did that.

Be careful Connie who you let know about this matter. It could mean your life.

I love you and am sorry that I passed on the gene to you; however, I am glad I had you. Your have been a blessing. Love, Mother Crystal, August 3, 1988"

It was almost midnight when they finished. Blane stood up. "These nine letters have worn me out. I guess you're going to write a letter?"

"Yes, I am. Brie will be home tomorrow. Shall we tell her then?" Connie asked. Blane frowned "Yes. She needs to know and now. Let's go to bed" He held out his hand to his wife. She gratefully took it, her heart at ease that he was not upset with her for her dilemma.

Connie was just drifting into a deep sleep when Blane spoke into the cold night air. "Connie?" he almost shouted. She turned over "What?" she whispered.

"Don't you get it? Every parent has died some sort of unnatural death? They have been murdered."

Connie put her arms up next to her husband. "Hold me. Keep me safe." and she slipped off to sleep as Blane lay there for a long time with wild thoughts until sleep took him.

CHAPTER FOUR

July 8, 2009   Albuquerque, NM

Hot air balloons filled the sky and more were being aired up and lifting off their pads. The locals were buying hot cinnamon rolls and walking in between the balloon crews and pads. A woman in her forties handed her seventeen year old daughter a cinnamon roll and they sat down on a park bench.

"Mom" Courtneay turned shaking her curly brown hair. "Why don't you know Grandma Judy's sister?" She did have a twin, didn't she?" "Yes. She did have a twin, my aunt Crystal. Something happened between them when they were seventeen. First their Mother died in a horrible accident and then their Dad just left and they never heard from him again. Aunt Crystal was taken in by their Minister and Mom was sent to live with some lady in Colorado Springs.

I told you that. Didn't I? Mom married Dad to get away from that lady. She didn't know then she was going to fall in love with him."

"I wish I had gotten to know them" Courtneay put her arms around her mother. "I don't think I could take it if you died." Windy held her daughter tight. The pain of losing her mother still stabbed at her heart whenever she was mentioned. Her Dad was never close to her, but his death still hurt too. She remembered vividly getting the call about their death just after she had married Blake, Sr. Someone had sneaked into their house and shot them both in their beds as they slept. The police said it was a robbery gone wrong. But, the murderer had ransacked the house like he or she were looking for papers as there was jewelry left in place. There were never any suspects found in that case.

"Hey, where's my roll?" a very tall boy with dark eyes and curly brown hair grabbed a pinch of Courtneay's roll. "Give me that Blake. Mom, did you see what Blake did?" Courtneay tattled on her brother.

"Here" Windy handed him a wad of dollars. "Go buy us all another one." "Yeah, like I already got one." He frowned. "Ok, then" she smiled at him "buy you two and us one. Now hurry, your Dad will be launching in a minute and I want to take pictures."

Blake, Sr. was head of his company's balloon team. They had one of the brightest and largest air balloons at the festival. He had a team of three and a ground crew of five from Jallostream Corp. "Weren't you supposed to be going up with him?" Courtneay asked her mom. "I would have if Andy hadn't insisted on going. And, the CEO has more clout than me, you know. But I'm ready just in case he breaks a leg or something." She winked at her daughter. "Mother!" Courtneay squinted at her mother's unlikely statement. "Just kidding" Windy insisted.

She really had wanted to go up with her husband. They had regularly gone up in balloons when they were first married. That is until the children came along and Blake, Sr. firmly stopped her going as the twins needed a Mother. He only got involved in the sport again when the company he worked for bought a balloon for advertising and community good will. His boss, Andy Levitt, insisted that he be in charge of the balloon as he was the advertising VP.

Blake was back quickly with the sticky goodness half in a bag and half all over his hands and some on his mouth. "These are good" he said with a mouth full. "I could eat a dozen." Courtneay took the bag and was about to pull out a roll when a big hand reached around her and caught the bag away from her.

"Daaad!" Courtneay yelled. "That's mine." "Was yours." Her Dad made a big display of taking out the roll and enjoying it immensely "mmmm".

Courtneay held out her hand "I will need much money to buy much more." Blake, Sr. pulled out a ten dollar bill and handed it to Courtneay. "Here, pig out." "Thanks Dad." She gave him a quick hug and headed for the stand. "What about me?" Blake asked.   Another bill appeared and was grabbed up by the teenager who like the other was off in a shot.

"Your children are pigs." Blake, Sr. told his wife as he reached over and took a piece out of her roll. "Yes, just like one of their parents. Hmmm? I wonder which one." She looked up at her handsome husband.

"Are you ready to ride?" he looked directly into her eyes. "Ride?" she answered with a furrow in her brow. "Yes" he emphasized "Ride.   Andy is a no show"   "Yes" Windy pulled her fist straight down in the air like one of her teens might do. "Yes" She whirled around "I'll tell the kids".   "Ok, but hurry, I'll meet you at the balloon."   Blake, Sr. took off in the other direction.

Courtneay was waiting with Blake in line for the rolls, when they saw their mother coming toward them with a grin that was the size of Texas.   Courtneay looked over at Blake. "She's going. Bet?" Blake leaned toward Courtneay. "Think?" Blake starting walking toward their mother.

"You get to go up, don't you? Courtneay beat Blake to the question. "Yes" Windy shouted. "You two going to be alright here until I get back?"   "Duh, let me think. No Mommy, I will get lost" Blake mimicked a small child. "Funny" Windy quipped.

Here, Courtneay, you hold my purse for me.   There are two twenties in there. Buy lunch.   Sandy will give you a ride home around four when she gets off work at the Sheriff's booth. Go tell her I went with Dad, OK?"   "Have fun" Courtneay and Blake said almost at the exact same second.   Windy kissed both of her twins on the face and turned and ran toward the balloon pad.

"Why isn't our Mother a fraidy cat like the other mothers we know?" Courtneay asked, not expecting an answer. "Let's go watch them off" Blake shoved her in that direction. "Stop" she complained but kept walking toward the balloon area.   "Wait" she turned around, "we have to tell Sandy first."   "You tell her. I'll save you a spot up front" Blake kept walking. "Ok, brat" she threw over her shoulder.

The sheriff's booth was surrounded by children waiting for the officers to pin a deputy badge on them. "Sandy!" Courtneay yelled over the crowd. Sandy looked up and waved. "Courtneay, do you want to help us?" she responded. "No," Courtneay yelled back "Can we have a ride home? Mom is going up." She pointed up to the sky. "Ok" Sandy smiled and waved "four O'clock…don't be late."

Courtneay turned sharply to go and ran into a man in a black coat with a cleric collar. "Oh" she stammered. "I'm sorry" "Are you alright Miss?" the man looked deep into her eyes. "Yes, I'm fine, thanks." Courtneay hurried off in the direction of the balloons not noticing the man was following closely behind her.

Scooting through the crowd, Courtneay saw Blake motioning for her to hurry up. He was pointing up. The Jallostream balloon was rising. Its brilliant purple top cut through the crisp air and seemed to light up the sky with the bright yellow sun and azure blue stripes on its middle. The crowd gasped. It was a beautiful sight. As the balloon rose, Courtneay and Blake waved to their mother who was waving madly down at them.

The balloon joined in what seemed like a huge waltz of beautiful dresses dancing across the blue sky. "Come on" Blake grabbed at Courtneay's arm "Let's go eat". "Eat? Already? You just had cinnamon rolls." Courtneay chaffed. "I'm still hungry. Come on, ok? It'll be Four before you know it and I want to eat before we go home" "Ok" Courtneay retorted, "But we have plenty of time."

Turning around, Courtneay felt a bump and looked up into the face of the man she had run into earlier. "Oh, gosh" she half whispered. "Sorry, again" noticing he had a purple scar going through his left eyebrow making a creepy looking cross over his eye. "My fault" the man said and turned fast and left.

Suddenly, people started screaming and pointing up. Courtneay followed their gestures at the same time Blake's eyes caught the horrific plummeting of his parents' balloon. It took only seconds but seemed like an eternity as the children watched the balloon crash into flames on the field amid sirens and fire trucks racing to the scene. Blake grabbed his sister's hand and they ran toward the crash site.

July 13th

Courtneay sat still in her dad's favorite chair as the mourners crowded throughout their house making small talk and eating from the huge array of food the neighbors and church had brought in after their parent's double funeral.

Blake assumed the head of the house and directed the comings and goings. Courtneay had not cried or showed any emotion since watching her parents fall to their death.

Their pastor, Rev. Grodin had helped Blake plan the funeral and Sadie, their father's only sister took care of the flowers and helping to pick out the clothing for the funeral. Aunt Sadie had never been close to the family, but she kindly stayed as close as she could to help them. Concerned about Courtneay, she had encouraged her to get cleaned up and dressed for the funeral. She had found a black dress of Windy's as Courtneay didn't have one. Courtneay cringed when she put on the dress but went ahead anyway. She kept her arms to her side hugging the dress that had been on her mother recently. Her stomach stayed in a sick shaking state as she watched the friends of her parent's move around her house.

Blake suddenly was by Courtneay's side. "Court" he whispered "Come with me. I have to talk to you." She didn't argue. She just followed him upstairs into his room. "Look!" He put his hand up onto his high school banner that was taped on the wall. It was blue with gold lettering. His fingers went across the lettering and suddenly his hand changed from its normal color to blue and gold matching exactly the color of the background and letters. Courtneay came closer "What are you doing?"

"I don't know" He almost shouted and then whispered. "I was down stairs and Sadie gave me a plate of food. I almost dropped it and my hand came down across the salad and then my hand turned the color of the lettuce and the tomato and the carrot strips. I blended into the salad." Courtneay just stared at him for what seemed like an eternity. Then she took his

39

hand and put it on his bedspread which was blue checked. His hand took on the colors so exactly they could not see his hand.

"Did anyone see this happen?" She kept her voice low. "No, I don't think so. I saw it, put down the plate and came to get you. Why?"

"I don't know, but I think Mom was trying to tell me something the other day. Something about us and that we might be different and that we might be in danger. I thought she was just going off on one of her wild stories and didn't really listen. But she did say she had some letters for us to read sometime." She shrugged her shoulders.

"Courtneay, look, when I moved my hand away from the spread it turned back to normal and now when I put it back and squeezed my hand tight, it didn't turn." "Well," Courtneay warned "keep your fist; we can't let anyone see this. They might take us away from here and I think that Aunt Sadie will help us stay right here at home. OK?"

Blake was just about to say ok when there was a knock on the door. "Hey, you kids in there?" It was Sadie. Courtneay opened the door. "Hi Aunt Sadie, we just needed to get out of the crowd for a minute." "I know what you mean sweetheart, but the people are starting to leave and I think you should go and say your goodbyes."

The kids followed her downstairs and assumed a position by the front door to shake hands with the mourners as they passed out of the house. Rev Grodin was the last to leave and stayed holding Blake's handshake a long time reassuring the boy that if he needed anything for him to call. "Blake, be careful here with your sister. Make sure no stranger comes into your home while you two are here alone. Alright?" "Yes, Sir" Blake said firmly "I promise and to call if we need anything. Thank you for all your help." "My pleasure" the pastor gave Courtneay a quick hug and joined his family in their car.

Now that they were alone with Aunt Sadie, Blake and Courtneay relaxed a little and had a bite to eat. "I have to get back home" Sadie announced, "but, I'll be back tomorrow and help you two straighten out all the paperwork that has to be done. And, maybe tonight you two can decide if you would like to come and live with me and John, or if you want to live here, I will help you figure out how. OK?" Both the kids got up and hugged her tight. "Thanks Aunt Sadie" Blake choked "We couldn't have made it without you. We will talk tonight and decide."

"Ok, then" Sadie picked up her purse and left. The kids sat in silence for a long time.

Then Courtneay got up "Let's clean up the rest of this mess. I am so tired." Blake started picking up the dishes that were left and together they made short work of the kitchen clean up.

It was so strange going to bed in the big house without any parents there; with just the two of them. Courtneay snuggled down into her covers and pulled her comforter up around her chin wishing it was all a bad dream and her mom would come walking through the door.

Just then, there was a knock at her door. "Court?" "Come in" she answered. Blake came through the door dragging his bedding. "I'm going to sleep here on the floor." He didn't ask if it were ok and there was no resistance from his sister. She was glad to know he was right there beside her. They both were very tired and sleep came quickly.

October 13th

"Courtneay, would you get the door?" Nellie called from the kitchen. Courtneay was in the living room deeply engrossed in copying her biology notes. "Got it Nellie" she responded going to the door with her mind still back in the book.

As she opened the door, her attention came to full focus at the tiny almost elfin-like Oriental girl standing in front of her with a huge plaid suitcase sitting beside her and a grey backpack hanging heavily off her shoulder. "Hi" the girl looked up at Courtneay "Are you Windy Tollison's daughter?" "Yes"

41

Courtneay looked somewhat shocked at the designation. "Can I help you?" she asked the girl.

"Well" the girl lowered her back pack. "I believe I am your cousin and I hope we can help each other." Courtneay was at a loss for words. The word cousin swam around in her head trying to connect in some sense to this obviously Asian girl saying the word cousin.

Suddenly Nellie was standing right behind her. "Who is this?" she asked Courtneay as she peeked around to get a good look at the stranger at the door. Nellie had been hired right after their parents' funeral to keep house and watch out for them.

They were seventeen and would be eighteen in December, but they needed help and Sadie arranged with the lawyer to get them a housekeeper.

Nellie Shultz was a large German lady with a no nonsense attitude and a take charge personality. It had been difficult at first, but they soon grew to love her. She protected but never told them what to do and was rewarded with their help and confidence.

"Well" Courtneay looked at her with her eyebrows raised "This is..." She started to say and then turned to the girl "What did you say your name was?" "I didn't" the tiny creature said in a smirky kind of way. "But, I am Dezza and I have every reason to believe you are my cousin. May I come in and explain?"

Courtneay didn't know what to say and Nellie came to her rescue "Yes, you may sit in the living room and explain to Miss Courtneay here. Just leave your luggage on the porch, no one will harm it." Dezza complied and came into the living room. Courtneay gestured to her to sit in the large overstuffed chair by the couch, but Dezza chose to sit at the end of the couch and patted the seat beside her "Please sit here, I have some papers to show you. OK?" "Sure" Courtneay responded.

"First" Dezza set the papers down on the coffee table. "Did your mother leave you some papers? I mean letters?" Courtneay's mind jumped to the steel box that was still in the back of her mother's closet. "Yes, we were going to read them and then just put it off." Courtneay felt a little scared. "You know, maybe we'd better wait for my brother. He'll be here any time now." "Your brother?" Dezza's eyebrows rose. "I only had your name on my list." "Your list?" Courtneay asked "What kind of list?"

Just then the front door opened and in walked Blake. He looked surprised to see Courtneay on the sofa with a strange girl. A beautiful Oriental girl at that. "Hey" he threw at Courtneay. "Hey" she responded "Come on in. I want you to meet someone."

Dezza stood up and held out her hand to Blake. "I'm your cousin, Dezza" she grinned at him.

Nellie came back into the room. She had been in the hallway and heard Dezza asking about letters. She thought she had better be in on this. "Can I get you kids a coke or some lemonade" she offered. "Thank you Nellie" Blake answered "I'd love a coke. She then turned to Dezza "What about you Dezza? Thirsty?" "Yes please, the same." She accepted.

Courtneay got up "I'll help you Nellie and exited with Nellie to the kitchen. Blake and Dezza sat in silence until the ladies came back into the room. He was trying to reconcile this cousin bit in his mind.

"Is it alright with you two if Nellie sits in on this with us?" Dezza looked a little troubled, but Blake quieted her fears "If we can't trust Nellie, we can't trust anyone. It's ok. Really Dezza, relax." "Ok" Dezza realized she had no control over this situation at least not right now.

"Blake?" Courtneay started "remember the day of the funeral we had a talk and were going to read the letters mother left us but we didn't?" "Yeah" he said, now wishing he hadn't asked Nellie to stay. "Well," Courtneay continued "Dezza has some letters she wants to show us and I think they may be connected somehow. We need to get them out now and know what's in them. OK?"

Blake nodded and then turned to Nellie, "You know Nellie, you don't need to stay, I think we can handle one little girl, don't you?" Nellie chuckled; relieved she did not have to go through a bunch of letters with some teenagers. "You're right. I have to get ready to take the bus to my sister's tonight. You remember I am going to be gone this weekend. Is there something you need before I scoot out of here?" "Not a thing Nellie. You deserve some time off. I hope you can relax at your sisters. Don't worry about us. I have been so hungry for pizza; I'll probably eat it all weekend" he grinned at her. "Bad boy" she quipped. "I have already made a casserole for tonight and it is ready right now and lasagna for tomorrow. Be sure to eat the salad I fixed, too." She turned to go "I'll get ready and come back in just before I leave. It was nice to meet you Dezza." Dezza nodded and smiled at Nellie.

When Nellie was out of the room, Blake offered "You know, Dezza, it would be better if we discussed this on a full stomach." "You never have a full stomach Blake" Courtneay teased. "I am hungry" Dezza said. "Do you think my bags are alright outside?" "I'll bring them in here" Blake jumped up. "You guys get the food out and I'll be right in."

Blake went to retrieve the bags and Courtneay took Dezza into the kitchen. In no time, the three were eating and waiting to really talk until they knew that Nellie was gone. After a few minutes, she came through, said goodbye and soon they heard her car pull away. They all seemed to sense a relief.

"Ok Dezza" Blake asked "What is this all about?" Dezza stood up and looked around the room. She was wearing a yellow short sleeve top and blue jeans. She walked over to the window and drew the drapes. The drapes were a deep hunter green with brown and white threads running through them. She put her back to the window and held out her arms. All of a sudden all Courtneay and Blake could see was a yellow shirt and jeans, even her hair disappeared. Courtneay gasped and Blake got up and walked over to her and stuck his arm down beside hers and they all watched as his arm assumed the same color and pattern of the drapes as Dezza's did.

"Wow" Dezza exclaimed "I knew I wasn't the only one. This is so great." She walked away from the window and her color came back. "Now do you see what I mean about us being related?" "No" Courtneay shook her head "I don't."

"Well, go get the letters Court" Blake urged. It didn't take a second urge to get her on her feet and running upstairs as fast as she could. In less than 2 minutes she reappeared with a small metal box. "Here they are. I think" She tried to catch her breath. "Clear off the table" she said as she approached. Blake and Dezza swept the table contents onto the bar leaving the table clear.

Opening the box, she laid out the letters. The letters were dated. There were ten. Dezza opened her suitcase and took out a large envelope and laid her letters beside theirs. She also had ten. Courtneay matched up the letters from Elizabeth, Nora, Jewel, James and Viola which were just like Dezza's.

"Ok" Dezza said "You read the letters you have like mine. Then, I will read mine from Sarah, Viola's daughter, on down and then you can read yours from her sister Mary, also Viola's daughter."

"Let's see" she pointed out "See, there is the one from Elizabeth, who started it all. I think we should take turns reading them. This might take awhile. I need to use your bathroom first." Dezza stood up. Courtneay got up too, "Come on let's go up to my room first. You can use my bathroom. Bring your suitcase and I'll grab your back pack. Let's get comfortable."

The girls turned to go. "I'll make us some coffee. Do you drink coffee Dezza?" Blake offered. "Everyday" Dezza smiled as she started up the stairs "Thanks, I would love some. I think we'll need it."

Blake had everyone a cup of coffee poured when girls reentered the kitchen in their soft pj pants and tank tops. Dezza took her cup and curled her legs up into the chair. "Before we start, I just want to say thanks. You two didn't know me from Adam. And, I don't exactly look like I could be your relative. But you are both so nice." She blushed. Courtneay reached across the corner of the table and patted Dezza's hand. "What do you mean we don't look alike?" I think we look exactly like cousins". They both laughed.

Blake was silently looking at Dezza "I understand we have to read these letters to understand what is happening, but then, Dezza, you'll have to tell us how you found us. This is very bizarre." Dezza smiled "You don't know the half of it. Wait till you hear my letters." She grimaced and shrugged her shoulders.

"Ok," Courtneay took the first letter. "I'll start with Elizabeth." Courtneay read Elizabeth's journal and as she got up to refill her coffee cup, Blake read Nora's letter, stood up and walked clear around the room.

"This can't be happening." He sat back down frowning. "Here" Dezza took the next letter in line "I'll read this one." She read Jewel's letter. Courtneay, who had been standing up, picked up the next letter and read to them all about James. "I'll do Viola's" Dezza said.

"After this one, our family tree splits." Blake had gotten a large sheet of paper and had the list of ancestor's written down in date order and in a family tree format as they read the letters. "Look" he showed the girls. "Now the tree splits into three; Victor, Sarah and Mary. "Dezza are you from Sarah?"

"Yes, but her sister and brother did not know about my line. You'll see."

Courtneay held out her hand "Can I do that list?" Blake handed her the paper and a pen "I was hoping you'd do it. My writing isn't wonderful" Courtneay made a face. "Thanks Bro, you know I love doing this stuff." She put the paper flat on the table.

Dezza picked up the first letter and started to read.

"My Name is Sarah, it is 1891. I am 13. I am going to have a baby and am going to give it to someone on a

46

passing wagon train. The father of the baby is Won Sing. He is 15 and the son of the laundry man here in Santa Fe. Won Sing and I played as children together in the alleyway outside our house.

When I was 12, Won Sing found me taking out the trash in the late evening and forced his way on me. I did not tell anyone and as I grew in the stomach, I started wearing loose clothing and ate as little as possible. As the family is a busy one, and my father out of town a lot, I was able to hide my condition.

My baby is about to be born and there is a wagon train stopping outside of town. My family is so distracted, they do not know I am off in a neighbor's closed up barn and about to deliver my baby. My best friend Juanita Santos is with me to help me. She has helped her mother have a lot of babies. I will wrap the baby up and put it in a basket. I will cover the baby with sandwiches I make to sell to the wagon train passengers. I am writing this and putting it with the other letters I have from my Mother and her mother so that if I get someone to raise my baby they may have the history of our family as they will know sooner or later that it can turn colors, I pray whoever takes my baby will be understanding and loving.

I just had a baby girl. She is so pretty and little. Please tell my baby her mother loves her and regrets having to give her away. I think the town people here might take her from me and do something bad, I do not know what, to Won Sing. Please don't be mad at her for turning colors. Please read the letters to her. Sarah Martinez"

Dezza stopped and took a drink of her coffee. Looking at both of her cousins, she asked "Shall I go on?"

"Yes" Courtneay leaned forward. "Please."

She began.

"For my daughter Willow: My name is Madeline Straumberg. I am a seamstress in San Francisco. When I came out West, I drove my own wagon as I am an able bodied woman. As we were going through Santa Fe, New Mexico Territory, a very young girl asked if I had children.   "No," I replied "I wasn't blessed that way. But, if I did have a child, I would have wanted her to be just like you."   She took a chance and told me. "Look, I am 13 and I have just had a baby and no one knows. My father will kill me. I have shamed the family"

"Well, child," I asked "where is this baby?"   "Here" she whispered, pulling back the blanket revealing a small beautiful little sleeping face.   "I fed her some canned milk and she is sleeping. There are some cans here in the basket. "Please, will you take her??" Without hesitation, I quickly and quietly pulled the rest of the sandwiches off the baby's blanket onto the seat beside me and lifted the basket down behind the seat and wrapped the remainder of the sandwiches into a scarf I had laying there.

Reaching into my purse, I took out enough money to pay for the sandwiches and then a 50 dollar gold piece. I handed the money to her and quietly and resolutely whispered "We will tell no one about this," I looked deep into her eyes. 'I will raise your baby as my own. I will love her and care for her. You are not to worry about her. She is safe."

I reached for her hand and drew her into my arms. 'Go and be good and don't be with a man again until you are married. Ok?'   She held me close for a moment and then drew back   'Ok.' she answered 'There is a box in the basket. Please read what is in it and then give it to her when she is big.' Then quietly and quickly she ran off into the surrounding bushes.

48

The wagon train left town that morning. I named my new baby Willow; as she was so frail but could scream so loud. The wagon people were so wrapped up in themselves they really did know if I had the baby there or always had the baby. It all went well.

I started my business in San Francisco and became quite successful. My Willow, that is you daughter, grew up very quickly and into a very beautiful Oriental lady.

As soon as you were twelve, you could change the color of your skin at will and after reading the letters that your birth mother gave me for you, we decided that you must control this curse or blessing. You are quite proficient at it. I need to add this letter to the others as one does not know the day or hour of their death. Madeline"

"Do you want me to read?" Courtneay offered. Dezza shook her head yes.

"For my son LuSong. My name is Willow Straumberg Ming. I married Cho Ming when I was fifteen. My mother died when I was fourteen and Mr. Lou Ming, who had been our landlord suggested that I marry his son Cho. I didn't have any other options, however, I had always admired Cho and he has been very good to me. I told him about my curse and he laughed and called it a blessing.

We did not expect to have children to pass on this trait to, but we were careless and now we have our wonderful son LuSong. LuSong and I play at our gift. We undress and play hide and seek. Cho plays with us and teaches LuSong to be brave and strong and has taught him to control his turning colors. He says it will help LuSong in many ways someday.

I am adding this to my letters from my ancestors that have come before me. I am learning so much about the honoring of parents and ancestors. I would love to have known my birth mother. I am very fortunate that she made sure to send the letters with my mother when she gave me up. I pray that LuSong uses his gift wisely and is not harmed by it in any way. Willow 1922"

Dezza picked up another letter. Blake sat as still as possible taking all of this in.

Dear Eric, I am writing this for your collection of letters containing the history of our family gift. We are Chameleon. We turn colors. I wasn't going to have you learn of this until you were grown, but you beat me to it. At nine, you were changing and controlling your colorings. I have had fun and sorrow with this gift. I am planning on doing research of our family. I want to know the family of my grandmother that was in Santa Fe.

Please read the letters carefully and don't let the world know what you can do. We do not fully understand what is happening and don't want to bring attention to it. Use it wisely son. Your father LuSong Ming

Dezza handed Blake a letter. He cleared his throat and began

"1980   My name is Crissy March Ming. I was married to the late Eric Ming. He has been dead now for five years. We have a daughter, Moonshadow. She is sixteen and is fully aware of her gift passed down to her from her father. The letters will explain much better than I can. I have tried to help her control her turning colors and she is very good at it.

I also leave this warning. I think that maybe Eric was murdered by someone who thinks that his gift is a curse or a witchcraft thing. I do not believe that Eric jumped off the Bay Bridge on purpose. He was much too happy with me and our daughter.

Be careful daughter and hide this gift. LuSong, Eric's father was found in an ally hanged by his own belt on a sign post. His body had been burned. There was a cardboard sign pinned on his shirt with a picture of a lizard in a hangman's noose. Don't let anyone know what you are. Your loving mother."

Courtneay started to pick up the last letter, but Dezza had reached a second sooner and smiled at Courtneay as she started to read, choked up and handed it back to Courtneay.

"1999   Dearest Dezza.   Can you forgive me for passing on this thing to you? You know, the changing of the colors. Ha. You are such a good girl and I am so proud of how you have mastered this thing and even that you can play games with it. But darling, you must hide it. I do believe that there is a group of people out there that are out to get rid of all of us that have this thing. I have done some internet searching and have many possibilities for us to check out to find your other relatives.

I know there are more of us out there and I think you need to find and bond with them. If anything happens to me, be sure you keep the letters for your children and find your relations. Be careful my darling. Your mother Moonshadow."

Dezza sat very still. A lone tear escaped and slid down her cheek. "My mother, Moonshadow, died six months ago. She" Dezza looked down "She was killed." Blake and Courtneay sat up wide eyed. "How?" they both asked at the same time.   "I came home from school and found her. She was just laying on the swing out back on the porch. I thought she was asleep, but then when I tried to wake her, I saw that she had a small hole going into her chest. I tried to hold her and I saw the big hole in her back. She was dead."

Courtneay came over and put her arms around Dezza and held her tightly for a long time. The two cousins together felt the sorrow of losing a mother in a horrible way. Blake felt the agony of the moment, his heart broken too. Dezza leaned back. "I found that we share an ancestor, Viola Martinez, me through Sarah and you through her sister Mary Martinez Roll to Beth Darnell to Mercy to Judy and her twin crystal. Then from Judy to Windy Weber and thus to you. I really lucked out several times. It would be almost impossible if I hadn't lucked out. Or like my Mom would have said if God hadn't helped me."

"Let's read ours" Courtneay got up and picked up their letters. She went to Mary Martinez' letter and started reading. Blake picked up Beth's and read that one and then handed Mercy's to Courtneay. After that letter, Dezza held out her hand and Blake handed her Judy's letter.

Dearest Windy, You have read the letters I have saved for you. You know that you must be careful not to tell anyone what we are. You must not have children dear daughter. I know that you will want to be a mother, but you must not. I fear for your life and it is a horrid life being constantly worried about your child.

Windy, I have stayed apart from my own dear twin sister because I could not take a chance on someone finding us and killing us. I felt it was safer never finding her as we have led a quiet and hidden life. My mother was shopping in a local supermarket when a car that didn't have a driver smashed through the front of the store and killed her.

After my mother's funeral, my father just disappeared. Pastor Jerry Barnes and his wife Cara took Crystal and I went with Sally Parks from church as she was leaving for Colorado Springs. I met your father at the junior college and we married and though I tried not to get pregnant, I did and I am so happy you are my daughter, but I live in fear for you and for myself.

There is a man stalking me. I have seen him a lot of times and each time I find he is looking at me. If I go to the store, he is there. I have seen him on my street walking by our house. He looks like some kind of preacher. He wears a collar like a priest. Your father tells me I worry too much. He won't take me seriously. But, you must. You must be careful. Love, Your mother, Judy Weber.

"Is there one from your mother?" Dezza looked up at Blake. Courtneay answered. "No, she said she was going to write us a letter, but didn't. Her mother was killed. She was found in the alley behind her house. It was after my mother had gotten married and moved here to Albuquerque. She had been strangled and burned. There was a strange picture drawn on the garage wall right by her body. It looked like a lizard with its head in a noose."

"You should write your mother's letter for her. For a record." Dezza told her.

Blake put his face in his hands and leaned his elbows on his knees. He sobbed quietly for a few minutes then he wiped his face and drew in a deep breath. "We are in a nightmare" he said softly. The girls sat silently holding hands. Blake walked over to a box of tissue on a side table and blew his nose. He turned and looked at the girls. "I am so mad right now. We have to find the others, our relatives. We have to bind together. We have to go after them." Courtneay's eyes got wide. "How? We don't know who they are. We don't even know who our relative's are."

Dezza got up and took Courtneay's hand then reached out for Blake's. Blake allowed her to take his hand. "Cousins" She looked into each one's eyes. "We can find family. We can. I found you."

She smiled then let go of their hands pulled off her pjs and disappeared in front of the drapery. "We can and we will find the killers." Blake and Courtneay quickly stripped and both turned the colors of the couch and chair they were in. Courtneay giggled "I did it." The room looked empty. "One for all and all for one" Courtneay chanted sticking out her arm, the only part of a person that showed. "Got body?" she asked in a silly way. Soon the scene looked surreal as their pjs started appearing on unseen bodies.

53

"I'm tired" Courtneay yawned. "Please, let's go to bed." Blake and Dezza nodded without speaking and the three went upstairs. "So much for modesty" Courtneay said in a half whisper. "Like the bikinis you girls wear conceal anything?" Blake asked in a sarcastic way, not expecting an answer. Courtneay made and "eeeuu" kind of face. If the state they were in wasn't so crucial, she would have been in utter dismay undressing in front of her brother. As it was, there was not one naughty thought. Self preservation kicked into their every thought.

CHAPTER FIVE

October 14, 1908 Santa Fe, NM

The passengers departed train 54 onto the platform near the Harvey House in Santa Fe, NM. It was the dinner hour and dinner was being served in the main dining hall. Sixty-three passengers slowly made their way to the doors of the Depot. One lone Negro woman was allowed out of the train when all the others had gotten off. She was instructed by the conductor to go to the rear of the depot where she would find dinner in the kitchen area where Blacks were served.

Luz endured the degradation and walked calmly to the kitchen's rear door where she was met by a Black porter that ushered her in and to a table where a large group of Black people were already seated. They were the porters and maids from the train. They had gotten on where she had boarded the train in the East. The atmosphere was friendly and the food was good. Luz Mason ate her dinner in silence trying hard to enjoy it.

She was still in a state of shock after seeing her husband Ben Mason, at the Docks of New York, board a troupe ship bound for a war which she did not understand why he had to go fight or what they were fighting for or for whom. She knew that Ben said he knew he had to join and go. She had no choice but to accept this. She was on her way back to San Francisco where they had a small one room flat.

Ben had been a barber in the Black section of the city and they met at a dance in the St. Regis ballroom. Luz was mad about Ben. He was arrogant and suave and charmed Luz the very night they met. They were married the next night.

That was only six months ago. Ben decided he needed to broaden his experiences and this war he heard about seemed to be just the thing. No matter how much pleading, Luz couldn't stop Ben, so she went with him across country to New York where he got on the ship. She didn't even know where he had gotten the money for the train trip to New York and for her trip back. But he handed her a ticket and thirty dollars when he left.

Now, he was gone and she felt a million miles from the earth. There was no one back in San Francisco and no one at the docks in New York. She felt sick. She needed some air. Luz couldn't stand the thought of getting back on the train.

Then a conductor came into the kitchen area and informed them that the train would be delayed until tomorrow morning; as a crew had to replace some track up the road. He also told them that they could sleep in their seats on the train or there were two hotels in town that would take Black folk. One being the Arnold Hotel and the other was the Gretchen Suites.

Luz walked out onto the platform and started to head back toward the train. It was deserted. A chill wind blew across her shoulders sending a shiver down her back. Not wanting to be on the train by herself, she headed toward the main street in town. She might look at the hotels. As she walked she noticed two of the maids from the train walking arm and arm laughing. She followed slowly behind them.

They turned a corner and headed toward a large two story house, white with green gingerbread trim and a green picket fence. The sign was large and the words Gretchen Suites stood out in fancy carved letters. Luz followed the girls inside and waited as they talked to the clerk and each were handed a key. The girls started up the stairs when one noticed Luz. "Hey" She smiled at Luz, "You're the lady from the train?" "Yes" Luz smiled back. "Well," She grinned, "You get you a room honey and meet us back down stairs here. You can go with us." "And, where might that be?" Luz asked carefully. "Oh, it's a club, honey. You'll love it. Oh and It's safe for a lady." She looked at the other girl. "Or else we wouldn't go." She turned and went upstairs.

The desk clerk looked up at Luz. "Room?" "Yes, please. How much is a room?" she questioned. "Two dollars" he turned the register book towards her and held out a pen. "Fine" she said "Do I pay now or in the morning?" "Now" his expression didn't change. "Ok" she said pulling out a fold of bills she had put in

56

her skirt pocket. She kept only four dollars in her pocket at a time for safe keeping. The other money she had tucked in her corset; laced tight. She pulled two bills from the fold and handed them to the man. He in return handed her a key. "Two twelve" he nodded toward the stairs. Luz took the key and hurried up the stairs trying to slow herself down as she suddenly felt scared.

Once in with the door locked, she surveyed the room. It was quite nice actually. A white chenille spread and white lace curtains complimented the golden oak furniture. There was a pitcher with water and bowl and a little nook with a fancy chamber pot. Everything looked clean and neat. Luz was relieved. She looked out the window onto the street. There were people walking here and there. It looked like a nice town.

She was just about to take off her hat when there was a knock at the door. Carefully, she unlocked the door asking "Who's there?" "Me, Irene. The girl from downstairs." Luz opened the door. Irene bustled into the room. "Aren't these rooms nice?" She chirped. "We would love to have you go with us. Please come. It'll be alright. I promise." She seemed so sweet Luz felt her nervousness fade away. "Ok, I'd love to. If you'll wait for me downstairs, I just want to wash up a bit." Irene whished out the door "Ok, see you in a minute. Hurry."

Luz washed herself and rearranged her hair. She took two more dollars out of her corset and put them into her skirt pocket along with her rouge locket.

At the foot of the hotel stairs, Irene introduced Luz to Delphina. Delphina was a plumb girl with deep dimples and a sparkle in her eyes. Luz couldn't help but like her. The three ladies walked down to the end of the street and turned the corner where beautiful street lights adorned a wide street with wide strolling lanes on each side. In the middle of this block, there was an alleyway that was lined with brick. They came to a large wooden door. Delphina pushed the door open and inside was a very large room with tables, a long bar and a dance floor.

There were some people at tables eating, some sitting at the long bar and others on the dance floor enjoying the small band's music.   Luz noticed that there were White people, Mexican people and Black people all having a good time. She felt happy she was there. "This is more like back home" She told Irene. "Where is home?" Irene responded.   "San Francisco"   "I know what you mean" Delphina chimed in. "Man, back east, its Black part of this, Black part of that. Wait until Whitey is gone then you can go. I love this town."

The girls sat down and shortly a waiter came. "What will you have girls?"   Irene and Delphina ordered beer. Luz asked for a whiskey.   When the waiter came back, he told them the price and each girl paid for her drink.   Before they could drink two sips, a large Mexican man came over and asked Delphina to dance.   She didn't hesitate.   Irene was next when a Black porter she knew came and took her hand.   Luz sat very still, fear gripped her heart. "Oh Ben" she thought a little angrily "Where are you?"

She took another sip of her drink and as she put it down, she looked up into the most incredibly serious looking green eyes. The man was beautiful. Big green eyes, dark black hair that was combed back against its nature as some hairs found their way free and came down across his brow. A grin flashed large perfectly even white teeth.   "Victor Martinez" he introduced himself.   Luz blushed, "Luz Mason" She offered back. "I'm a married woman" she abruptly announced.   "Fine" he responded "I'm married too and I am not looking for a lover, just a dance partner."   Somehow she felt comfortable. "Fine" she said back "I would love to dance with you, but that is all, dance."

He took her hand and led her to the dance floor. A waltz had started and he held her close and they moved smoothly around the room. Luz melted in his arms wondering how he could smell so good.   His whole atmosphere engulfed her in a magical way. They danced four dances talking continuously and when they went back to the table the other girls were gone.

"Oh, my" she looked around the room trying to spot them, but they just weren't there.   "I have to go." She started for the door. "Come on" he took her elbow, "I'll walk you back to your room." She didn't resist. She didn't want to be alone. When

they got to the hotel, there was no one in the lobby.
turned to tell him goodbye as he had bent over to give
kiss. Their lips met and the world stood still.

Luz's eyes opened wide at the loud knock on her door. "Desk
clerk Mrs. Mason. The train will be leaving in an hour."
"Thank you" Luz replied looking around the room. "He's gone"
she thought relieved and mad at the same time. "What have I
done?" she chided herself. She quickly got up washed and
dressed and headed for the train. As she walked along the
street she expected to see him. But she didn't.

She boarded the train and as it pulled out of the station, she
turned looking back for as long as she could see the town.
Tears didn't stop rolling down her cheeks for a long time then
she fell into an uneasy sleep as the train screamed its way to
the West Coast.

October 10, 2009 Berkeley, California

Richard Bell stared out at the drizzling rain from his second
story college Dorm. Berkeley campus had rain water running
down every drain, over the sides of most gutters and some
lower elevation buildings were sand bagged against the
flooding. His fifth phone call to his Mother in Flagstaff didn't go
through. He knew they were being hit hard with an early snow.
Maybe their phone line was down.

He had just received a package from his mother and was
waiting to open it when he had her on the line. She loved to get
excited about him opening a present. He turned nineteen
today and although he talked to her almost every day, he
especially wanted to talk to her on his birthday.

His mother, Dawn Bell, had raised him alone since his father
Ron Bell was killed when he was 5 years old. Ron had gone
fishing with Dawn's father Bill Brown. They had gone to Lake
Mary, where, when reported missing, only their boat was found.
No bodies were recovered. It was never a closed issue with his
mother as she expected to see her husband and her father

come through the front door at any moment. He sat the package down and decided to go to the cafeteria for a bite.

As he entered the side door of the cafeteria a flying girl came barreling around the corner and ran straight into him. "Ouch!" he stepped back as the girl crumbled at his feet. "Ouch?" she yelled up at him. "I think I'm the one hurt here." Her short curly black hair framed a beautifully chiseled African American face. Her eyes were large, extremely green and seemed to crack lightening as she glowered up at him. "Here" he reached down his hand "Let me help you." She looked demure and reached for his hand then her demeanor changed in the twinkling of an eye. "Oh, thank you!" with that she grabbed his hand and at the same time swung her leg around and tripped him sending him sprawling against the wall of the hallway.

She was just about to get up and run when she saw his hand disappear. There, where only she could see, against the wall, Richard clear up to his rolled up sleeve, had turned the pasty yellow color of the wanes-coating. Even the pattern of the wall was on his arm. She squinted hard and looked again. He, quick to her gaze, tightened up his arm and it returned to its right color. Richard stood up quickly and turned to leave the building, "It's been fun running into you, whoever you are. Goodbye" he threw over his shoulder. "Wait!" she yelled at him but by now he was running across the courtyard and into his dormitory.

She followed him in but there was no one there. He had taken the stairwell up to his floor and quickly entered his room and locked the door, chiding himself for letting his color change. "Man, I hope she forgets what she just saw" he thought angrily at himself.

Just then the land line rang. "Hello" he answered. It was the Dean of Students asking him to please come to his office. Thinking that this girl had gone to the Dean, he put on a long sleeve shirt and a jacket and left by the back staircase. It only took two minutes to cross over to the administration building. "Yes sir?" he asked as he entered the Dean's office. "Hello Richard" the Dean stood up and made an indication that Richard should sit on the large soft sofa that he had against the wall. Richard looked at the chair at the desk and then the sofa. He shrugged his shoulders and complied. When he had settled into the big overstuffed couch, the Dean came over and sat in the chair beside the sofa. "Richard" he started looking him straight in the eye.

"I have some bad news for you." Richard started to get up. "No, no, just sit there" the Dean said softly. Richard's eyes connected with Dean Simmon's eyes as he heard this kindly man tell him that his mother was dead. "How can this be?" he thought "It's my birthday. She isn't dead. She can't be".

"What?.. I mean what happened?" he put out his hand in the air. Simmon took his hand and gently laid it back down "Richard it seems there was a house invasion. The police told me it looked like someone broke in and tried to assault your mother. She fought back but she was killed. I need to know who it is that you will have back in Flagstaff that can help you take care of your mother's funeral and estate."

"Just me" Richard looked up into the dean's eyes. "Just me. My father is dead too."

"Ok, Richard" the Dean went back around his desk. 'I'm going to arrange for you to get out of classes and take care of whatever you need to do. Do you have a friend here that can go with you?"

"No, no one that can spare time off."

Richard felt surreal and he sank back in the sofa. He looked down at his hand. His fingers had turned a beigy color with white streaks across them. He quickly put them under his leg. "Not now," he told himself, "Not now." He couldn't let the Dean see him color. He had to stay strong. He could cry later. He stiffened himself up inside.

"I'm sorry Richard. If there is something else you need, please just give me a call or come by." The Dean held out his hand. Richard got up and shook his hand and numbly left the office.

Not remembering how he got back to his room, he looked at the telephone and realized he would never be able to call her again. He had to get home. He had to find out what happened. He threw some clothes and his toiletries into a small suitcase and sat down to call the Amtrak Station. He found out that the train would leave at six in the morning and take until the following morning to get home.

He called the Flagstaff police department and found out where his mother was and that nothing would need to be done until he got there the next day. Richard just sat on the bed for several hours feeling the loss and the emptiness. He then watched the news and whatever else was on he didn't seem to know, he was in a state of shock. They had been so close, everything to each other.

Morning found Richard, sitting at the window, waiting for it. The room soon filled with the sun's brightness. He had not gone to bed and had been sitting there in the darkness with the package his mother had sent laying on his legs. As the room brightened enough for him to see the writing on the package, he took out his pin knife and carefully cut the tape from the package. Laying back the wrappings, he found a plastic box with letters inside. The first letter he pulled out was in his mother's handwriting.

"My Dear Richard,   This box has the letters from your ancestors. There are nine letters, other than my own. Please read them carefully and keep them in a safe place for your children. Read them first, then finish this letter."

Looking through the letters, he made sure of their order, and then turned the letters upside down on his knees, the last being his mother's. He turned the first letter over. It was Elizabeth's journal. Then he read Nora's letter.

Glancing at the clock, he put down the letters and hurried and got dressed, put the letters into his overnight bag, grabbed his jacket and left for the train.   It took him just twenty minutes to get to the Amtrak station. He went to the line for tickets being picked up. Soon he was on the train. He found a seat at the end of one of the cars that only had two seats facing the wall of the stairwell. He put his back against the window and his feet up on the second seat to assure his privacy.

After the train had pulled out of the station and he was sure he wouldn't have another passenger sitting near him, he went to the snack bar and bought several sandwiches, two sodas, two bags of chips, a candy bar and a bag of peanuts.

Settling into his seat he pulled his bag up on his lap and pulled out the box of letters. Gently he placed Elizabeth's and Nora's letters on the bottom of the stack and read Jewel's, James' and then Viola's letters.

He was engrossed in the letters when his stomach growled rather loudly. He rested the letters on his lap and began to eat his food stash. After downing the first soda and eating the sandwiches and one bag of chips, he picked up the letters. The next one was on a faded brown coarse paper and it was signed Victor Martinez.

"To my Daughter Lillie, As I have told you over the years little one, you are a Chameleon and have to be very careful with your gift. There is someone out there that wants to kill us all. I haven't got a grip on what is going on.

My mother, Viola, had gone for a visit to see my sister Mary. She and Mary were somehow locked in Mary's clothing store and it was set on fire. Someone did this purposely. There was painting on the sidewalk in front of the store and words that said "Die Witch." The painting was of a hanging lizard and there were two initials J.W. beside it. Mary's daughter Beth gave me this information. The police have no clues who did it, but Beth and I both think that it was murder and because they were both Chameleon. Yes, that is what we are. The only initials I know of, that are J.W., are in our great Grandmother Nora's letter. Joshua Wells was the preacher that had her hanged.

Pass these letters on to your children if you have any. Learn to control your gift even better then you have in

63

the past and tell no one of it.   I had another sister Sarah. Sarah did not have any children which I think a blessing. It would have been hard on a child as Sarah hanged herself. Her husband said she was always sad but did not agree that it was suicide.

Your father Victor Martinez"

He pick up the next, it was on a light blue silky paper.

"To my dear Son Rudolph.   You are getting married tomorrow and I need to put these things in writing to you along with the other six letters.   They have to be kept together and passed on to your children.

I know your Sarah will be accepting of your Chameleon traits and I pray she helps you conceal your abilities and teach your children to do the same. My father was always watching and waiting for something bad to happen to us.

We stayed away from any church where the pastor wore a clerical collar.   We did go to a little church called Wayside Chapel where the preacher was a woman.   It was a good time in the fellowship of the people of that church. I urge you to go to church, but be very careful to find out all about it.   If they have any secret type of society, beware of it.

My father moved us to Arizona when I was only four and he became a lumberjack in the White Mountains. When I was sixteen, my father was killed in a logging accident. Somehow the straps of the truck holding the logs he had just loaded were severed and they all came down on him. The foreman told my mother that there was a stranger looking around the property that day; a man wearing a clerical collar.   There was no other information.   But my mother and I are sure he was murdered.

They taught me well how to use my gift and I have strived to teach you the same. I am sorry if I seemed overly harsh, but I love you so much, I had to make sure you never let anyone see what you can do. God gave us these gifts maybe for a trial. Be sure it is used for His good and not for worldly gain. We are not witches, we belong to God. We must be the good people. Use it well. With all my love, Lilly Brown."

Richard yawned and stretched but hurriedly picked up the next letter.

"To my son Bill… As you have read in the other seven letters, you are what we are and were. I know I am hunted as my ancestors were hunted and at some point, upon carelessness, I might be killed. My mother was murdered as she stepped outside to pick up the morning paper. A car drove by and someone shot her. A neighbor saw the shooter and said it looked like a preacher with a clerical collar.

So I write my letter while you are still a baby. I will teach you and harshly as my mother taught me, how to use your gift and how to conceal it from the world. If I don't live to see you grown, these letters will be in safe keeping for you. Be on the offensive son. Start trying to find out who it is that is hunting the Chameleon.

That is us; a clade, a certain sect of the animal that bit our ancestor Elizabeth. There must be a lot of us. I know that my Grandfather Victor had two sisters; Sarah and Mary. I don't think Sarah had children, but don't know that for a fact. Mary had children. Find her family. Get together with others of our kin. See if they are Chameleon. Don't let them get our family. Go after them; whoever they are that are killing us. As long as I live I will try to gather information of our family. I don't know why my father and grandmother didn't leave anything of our family other than the letters. There must be a way to find them. Try Bill. Your father, Rudolph"

After Rudolph's letter, Richard sat looking out the window eating a candy bar. When he finished he pulled out a typewritten letter.

"Dear little Dawn, It's you and I daughter. You are just two days old. Your mother, my sweet Jeanie is gone. She tried hard to live and be with you, but her heart just couldn't do it. The doctor said she shouldn't have gotten pregnant. We did not know. We thought long and hard about having a child, because of the Chameleon trait on my side of the family, but she so wanted a baby and was understanding about the gift. It is a dangerous gift and I selfishly wanted a child.

And now sweet daughter, you are not only without a mother, but you have a gift, or is it an affliction and a dangerous sign on your back? I have found out a lot of things about our family that was not shared in the nine letters that I have saved for you. I have found out that my Grandfather's sister Mary's daughter Beth had a daughter Mercy and Mercy had two girls, Judy and Crystal. Crystal lives in Sonora, California. This took a lot of letter writing to the newspapers and county court houses.

Someday, I hope you find out. My father lives in fear for his life and though he is still alive as is my mother, I fear for them and myself, too. We live two houses apart and will share in raising you. I will keep trying to find out more about our family tree. Your Daddy, Bill"

Richard then tenderly returned to his mother's letter and began to re-read her letter. A tear carved a shiny streak down his cheek. He didn't notice. His eyes reddened by the sentiment were vibrantly green; a mirror image of the eyes of the girl who had ran into him in the cafeteria.

My Dear Richard, This box has the letters from your ancestors. There are nine letters, other than my own. Please read them carefully and keep them in a safe place for your children. Read them first, then finish this letter. You already know all of this, but you need to have these things written.

There is evidently danger being one of us. Our ancestors have been killed for being Chameleon and someone or ones are out to exterminate us. It is someone who represents the church or is using the church clothes to trick the authorities.

My Grandfather Rudolph was killed when his foot slipped on a curb in the city and he fell under a bus. Or, was he pushed? We don't know. I don't know for sure, but am suspicious of your father and my father's death. I don't say disappearance anymore as I know they are dead. If they were not they would have come back. I think they were killed. Several weeks before they went fishing, a man came to our door saying he was a preacher and was wondering if we would visit his church. He asked questions that seemed out of the ordinary. I felt very uncomfortable even though he was wearing a clerical collar. He kept looking at my arms and hands. I was very careful not to tell him anything personal, and was quite aware of knowing I must not turn colors. He had evil eyes. You must not let anyone know about your abilities.

I did find a Connie Benson in Wyoming. I wrote to her, but as yet did not get an answer. You can use your computer to find her and see who else is in our family and if they are Chameleon. Your Grandfather said to be on guard. I urge you to be on the defense but then to find out who is killing and stop them. Find the other members of our family, our Clade. Find them and band together. Don't be a victim. Our ancestors did not know what to do, but you are smart. Figure it out.

I felt I must send you this bunch of letters now as I don't know what the future will be. I feel God is leading me. I pray always for you, Son, and I wanted you to know, today, how very much I love you. Be brave and stay alive.

67

Your mother and sincerest friend, Dawn"

Putting the letters back into the box, he carefully placed the box at the bottom of his overnight bag. He took out his iPod, put on his earplugs and lay back listening as the sweet loudness of the Concord Blue Devils Drum Corps covered every thought of the letters. The drums rolling and the horns screaming washed away time and space making the trip to LA go fast.

He boarded the cross country train and soon was settled in a comfortable lounging-type seat for the trip from LA to Flagstaff. He looked forward to sleeping and forgetting. Too much for him to think about. Too much to consider and sort out. He already knew a lot of what he read from his mother telling him all these years, but he never had them all converging on him at one time. He felt sick to his stomach. He decided to take two antihistamine pills to help him sleep. He had some pizza at the train station and was feeling comfortable and was getting sleepy before they even got out of the LA station.

As his body relaxed and his head was just making a comfortable agreement with the pillow, a voice intruded his reverie. "Is this seat taken?" He didn't even look away from the lights outside winking as the train sped by. "No". He murmured. He was aware of a presence sitting beside him, but he didn't want to move away from his comfortableness to find out who was sitting by him. He kept his eyes closed and was just starting to drift off.

"Where are you going?" a small voice seemed to whisper loudly to him." He took a deep breath, sighed and turned toward the voice. "I…" he was looking into the same finely chiseled face of the small Black girl that had flattened him in the cafeteria yesterday. "Me. I'm the girl who ran into you." He smiled as he realized how small and gentle she seemed now against the whirlwind Kung Fu fighter she was yesterday. "Yes, I know. Am I dreaming, or are you on this train going to Arizona?"

"I'm here" she smiled and reached over and pinched his arm. "See?" I'm here" Her little Cheshire smile seemed to calm his being. She seemed familiar. He took in the sight of her. Petite, that's what he would call her and then he thought of the awful thud in which he hit the cafeteria floor under her Karate-type tactic.

"Where are you going?" he asked.   "With you." Now her smile seemed a little mysterious. "With me?" he smiled back at this ridiculous statement. "And where do you think I'm going?" he questioned her.   "Flagstaff" she said quietly. Then she bent over toward the aisle and looked both ways very slowly like she was expecting to see someone. "How did you know that? Who are you?" he asked

She reached out her tiny hand   "Hi, I'm RuDee and I'm your fourth removed half cousin." She sat back keeping her eyes on him.   He just stared at this incredulous statement. "Fourth removed half-cousin" he said very slowly. He held out his arm "I'm White. You look like you're Black. Are you?"   She put her hand on his arm. "Your great-great-great Grandfather was half Mexican.   He is also my great-great-great Grandfather Victor Martinez. His wife, your third great Grandmother was White and my third great Grandmother, his one night stand, was Black. Thus, you be you and I be me" she said in an exaggerated slang.

Richard sat back, drew in a big breath and sighed. "Why not?" he thought.   Everything else sounds like a fairy tale."   He looked at her. "I suppose you have letters?"   thinking of his. She grimaced and nodded.   "Just five, but I am guessing you have more. Is that right?"   He nodded, his head swam.   He felt exhausted.

He wished he hadn't taken the antihistamine. He wanted to go to sleep and at the same time he wanted to be alert and ask questions.   "I took some antihistamine…" he started when she interrupted "Let's sleep awhile, ok? I am so tired. We can talk later."   She unrolled a large puffy quilt that miraculously had been folded down into a very small space. "Here" she said as she spread it over the both of them. "I hate trains, they are so cold."   He didn't resist. It felt and smelled incredibly good. He closed his eyes and sleep rescued him from the mindboggling day he was having.

"Come on" a familiar voice brought him into consciousness. "We are at the station." Richard looked up in to the friendly green eyes of his 4th removed half cousin. He chuckled at the funniness of it all. He grabbed his bag and followed RuDee down and out of the train onto a snow covered platform.

"Burr" she complained as she slipped into her coat. "Don't you have a coat?" she asked him. "I left in such a hurry. I'll have one at my house. Come on." He led her into the terminal. He went over to the ticket agent. "Could you call a taxi for us?" The station master pointed at the front doors. "They're out there."

RuDee followed him out to the front entrance where he waved at a driver who immediately got out and opened the door for them. As they climbed in, Richard told him "its 4881 LaMont." The cab driver nodded and they took off. RuDee kept quiet as the driver enlightened Richard on the weather forecast and what had happened.   It seems like an early winter had descended on them leaving a foot of snow way before they were used to snow.

Upon exiting the cab, Richard paid the driver and walked up and past the front door to a bush and bent over, uprooted a large red clay pot and pulled out a mud coated key. After carefully wiping it off on a patch of snow, he inserted it in the door and led RuDee into a dark hallway.

The house seemed immense to RuDee.   It was a two story house with the entrance and living room two stories high. The bedrooms and an open hallway were on the sides of the house with Swiss Chalet looking windows and archways looking down on the living room. A round stairway in the side of the living room was evidently the way upstairs.

The house was cold and dark. Richard found his way to the switches by the door and light flooded the premises. "Wow" RuDee exclaimed "This is beautiful." Richard smirked hiding his real thoughts of hurt and pain of his mother not being there.

It was still dark at 6am. The sun would be peeking over the houses soon. "Come on." he led her into the kitchen. "Let's

make some coffee."   RuDee didn't wait to be asked, she
spotted the coffee pot and started to figure it out. "Here"
Richard said   "I'll do it." He pulled out a canister and filled the
top with coffee and then put water in the carafe and poured it
into the coffee maker. Soon the aroma permeated the air. He
then went to the fireplace and put a match to the papers under
the logs. The fire had already been built. His heart hurt thinking
that his mother had made that fire. The papers lit instantly
throwing flames on all sides of the logs and soon a roaring fire
warmed the room and the fireplace fan seemed to send it
hurdling through the house.

He turned and went to the refrigerator. "Well," he thought out
loud "we have breakfast foods here."   "I can cook Richard."
RuDee said. "Will you let me? Then we can talk." He nodded.
"I'll be back, I need to look at some things."

"Go ahead, I'll get the breakfast. Where is the bathroom?"

He pointed to the area behind the kitchen and then headed up
the spiral staircase.

Entering his bedroom, he put down his bag and used his
bathroom. Then he went to his mother's room but the door was
taped off. He started to tear down the tape and go in, but
something stopped him. He turned around sick to his stomach
and went back to the kitchen.

"RuDee" he said as he watched her pile a huge portion of
scrambled eggs on two plates already sporting toast with butter
and jelly. Juice had been poured and two cups of coffee sat by
the plates. "My mother was murdered here, just day before
yesterday. Do you or can you stay here? "   RuDee came over
and took his hand. "Richard, I came here for a purpose. I am
used to tragedy. I am here on a mission. Of course I can stay
here and I am going too, until we figure out what to do. OK?"
He nodded and she indicated he should sit. His hunger took
lead over his queasiness and he ate.

Their empty stomachs taken care of, RuDee and Richard sat
back with a second cup of coffee. "Ok RuDee" Richard
started, "Why are you here?"   "I have these" she reached into

her large sack-type purse and pulled out a large zip-lock bag of papers. These are my letters. I felt confident you had letters. We need to share our letters. We need to bind together Richard, or we are going to die." A shudder when up his spine. He had really never felt scared of anything, but her voice, his mother's death, his family background all fell in on him. "Ok. I'll go get mine."

He bounded up the stairs and in a moment was back with his box of letters. "Ok" he asked" Where do we begin?" "Well," RuDee started "How far back do your letters go?" "To the beginning" he said rather softly.

"And how far back is that?" RuDee asked her demeanor looked drooped. In fact, Richard thought she was going to cry. But then she straightened herself. "It began with our Ancestor Elizabeth Stockton Norris. She was bitten by a Chameleon." He made a mock Arabic bow "And thus, we are." His brow furrowed "You are, aren't you?" He realized she had not said she was a Chameleon." RuDee reached out and put her arm next to his and almost instantly it turned the light color of his arm exactly. He seemed to see two of his own arms. She made a fist and her arm turned back to the black skin that was her's. "Ok" he breathed in deeply "I take that as a yes. So," He pulled out his letters "We will start at the beginning.

Tears were coming down RuDee's cheeks. "It's like putting a piece into a puzzle, a piece that you thought you would never find." Richard relaxed in her presence and reached for her hand. He held it tight for a moment. "Listen, little cousin, we are together; at the start of putting a great puzzle together. One that our Grandfathers have insisted we do." They grinned at each other taking in the awesome feeling of family just found.

"Come on" Richard picked up all his papers "let's sit by the fire." RuDee followed him into the living room with her's. They got comfortable on the large leather sofa. RuDee snuggled in close. It was strange how they felt so comfortable with each other; like they had known each other forever. Richard put Elizabeth's letter on top and started to read. RuDee sat as still as mouse as he read that letter and then when he got through reading Nora's letter, tears were streaming down all four cheeks. It was a feeling that only a handful of people will ever feel, reading the testimony and letter of someone who was hanged for changing colors.

"How about a coke?" Richard put down the letters. "Ok" RuDee answered "I need a small break from this. It's almost too much to take." Richard was gone only for a moment and he returned with two large mason jars filled with ice and coke. "Thanks" She gratefully accepted the drink. "RuDee, what about you? Can you tell me about you?" She grinned. "Let's wait, ok? Until we finish all the letters and then we can tell each other our own stories. Is that ok with you?" "Yeah" Richard nodded and settled in with the letters. "Here goes."

He picked up Jewel's letter and handed her James'. "You can read the next one after I read this one." He read Jewels and then RuDee read James'. Viola's letter was next and as Richard finished, he handed Victor's to RuDee "Here, this is where we get tied together." He laughed "This is so weird. If I smoked, I would probably be pacing back and forth lighting one after another. However, since I don't have that vice, I'll just drink coke and coffee one after another." RuDee laughed at the silliness. It was needed in this awkward crazy moment. She took the letter and read it. "He didn't even know about my great great Grandmother. Not even a notion that he had impregnated the lady he took to bed that night." Richard raised his shoulders in a hopeless sign.

"Oh well," She sighed. "Ok, yours or mine?" "Yours" Richard sat up. "I think you have known much more about me than I have about you." "Ok" RuDee pulled her letters out of the bag. Here is the first one.

"To my daughter Martha, I know I have to write the truth to you. I hope I don't have to be alive when you know it. But, if I am , I am. You were born in 1909. You father Ben Mason is not your real father. Ben went off to war and I saw him off. Then on my way home to San Francisco, I stopped in Santa Fe. We had to spend the night as the train was waiting on track to be laid. I went to a dance hall with several other women, just to have a drink and maybe dance. I was feeling so lost and lonely, not knowing if my husband, Ben, would ever come home. The girls I went with seemed to disappear and suddenly a large beautiful Mexican man with beautiful white teeth was there asking me to dance. I told him I was married. He said he was married too, but just wanted to dance. I was pulled to his person like a giant magnet. He made me forget my loneliness and nothing in the world seemed to matter with his arms around me. If he had asked me to go off into a foreign land with him right then, I would have gone. Right off a cliff, I would have gone. Instead, we went back to my room where we spent a magical night together. Two strangers and yet we felt more like one person than any two people could feel.

When I awoke, he was gone. I looked for him all the while I walked back to the train, but he was nowhere. I left and went back to San Francisco my whole being still warm with his touch. It was only a month later that I found out I was pregnant. Not knowing who the father was until I had you. Then you were here and there was that incredibly deep dimple in the middle of your chin and those fabulous green eyes.

Ben didn't come back from the war until you were two and after many letters I had written about you, he was excited to be a Papa. He always said you had a dimpled chin because you were kissed by an angel before you came out of the oven. He loved you so much. Even when you started to turn colors, we both thought you had a serious ailment, but our doctor said it was a rare skin pigmentation disease. He thought he had heard of a similar case in San Francisco, but wasn't familiar with the case. He said it didn't matter as you were healthy. I watched as you would get mad or excited or even happy, you would turn the colors of whatever you were near. One of the old women on our street said that it was a sign of the Devil, but we told her she was crazy. We worked with you until you were able to control your ailment and you were quick to learn and loved to tease us with it. You would strip down and hide from us. It was fun, but scary.

Once a teacher in your school told me that a man, a pastor of some kind came asking if any of the children could turn colors. She said she told him "No, of course not." She said she did not like his eyes and she did know about you turning colors and thought it was better that he did not know anything about you or any of the children, for that matter.

I am also writing this letter because you must have inherited this trait from your real father. His name is Victor Martinez. He doesn't even know you exist. If something happens to me, you could probably find Mr. Martinez in Santa Fe, New Mexico. I am sorry you had to learn about your heritage this way. I did not even write this letter until after your Papa died. He would have been crushed. I think that you might have some half brothers and sisters somewhere and sometime you might want to find them. However, I do ask that you be careful and not tell anyone about your ability to turn colors. You Mother, Luz Mason."

"Wow" Richard bent toward her to see the letter. "My third great Grandfather was a womanizer. That old goat." "I think my third great Grandma had something to do with it too." RuDee smirked, "They sure had a one night stand to beat all one night stands. I guess we had better not put blame anywhere." She frowned, "Want me to go on?" "Yes" Richard stood up and made himself comfortable again. "We can't stop now.

RuDee started

"Dear Daughter Rita, My little lizard. We are a couple of lizards, aren't we? We have had fun with this trick we can do. I am writing this my Rita so that you can have a record and pass down the letter along with your Grandma's letter to your children. It is an interesting life we lead and you will lead. But, you must be careful who you let know about the trick. Someone might think you are evil and do something bad to you.

Read your Grandma's letter and mine and make a letter for your children. We are not evil. We love God and He loves us. Do good with your ability to change color. Don't ever use it for evil my dearest little girl.

My Papa died when I was 10 and then my mother took the Diphtheria and died when I was eighteen. I married your father Sam Tyrell and we had you. Sam was very sweet to us and was not angry or upset about what we can do. But he did warn us that he had heard of someone looking for people that could turn colors like a Chameleon lizard. He said the man wore a clerical collar and told people he would pay twenty dollars for the identity of anyone who could or did do that. One day as I bought meat at Oldson's meat market, I saw a man with a clerical collar watching me. I was very nervous and my hand turned the color of the ground beef that the butcher had put up for me to inspect. I quickly righted myself and the color went away, but the man saw it. He didn't say anything. I hope he did not really see it. Be careful as it could happen at any time. Be on your guard. I love you, your mother, Martha."

RuDee picked up another and continued

"Dear Shirley, This is a letter to be kept with your other letters and given to your children. You shouldn't have children, but you probably will. You already know your gift and have mastered it well. I must reinforce, that you must not let anyone know. It is dangerous. There is someone out there that wants us dead. That is we Chameleon people. Don't let anything make you think you are evil. It is nothing that you did. We just have a genetic quirk and that is all, however, some don't think so. I think they are the ones that killed my dear mother. She was walking home from shopping when she was struck and killed by a car that disappeared. No one was found. My father said that he was sure someone was out to kill her and maybe me. He made sure that I did not display my gift and that I was tough enough not to fall into using it. He changed our names and address to keep me hid. We used to be Radcliff, but then we went by Johnson. I don't think whoever killed my mother knows about me or where I am. Be careful and safe my sweet one. Your mother, Rita."

RuDee continued

"To Bob, You are a marvel to me, son. You can manipulate your gift so well. I have enjoyed raising you and having fun with our gift. You have somehow had the savvy enough to know it is a dangerous gift and that someone wants to wipe us out, even though it is just something in our system. Your father is in agreement with me. He has been my tower of strength, after God that is. I expect I will be killed, it seems like all of us get killed. My great grandmother, grandmother and mother were killed. My mother was found dead in her car in the garage.

The Police said it was a suicide, but we know better. She wouldn't do that. And she wasn't strong enough to pull the garage down shut. Dad always had to do that. I hope we can keep secret enough to escape the wrath of whoever this is that is killing us. As you read in the letters, our family tree is unknown to our great great great Grandfather. I know that he must be the tie-in to this phenomenon.

I hope you find your half cousins and band with them for safety. I don't know how to start to do this, but I am sure you can somehow. I know you are smart. Try to find them and to find out if anyone knows how this started and if they are still alive or if they too have been killed. I think you should be aggressive in finding these things out. You are the hope for our future children. Please be careful with yourself and remember that the God who made you doesn't make mistakes. Do good for Him. Love, Mother, Shirley Tyrell Swann."

Richard gently took the next letter from her hands and began.

"To RuDee. Dear One. Your mother and I are leaving you with Mrs. Marshall. I can't take the chance of bringing the killing force near you. I wasn't able to save my mother. You know she was found hanging from a bridge and her body had been burned. I am afraid I won't be able to save you, being with you I will only draw the evil to you. You are still so small, but you do know your genetic twist. I have been purposely hard on you. I have instructed for you to take the martial arts. You must be able to protect yourself from the enemy. Also I have left funds for you to take serious computer skills so you can find our family and bond with them for safety.

You have the letters and know just what we know. I will keep in contact with you, but carefully. You must be strong and take charge of your own safety. Mrs. Marshall does not know you can change colors. I hope you never let her in on our secret. You must keep the secret RuDee. You must be strong. Watch out for men in clerical collars. Go to the church I have taken you to or one that has no secret societies within it. Remember, the Gospel has no secrets. It is all out in the open. Stay close to your friends, but never let them know what you are. Never. I tried to find out more about Victor Martinez in New Mexico, but haven't found anything. It is up to you. Do not have children. Don't... Your Father, Bob Swann"

"There it is" RuDee turned and laid her stack of letters on the ones that Richard had laid down. "What happened to your father, RuDee?" Richard asked. "I don't know" RuDee answered, tears coming to her eyes "He and Mom just left me there and I haven't heard from them since."

Richard patted the paper and pulled his from underneath her's and sat down on the floor beside them. "Ok, I'll read the ones I have. He proceeded to read his letters to RuDee. When he finished his mothers, RuDee leaned into his chest and he put his arm around her. "Well Cousin, we begin the offensive, I think." RuDee nodded her assent. "Come on Cuz" He changed the mood to a lighter note "Let's take a walk, then, I have to go to the police department and see about my Mom." Somehow, having RuDee there made the pain lessen as he thought about his mother.

RuDee sat on a park bench just across the street from the police station waiting for Richard to finish up his business regarding his mother. She had purchased a local newspaper and was enjoying an apple she had brought from the house, when she noticed a man standing at the corner by a mail box at the foot of the police station stairs. A shiver went up her spine. She shook her shoulders, regained her composure and lifted the paper up to her face pretending to read.

The man didn't seem to look her way at all. Comfortable in herself that he would not put Richard and her together, she stayed in the seat and waited for a few minutes, then carefully folded the paper, threw away her apple core into the trash can near the park bench and slowly crossed the street to the drug store.

Once inside, she walked over to the magazine section in front of the store. She could see the man clearly without being spotted. Her mouth became very dry. A small boy about seven was looking at a comic book next to her and when she looked his way she noticed his eyes pointed directly at her hand. Looking down, she saw that her hand had turned the color of the Ladies Home Journal she had been touching.

Quickly, she stiffened and the color went away. The boy started to walk toward her when a lady grabbed his arm "Don't you ever walk away from me in a store" she scolded "You know better than that." "Mom" he squealed "I saw something. " "Come on" she pulled harder as her step quickened, completely ignoring his statement.

RuDee looked back across the street. The man had disappeared and Richard was just walking out of the station and coming across the street to the park bench where she had been. She didn't dare go out. She scanned the street and saw a green car sitting just around the corner opposite the store she was in. It looked like the man she had seen. Richard looked around for a moment then started walking north in the direction of his home. The green car drove slowly by him and continued on down the street.

When she was sure that the man in the car couldn't see Richard anymore, she quickly ran and caught up with him grabbing his arm "Come on" she whispered urgently. Richard caught the tension in her voice and followed without question. RuDee pulled him into a clothing store that was full of teenage girls and guided him to the back of the building. Grabbing a couple of blouses, RuDee asked the counter girl "Can I try these on?" The lady nodded and pointed to the dressing rooms.

"Come on" RuDee still had his hand and drew him into the stall with her. "I can't come in here " he objected. "Shhh" she put her finger to her lips. She sat him down on the stool in the dressing room. "There was a man watching you" she whispered "with a clerical collar. He drove by you, too." "Did he see you?" Richard's eyes had widened "No, I really don't think he connected the two of us. We have to get out of town Richard. He knows who you are. He was probably the one who killed your mother."

Silence engulfed the stall. RuDee peeked through the crack in the door and immediately her hand in an uncontrolled reflex pushed Richard, stool and all, into the corner of the stall. "It's him" She mouthed. Richard stayed in the corner of the stall with his feet up on the sides of the stool.

RuDee stood in front of the stall door, which was a good foot above the floor. She let one side of one of the blouses hang down from her hand and she scuffled about like she was trying on clothes. She turned and peeked out carefully just in time to see the man leave the store. "Boy, that was close" she whispered.

"We have to go Richard." RuDee stuck her head out and motioned to the clerk to come and when the lady had come to the door of the dressing room, RuDee screwed up her face and in a timid little voice "Hi, I have just had my monthly time surprise me and I have a big spot on my jeans." The girl showed signs of sympathy. RuDee continued, "Is there a back door? My boy friend can walk behind me. I am so embarrassed." She looked at the lady in a pleading way. "Sure, honey" the lady comforted "Just go through that back door when I wave at you. I have to go up to the counter to push the release button on the lock. You stay here until I do. And good luck." She winked at RuDee. RuDee thanked her and shut the door but kept peeking out. As soon as she saw the lady hold up her hand, RuDee scanned the store. No man. Then she walked out toward the back door with Richard following a couple of inches behind her.

Once outside in the alley, Richard took over. "Come on, I know this town." He led her up the ally and through a fence that led in to an automotive repair shop that had been empty for years. Crouching down they went around the side and after checking the vicinity he grabbed her hand and whispered loudly "Run" they ran across the street and down into another alley. This alley turned off into two alleys. Richard led her in and out of alleyways, backyards and soon they were in the alley outside his house. After carefully going through the back fence gate, they went to the side of the house that was covered with shrubs and unkempt bushes. Peeking through, RuDee spotted the car parked in front of the house about three doors down.

"There he is." RuDee nodded up the street. "Ok" Richard whispered "We'll sneak in and get our stuff then we'll push the car out of the garage and go down the alley. Then, maybe we can decide what we're doing." On hands and knees without turning on a light, Richard went from room to room picking out papers, treasures and things he thought he might need. They methodically piled their things by the back door occasionally checking on the man in the green car. He seemed to be settled in and waiting for Richard to get home.

"Richard" RuDee whispered "we need to strip down in case he comes up to the door. We have to hide from him." Richard nodded. Quickly they took off all their clothes except their underwear. "Start turning" he whispered. RuDee grinned and almost immediately disappeared from his sight. He squinted and was able to just see her black panties which were skimpy at that and a small sliver of a bra that looked like it was laid against the wallpaper in the dining room. "Good" he said admiringly as he himself disappeared from her sight as she could only see the hallway. 'You too" she whispered. "Let's hurry."

Richard took his mom's jewelry, cash from where she always kept a stash, his favorite clothes and a package of papers. RuDee had put her stuff together along with both of their letters. RuDee watched out the front at the man who was still sitting in his car. He was eating and she could see a large soda cup sitting on his dash board. He was intent on staying there to watch the house. Richard, while she watched the man, took all of their stuff to the car through the back door and the garage side door that was hidden from view of the street by the large heather and some butterfly bushes. Luckily the garage's driveway slanted down as it entered the alley. Putting the car in neutral, he pushed and turned the wheel directing the car into the alley.

RuDee took one last look and feeling confident he did not see them, went out the back carefully closing and locking the back door of the house, going through the garage door and then locking that door. As she exited through the open garage door, Richard reached up and quietly and slowly closed it. They pushed the car to the end of the alley; the opposite end of the street from the enemy's vehicle. Then pushing the car onto Beaver Street, they jumped into the car as it coasted down the street and Richard turned it on another street further away and completely hidden from the street his house sat on. They coasted two more streets and then Richard started the car and he headed for the freeway with RuDee looking back all the time. "I think we did it" She smiled at Richard. He looked over at her and then they both began to laugh.

"Yes" she blushed, "We should dress."   She climbed over the seat and got into her bag and had on jeans and a tee shirt in no time. "You'll have to pull into an alley" she said "or we might get arrested"   Richard pulled in behind the Wal-Mart store and took the clothes she handed him. As soon as he had donned his jeans and shirt he got back behind the wheel. "Ok" he turned and looked at her "Where to?"

"What about your Mom?" RuDee looked him straight in the eyes. "What did the police say?"   He shrugged. "They have her at the morgue" He looked away "They won't release the body until after an autopsy and investigation." He choked a little "I don't want to leave her this way, but I don't know what to do. Maybe we can hide somewhere for a while. I'll call the police from somewhere. And I have a friend Jason who can board up my house until I know what to do with it. I'll call him in a day or two. What do you suggest?"

RuDee just sat still for a few minutes "Well" she started "You know this country. What do you want to do?"   He leaned back and took her hand "I don't think I should go back to school for a while. I don't know if he knows I go there, or if there are more of him. I think maybe we should go somewhere and try to find the other members of our family.   There are more out there. Right?"   "Right" She said slowly "But where?"   "How about Santa Fe?" he threw out to her "That man will think I went back to California, I hope."

RuDee pulled the bag out of her pack that had the letters. "We need to get going, but we do need to find them and I think you are right; start at Santa Fe and Victor Martinez." She pulled out her wallet "Shall I sneak into Wal-Mart and get us some food?" "Good idea" he looked at her while reaching for his wallet in his backpack. She put her hand up in a stop gesture, grinned and got out of the car. "I have some money. You stay here out of sight. I'll be back in a few minutes. Anything you don't like?" she asked. "No, I like it all" he raised his eyebrows and smiled at this captivating young lady. RuDee quickly slipped onto a loading dock and into the employee loading entrance where some workers smiled at the pretty young lady as she acted like she owned the place.

Richard was just thinking he was getting a sick stomach when out of nowhere RuDee slipped into the passenger side with two large bags which she slung onto the back seat. "Let's go" she said "I think I saw his car in the front of the store." Richard needed no urging, he went down numerous streets, up back alleys and criss-crossed his way across the town. He stopped at a gas station and filled the car. He felt sad as he used his mother's gas card. The one she had left with the stash of money for him. "She must have known I'd need it someday" he thought tenderly. Then he angered and stiffened inside "Why should I run from them? I should take him out" he thought, surprised at his aggressiveness and fury.

As they entered the freeway at the last entrance of the town, Richard started to tell RuDee that they should stay and fight when he realized the idea was not a good one. They needed to know who and what they were fighting first. RuDee seemed to feel his mood change. "I know" She looked down "I want to take him out too." Richard frowned at her "You a clairvoyant too?"

She just smiled and opened a bottle of water and handed it to him. "Here, you need to keep hydrated." Then she laid out a feast of goodies on the console between them. "Wow" he lightened "I've always wanted to eat that much junk at one time" "Now's your chance" she giggled.

The two orphans comforted themselves with the array she had bought. Jerky, candy bars, potato chips, cookies and peanuts. She even opened a bag of gummy bears. "I needed this" she said as she stuffed a handful of peanuts, some gummy bears and half of a Snickers into her mouth. Richard almost choked from laughing. RuDee ate but never took her eyes off the cars behind them.

They had driven for several hours without talking. When they were passing the town of Holbrook, Richard broke the silence,

"You know, maybe we better get off the track for a few days before we go to Santa Fe." "Good idea, but where?" I know just the place" as he turned his car off the freeway at the town's last exit, took the frontage road back through the middle of town and turned south. "We'll go through the White Mountains into New Mexico. "We'll stay in Pinetop tonight."   "You're driving" RuDee sighed grateful to be off the freeway and into seemingly safe territory.

As they drove toward Show Low, RuDee commented that there was no one else on the road but them and that was making her feel a little better after all they had been through. "We'll stay at the Casino in Pine Top. Lots of cars, lots of people and I think we won't be spotted."

CHAPTER SIX

"Are we ready?" Ron shouted from the front seat of the Expedition EL. "Yes" the trio with him answered in unison. "Ok then, we're off." He looked around to the back seat. Jadin and Autumn were already snuggled into their pillows with their iPod speakers firmly in their ears. Susan was putting on her eye makeup in the passenger side mirror. Ron was excited. He was finally going to Wyoming. He had promised himself that he would go back and see it someday as his father had grown up on that ranch and had told him so many tales of his wild cowboy days. His Dad's parents had died when he was in college and his aunt Clarissa had stayed on at the family ranch. She had passed away last spring and they had not been able to get away to even go to the funeral.

Jadin and Autie were not happy they had to go to Wyoming and leave school for a week, but Ron had insisted they share this family experience. Susan, too, thought they should experience this trip and besides she told them their hard work all the other years would make their senior year a breeze with or without this week in school. Once they had settled in their minds there was no way out of this trip, they settled in and were actually looking forward to some new scenery.

Since finding out they were Chameleon, they had become very close. All the sibling rivalry had somehow disappeared and they enjoyed being together speculating on this phenomenon. They had quickly become proficient in controlling their changing colors. They played games hiding from each other and sometimes actually stripped down and became a part of the house's woodwork. Once at midnight, Autie convinced Jadin to walk along the cement wall that ran beside the houses in their neighborhood. They were having fun until they convulsed into laughing and a driver passing by almost ran out of control as he evidently saw the wall move. They quickly decided that wasn't a good thing to do. Susan sometimes joined in their antics to be close to her children; to help them with their gift and to keep them from going to an extreme.

As they entered Wyoming, the sites were incredible to the desert dwellers. "Do you think they will have mustangs on the ranch?" Autie asked. "I don't know" her dad answered "I know there is a man taking care of the ranch, but I don't know if there is any live stock or actually what is going on there. I just have his name and number."

October 14 Wyoming

It had been months since Brianna had been told about her Chameleon traits. She had been very upset with her mother for not telling her sooner as she had on several occasions thought she saw her hands turn colors but she would not let herself believe what she was seeing. She made a decided effort to not believe it and the colors seemed to disappear. After this revelation, Brie let the color happen to see just how far it would go. She was used to spending a lot of time alone as they lived on a large ranch and she shared in the chores with her parents of taking care of wild mustangs that were sharing their mountain country ranch.

Brie was a tall very strong girl with chestnut hair that she pulled back in a tight bun to accommodate the cowboy hat that she wore daily. Her enormous hazel eyes changed from varying shades of green to a deep gold depending on what she was wearing. A strikingly beautiful girl, Brie looked much older than sixteen. She had been a responsible help for her parents from childhood. She got her first horse when she was two and rode like a grownup from the very first time she was seated on Gull Buckets. Gull Buckets had been retired now for three years when she broke her leg stomping a snake that was inches from Brie. The hero horse shared a meadow with several other older horses that Brie's Dad felt deserved a good retirement.

Brie's present horse, Chieftain, was a large chestnut American Saddle Bred about sixteen hands high. His color echoed Brie's own mane. Since she found out she was a Chameleon and when she was out on the range with Chieftain, Brie would play with the horse by trying to hide from him. He was never fooled. He would sniff the air and find her. She especially liked lying in the water of the lake near her home. It seemed somehow more magical to turn the shades of the water. She called the gift her "inviz."

She had read all the letters that her mother had plus the one that she wrote to her. It was a little concerting that all of her ancestors that had this trait had been killed, even her Grandma. She thought Grandma had just died of something. It was unthinkable to find out that that she had been shot, hanged and burned. It made her so mad she kicked the side of the barn with her boots. "Boy" she thought "if I could just find them." She shook her head "No, I am going to find them."

Brie signed up for computer lab instead of a study period. She was determined to do some genealogy and try to find the other members of her "clan" as she called it. There must be some. Especially since her grandmother had a twin. She knew that her Grandmother's twin went to Colorado Springs in Colorado. She would start looking at records where and whenever she could. Brie had a boy friend. A friend, nothing romantic, but a good dear friend name Jed. Jed was a computer whiz. He was helping her learn her way around the internet but she was careful not to tell him anything. She knew the Law of the West. It was hard and cold and she had to survive. She could and would not trust anyone that probably couldn't understand what she was going through.

It was Friday and as Brie left the school Jed ran up. "Hey" he grabbed the strap on her back pack. "Wait up". Brie jerked the strap out of his hand "Hey, yourself." "Let's go to the DQ." He responded cheerfully. "I don't want to go home yet." He whined. "Ok" Brie decided "Just for a while though, I promised to clean out the water truck tonight. Dad hurt his arm yesterday and I want to help him." As they sat in the crowded tiny area where they had a few picnic tables, Jed leaned in close. "Brie" he half whispered "What is going on with you? You haven't been the same person lately." Startled, Brie just shrugged her shoulders "Just growing up, I guess" she retorted. He shook his head "No, that's not it. All this getting info off the web. You're looking for something with a vengeance and I want to know if there is something wrong and if I can help." Brie looked deep into her friend sky blue eyes. "Jed, I can't tell you. I mean, maybe I will tell you sometime, but not right now. OK?" she begged with her eyes. "Yeah" he answered "Just want to help." She squeezed his arm "Hey, I promise to tell you, but not now. I really have to go." She got up leaving him to finish his soda.

As she drove her pickup into the ranch driveway, she saw her parents getting into their truck. They stopped and rolled down their window. "We're going over to the Tanner place. We need to open up for Clarissa's nephew. Do you want to come with us? I'll let you drive" Her father appealed. "What about the water truck?" Brie had gotten out of her truck, leaving it over to the side of the lane. "That can wait. I would like your Mom to stay here to answer the phone in case they get lost." "Scoot over" she teased her Dad as she opened the driver door. As he slid over, Connie, her Mom, slid out the passenger door and started back to the house. "You two don't stay to long. If you'd like, you can bring them back for dinner. I'll get the bar-b-que ready and do up a salad."

As Brie steered the truck into the Tanner place her eyes were magnetically pulled to the handsome blonde boy that was standing by a large SUV. He was muscled and tan and stood out like a sore thumb in her wild cloudy world. As she and her Dad got out of the truck the rest of the Tanner's exited their vehicle. Brie did a double take as she saw a blonde girl, who looked like a shorter feminine version of her brother, walking toward her. Then her eyes caught sight of Mrs. Tanner. If the hair had been a shade darker she would have looked like her mother's twin. The deep dimple in their chins were exactly the same. She looked at her father and noticed the frown and surprised look on his face too.

Mr. Tanner extended his hand "Hello" he said "I'm Ron Tanner. This is my wife Susan and our son Jadin and our daughter Autumn. Thank you for coming over."   "Blane held out his left hand "Sorry, I damaged this one today" He indicated the right arm. "Oh, sorry" Ron sympathized.   Blane walked by the group "Let's open the house."   Then he stopped and introduced his daughter to them.

It was dark and cold in the large rambling ranch house that had been closed up with boards on all the windows. Blane walked into the house alone and soon the light flooded past him to the group just entering. "Well, it looks like the power company did their job. I was worried they wouldn't have it turned on yet. Let's get a fire started." He went over to the fireplace that had already been prepared some time ago. There was even paper underneath the logs and upon contact with Ron's match it burst into large welcoming flames.   "It'll take a while to heat this cavern" Ron grimaced   Susan was hugging herself and shivering. "This isn't Bakersfield, Is it?" she joked.   Blane turned to this woman who looked so much like his wife. "My wife is making dinner for all of us. I hope you will come home with us for dinner. We'll leave enough logs on and by the time you come back here, it will be warm and comfortable."   Susan shook her head yes even before looking at Ron for his okay.

As Connie watched the two vehicles come to a stop in front of her house, she looked over at her table hoping it looked nice enough for these California people.   She had used her mother's Real Old Willow dishes and the centerpiece was a cobalt blue bowl with some yellow field daisies gathered in it. She hurried to open the door and Susan was ushered in first. When their eyes met there was a moment of silence.

Blane came forward   "Mrs. Tanner, this is my wife Connie." "Please" Susan held out her hand "Susan."   The troop followed and after all the acquaintances were made, Connie seated everyone at the table and the meal began.   Brie was having as hard a time keeping her eyes off Jadin as he was keeping his eyes off of her.   There seemed to be a strong chemistry between them. Ron and Blane were having a problem too. They kept sneaking looks at each other's wife.

Autumn was taking this all in. Finally, she broke the silence and mystery. "Mom" she said rather matter-of-factly "Do you realize how much Connie looks like you? I mean you look like her?" Everyone stopped eating and looked at this brave young lady. "Look" she continued. "You two have the exact same dimple, the same shape of face and the same body. I mean, well, you do." she stammered, feeling embarrassed.

Susan rescued her daughter. "Yes, honey, I did notice how unusual this is." She smiled at Connie. "Maybe we're some long lost relatives or something. Probably just a kind of look alike. However, you are much prettier and I wish I had your nose." Everyone laughed.

Connie was staring at Susan. "Well, thank you, but, I think our noses are the same too. This is hilarious. What was your maiden name Susan? I don't even know if that would make a difference." It was getting funny now and the men started to make little jokes at the women. Suddenly the room was filled with a warm family feeling.

Brie sat back taking this all in. She looked over at the twins. "Could they be related?" She thought. "Could they be Chameleon?" she shook her head to herself. "No, that's crazy." Just then she looked down at Susan's hand as she was sitting right next to her and she blinked twice not believing what she saw. The end of Susan's little finger was the exact color of the blue napkin she was holding on her lap. Brie's reaction made her cough. Connie jumped a little "Are you alright Brie?" Are you choking?" Brie shook her head "no" but got up from the table feigning a cough. "I'll be right back" she coughed.

Susan looked down and saw her finger was blue. She stiffened and it corrected. "I wonder" she thought as she watched Brie through the pass-way window into the kitchen. Brie was just standing by the sink, not coughing now.

The evening was pleasant and the women seemed to be thrilled they looked alike. Autie and Jadin sat mostly quiet enjoying their parent's chatter with this other couple. They hadn't seen them interact with other parents much. They did wonder if Brie was always this quiet or maybe she didn't like them. That was Jadin's fear. Autie wondered if she were stuck up or just shy.

After the women had the kitchen back in order, the two families said their good nights and the Tanner's left to go back to their ranch. Brie offered to lead them, but Ron said he was sure he could find it.

A rooster crowed bringing Autumn to a state of awake. "What?" she said aloud. "We have chickens?"

She pulled the quilt around her and walked into the living room where her dad had just put fresh logs on the fire bringing it back to the comfortable roar that they were beginning to enjoy. "Hey, sleepyhead" her dad gave her a big hug. "Hear that rooster? I wonder if he belongs here or is just visiting." He laughed. "Come on in the kitchen, I made coffee. Maybe if your mother gets brave enough to come out from underneath all those quilts, we can have breakfast."

Just then Susan appeared wearing a coat over her bathrobe. "Brrrr" she complained "I'm a hot weather gal, you know. Did you bring in the food last night?" she directed at her husband. "Yes, dear we did. I think you had a glass to much wine last night." "Who needed wine?" She quipped "I was intoxicated with the company. Can you believe we look like we are from the same family? Me and Connie, that is. That was so cool." She sounded like a giddy teenager. "I think I'll make pancakes. It seems like a warm comforting food for this climate." "I think I could eat a huge stack of those" Jadin poked his head around the corner.

Autumn was sitting still in a chair she had pulled up to the kitchen's side window. The blanket hid her from the others. She was watching a brood of chickens scratching up the ground near an old shed. The shed was red with its peeled surface revealing several layers of other colors it had been. Suddenly the chickens scattered. She thought she was getting dizzy as she watched the shed's boards waver and seem to move in a way that it would look if it were behind a large spray of steam. All of a sudden she drew in her breath hard. "No" she thought "It couldn't be." She stared harder. It was still. She kept looking, not moving. "I'm dreaming" She shook her head then placed her head on the cold pane to steady her eyes. The boards were not moving. Her eyes followed a small red hen as it walked toward a tree. It had started pecking the ground and then jumped several feet up in the air with a hysterical cackle. It turned in mid air and ran off in the other direction. Autie looked hard at the tree just in time to see its mid-section waver and then the grass off to its right was moving like a football game wave.

"Jadin" she said in a loud whisper as she slid off the chair onto the floor with a plop. Everyone looked around. "Autumn" her mother yelled. "Are you alright?" Her father was by her side in a second helping her up. "How did you manage that?" he laughed. It looks like a sturdy chair to me." "I thought I saw something out there. Something strange." Autie started to blurt out what she saw then changed her mind. Her mother didn't really like to talk about "strange".

Susan had just collected the first pancake from the pan onto a large platter. Her mind didn't grasp her daughter's situation. She was trying to concentrate on the breakfast and her mind was on Connie. "Maybe" she announced as she sat the platter in the middle of the table. "Jadin, pour the coffee. I think everything else is on the table. Maybe, I am related to Connie." Jadin took his eyes off his sister and obeyed his mother's command. Autie pulled her chair over to the table and acted as if she had said nothing. Her Dad and brother seemed engrossed with the immense layout in front of them. Susan had also scrambled eggs, put out orange juice and syrup. She had even put the butter in a pan near the stove and it had softened into an irresistible lump. Susan, too, was hungry and her talk about Connie took back burner to the hot breakfast that lay within their grasp. The conversation stopped as the Tanner family enjoyed their feast; their appetites whetted by the brisk cold Wyoming atmosphere.

Over at the Benson ranch, Connie was washing up their breakfast dishes when Brie came in the back door. "Where have you been?" she asked her daughter "I left some breakfast on the back of the stove." She didn't wait for an answer Brie was usually late for meals and sometimes didn't show up at all for them. She had always let Brie have a free rein with her comings and goings as her daughter had always been a faithful help and always completed her chores and most of the time some of theirs. Looking down at Brie's feet, she made a face. "Your shoes are muddy." Brie looked down and backtracked to the door where she stepped out of her low cut tennis shoes. "Oops" she grinned at her mom and reached around the outside of the door and pulled the mop in and wiped up her prints. "Sorry Mom" she put up the mop and hugged her mom. "Thanks for saving me breakfast, I am hungry. I'm taking this plate upstairs, OK? I have some homework I have to do." She reached into the refrigerator and pulled out the milk bottle. With bottle in one hand and plate in the other, she made her way up to her bedroom.

Sitting down at her desk, she picked at her food and ate slowly going over that morning's events. "I am so stupid" she scolded herself. "Why did I go over there? I know she saw me." She mulled the scene over in her mind. She saw Autumn staring out at her, staring hard. And then when the chicken jumped, Brie had felt her heart go through her head. Shaking herself out of this state, Brie quickly finished her math paper, put on her nice jeans and turtleneck sweater, grabbed her Levi jacket and headed for school.

As Brie entered the school building, Jed was waiting. "Hey" he leaned into her ear. "I have something to tell you." "What?" she said as she kept her fast pace. "I'll tell you at lunch. It's too complicated now. Oh, yeah. Mom let me get a 24 hour pass for Findmyfamily.com. I tried it out last night and I found my uncle in Seattle. It is so cool. Maybe we can get on it in Lab today." "Sure" Brie looked at Jed trying to concentrate on what he was saying. Her heart had not calmed down since this morning's episode. "I got to go get a hall pass. Mrs. Murphy caught me out of lab last week and now she insists I be shackled." "Ok" he responded "see you later"

The cafeteria was packed. Seemed like no one brought their lunch. Elbows and hands were everywhere as Brie tried to pick out her food. The line was pushing on much too fast to consider what might look good or not. She grabbed a hamburger, some fries and a large Jell-O parfait. The whipping cream was sliding down the side of the plastic cup when she found her way over to the last table where she, Jed and a group of their friends always sat. Wedging herself between Jed and Scarlet, she almost dumped the tray. Jed's hand flew out and caught the edge. "Whoa" he exclaimed "Slow down girl."

Scarlet leaned over and whispered "Did you see that boy over there by Cassandra? He is so "karat". Brie's eyes followed Scarlet's nodding. The boy was new all right and very "karat". His hair was immaculate, almost too perfect. He looked like a person modeling in a catalog. He was clean shaven, a contrast to the cowboys in the school who all seemed to sport five o'clock shadows or maybe two or three day beard growth. Cassandra was talking to him a mile a minute but his eyes were scanning the cafeteria like he was expecting to see someone. When his eyes came in Brie's direction she noticed they were beautiful eyes that stood out from his face and piercing. So intense. She quickly looked down at her food.

The chatter seemed to dance around her head as she tried to concentrate on eating, hear what her friends were trying to say and to wonder about the Tanners. Now, that new boy was crowding his way into her brain too. "Got'ta go" She stood up with her tray "I'll see you in lab" she looked down at Jed.

After depositing her tray at the tray window, Brie went into the bathroom and leaned against the cool wall of an empty stall. Standing there just trying to calm her heart. "Brie?" She heard

Scarlet's voice "Are you in there?"   "Yes, I'll be out in a minute" "You alright?" her friend continued.   Brie opened the door "Yes, I'm fine. Why?" she questioned Scarlet. "Well, you didn't eat much and ran out so fast...."   "I've just got a lot on my mind" she interrupted. "I'm ok, really."

In Lab, Brie put her books down on the desk with the newest computer. She had to get there early to get it. Everyone wanted to use the new one. Jed came in and dragged his chair up to her desk.

"Ok" he whispered "Here is the site and my password. I know you want to see about your ancestors and all. I'd stay and help you, but Jenson wants me to help the new guy get oriented." Then he poked her shoulder "And, since you have the best computer, I'll have to show him how on a dinosaur." He laughed and walked away. Brie watched as Jed went back to the door where the new boy stood. They went over to the far side of the room and Jed started showing him the ropes. Brie opened the website and put in Jed's password. Then in the search line she typed Susan Tanner".

As Brie was leaving the school, Jed ran up. "Hey" he grabbed her shoulder. "Did you find out anything?" Brie shrugged her shoulders "A little, I guess. I'll try tomorrow. OK?" "Sure" He responded "That new guy wants to meet you. Can I give him your number?" "What?" Brie was taken by surprise "Me?" she pointed to herself.

"Yes" Jed continued "He seems like a great guy. You should see his tattoo. It is so cool." "Tattoo? Ugh" Brie reacted. "I hate tattoos. I think the body has enough color in it."   "This one is really different. He doesn't know I saw it. I think he doesn't want to show it off. We went to PE right after lab and he took off his shirt to wash his hands and arms. He got some grey gucky stuff on them from that old computer. Well, He started to wash and as I walked over he quickly turned and put back on his shirt. But you know old eagle eyes here. I saw it. Pretended like I didn't, but I did."   "So what?" Brie was getting impatient to get home and do the chores. Jed looked hurt. "Well" she corrected her attitude. "What was it?"   He got really close to tell her. "A hung lizard, or is it hanged?"

"A what?" she said rather loudly. He directed her into her pickup. Once inside he said it louder. "A lizard that was hanged. It was a cool design. A rope curved like a Christmas tree hook with a loop and a lizard hanging with his head through the loop. Or, is it hung? Anyway, it's underneath the top part of his arm."

Brie felt like she had been hit in the stomach. She wished she could tell Jed she was a lizard. 'That's disgusting" she said. "I hate lizards." "I thought it was cool" Jed looked at her kind of funny. "Are you alright?" "Yeah. I'm just in a hurry to get my stuff done. We're having company again and I promised to help." "Ok" Jed got out of the truck. "See you tomorrow" Brie threw him a kiss. She felt sick all the way home. It changed her whole thought of this new boy. He was good looking, but a hanging lizard? "Why that tattoo?" she asked herself.

"Connie wants us to come over again tonight" Susan announced as she put her cell phone back in her purse. "I told her ok, but that we were having an early dinner. So we will go over about seven for dessert."

Jadin had been with his father most of the day walking the perimeter of the ranch and looking over all the equipment. They had talked about how it might be if they moved there an actually ran the ranch instead of living in Bakersfield.

Autie went with her mother into the small town and they enjoyed looking in all the little shops. The store itself was an adventure as there were so many homemade items and canned foods made by the local residents. In the Western clothing store, Susan bought them all a denim jacket that had a quilted lining. There was a man standing outside by a huge bar-b-que, cooking chicken and roasts. When they were through looking and buying, they picked up some meat from the man and went home and put together a nice dinner. Autie had put the morning's event out of her head. It seemed like a dream anyway. Probably the altitude she thought to herself.

When the Tanner's arrived at the Benson ranch, Brie was still out feeding the stock. They were all sitting around the kitchen table having pie and coffee when Brie came in the back door. She was about to walk on in. "Shoes" her mother called out. She stopped and backed up and slid her shoes off and onto a mud rug.

"Sorry" Connie said to the crowd, "She muddied up the kitchen floor this morning." Autumn's eyes jerked toward Brie with Connie's statement. "Brie?" she thought wildly. Brie was looking down and didn't seem to notice the statement. "Here is your pie sweetheart" her mother handed her a plate. Jadin got up and pulled a chair up close to the table. "Here" he gestured "Sit here." Brie followed his direction and sat down as she was handed a cup of coffee and her pie.

The group was seemingly having a good time getting acquainted. "What year are you in?" Autie asked Brie. "Jr." she answered after she had swallowed what was in her mouth. "You?" she looked at Autie and then at Jadin. "Senior" he said almost choking. Silence followed. The grownups had decided to play a card game and the kids declined one by one. Brie asked them if they would like to come up to her room and watch TV. The twins replied in unison "Yes."

Entering Brie's room, Autumn's eyes got big and she giggled "Ha. You have my bedspread. And my curtains." "What?" Brie asked confused. "I have the exact set." Autie answered "But I don't have that lamp. Mom wouldn't let me get that." "That is funny" Brie wrinkled her nose. "I thought I was the only odd ball that liked this crazy pattern." Jadin kept his mouth shut as he had told Autie how lame he had thought it was when she had it put in her room.

The flat screen TV on Brie's wall became a center focus for the group as they huddled on her leather loveseat that sat right in front of the TV. "I love these ranch houses" Autie announced "They are so big. You couldn't get a couch in my room. My bed hardly fits."

Brie flipped through the channels then stopped "What do you guys like to watch?" she asked turning sidewise to see their eyes. She accidently bumped the pillow that Autie was holding on her lap and it bounced to the floor. "Sorr….." Brie started to say as her eyes saw Autie's hand suddenly turn the color of the distressed brown leather love seat. She sat quickly down and looked deep into Autie's eyes "You turned colors."   She said matter-of-factly. Autie and Jadin both froze in their seats their eyes locked on Brie's face. Autumn had stiffened and the color had returned to normal.   "What?" she asked like she didn't know what Brie was talking about.

Brie all of a sudden felt mad. And she never felt mad. She stood up and almost in tears "You know what I mean… Here." She quickly knelt down and laid her arm across Jadin's knees on his camouflage pants. Her arm disappeared. Jadin jumped back a bit and Autumn sat like a statue. Jadin out of reflex grabbed her arm off his knees. As he lifted it, it turned back to Brie's normal color. He kept hold of her arm.

"You're a Chameleon?" He asked already knowing the answer. She nodded silently.   Autie stood up. "It was you this morning out by the shed. Wasn't it?" She pointed at Brie.

"Yes" Brie answered. "I know you saw me or saw something. I have been worried about it all day.   I looked your mother up on a website about genealogy. You know, ancestors. Well, I got a few families back. To a Mildred and Bill Jones. But that was all. I thought maybe we were related. Look at our mothers. They almost look like twins." "Yeah, I know" Jadin started speaking "We have to be related, somehow. We have letters telling us about our ancestors. Maybe the two families tie in somewhere. Do you have letters?"

Brie nodded "Yes, My mom has them in the safe." Brie sat down on the floor in front of them. She had tears coming down her face. "I, I mean,   you don't know what this means to me. I have felt so alone with this thing, this gift shall I call it?"   Autie put her arms around Brie and held her tight.   "We know how you feel. We just found out this year."

"Then you know we are all in danger?" she looked at the twins. "Danger?" Jadin asked "What do you mean danger?"   "Well" Brie continued "You must know that someone out there is trying

99

to kill us and our families."   Autumn frowned and shrugged "That's crazy" she said "Who and why? And who knows about us anyway? Only my mother and Dad know about this." "What about your grandparents?" Brie asked "Where are they? Are they alive."   "My Grandmother is living" Autie said "In Colorado" My grandfather died of a heart attack last year and Grandma is fine. She can turn colors, my mother said, but she won't. Why do you ask?"

"Why do you think we are in danger?" Jadin asked again. "Well," Brie continued "My letters all tell of how each writer's parents were killed in a strange or bizarre way. Don't yours?" The twins were shaking their heads "No",   "Where are your letters?" Brie asked. "Back home" Jadin answered.

"None of our letters tell of danger. Just that we should be careful that no one thinks we're witches." Autumn stated. "However." Jadin stood up this time and paced around the room. "Remember Autie, the first letter from Hattie? Was it? She said she and her twin thought they were witches. She was stolen and did not know much about the affliction" he shrugged his shoulders "or gift?"

"Let's tell our folks" Autie said loudly.   "Ok" Brie agreed, "We really need to. I think one of my grandmothers tells of a sister that was stolen. It must be that one."   "What did you say you found out about my Mom today?" Jadin asked Brie.   Brie went to her backpack and pulled out a sheet of paper. "Here" She handed it to Jadin. He took it and read it. "That's right, My Mom and her parents and her grandparents." His eyes narrowed. "This is dangerous Brie"

She nodded her head and her eyes narrowed too.

"I think we need to know about your letters" he walked over to Brie. "Could we? He asked. "Of course" Brie answered him "I think we need to include our parents, don't you?"   "Yes" Autumn intruded and Brie nodded yes. "Let's go."

CHAPTER SEVEN

October 14 Albuquerque

Dezza walked into the kitchen of Blake's and Courtneay's house in Albuquerque the morning after they had read their letters to each other. Blake was sitting at the table already drinking coffee and eating a huge Danish roll. There was a box in the middle of the table with Danish rolls and donuts. "I thought we could use some sugar after last night" Blake grinned up at Dezza. "Help yourself cousin." Dezza crossed over and poured herself a cup of coffee and sat down beside Blake. "Thanks, I need sugar. I don't usually eat any carbs, but you're right, I think we need them this morning." As she put a large chocolate donut on a napkin in front of her. "And chocolate is good for my nerves." She laughed.

About that time, Courtneay came into the kitchen and exclaimed "Donuts? I need a donut." She grabbed a large sugar donut and went to the coffee pot and poured her a cup. As they devoured over half the big box of donuts, they started to feel a little silly over their antics.

"You know" Dezza stood up. The twins looked up at their new cousin. "We have to find the others. I really believe we need them." Courtneay and Blake nodded in agreement. "But how?" Courtneay asked. "Well, I found you two by going to the Santa Fe court records of births and deaths. I tried to go on line to get them, but couldn't, so last November, I took a trip to Santa Fe and did some digging. I found my great great Grandmother, Sarah Martinez Barnes. Then I looked for her siblings and found your great great Grandmother Mary Martinez Roll and our 3rd great Grand Uncle Victor Martinez. Then I went back to San Francisco and found Beth, Mercy and Judy. Then I came here and found Windy" She shrugged her shoulders and pointed to the twins "Thus… you. If I can, we can. OK?"   "Ok!" both Blake and Courtneay said at the same time. "Where do we start?" Courtneay added.

Dezza pulled a notebook out of her bag "Here" she handed the book to Courtneay. "We start in Sonora. I believe that is where Crystal, Judy's twin sister was. I think we should try on line first. It's a long way from here." "Ok" Blake started "Let's get busy."

Courtneay and Dezza cleaned up the kitchen while Blake got his computer and printer set up on the kitchen table. "We'll work here" he announced "So we can all see."

Just then there was a noise at the front door, they all froze. They could hear the door being unlocked and the knob turning. "Hello" a familiar voice announcing her entry. "It's me, Nellie." Courtneay breathed a sigh of relief. Dezza couldn't seem to catch her breath. She reached over Blake's shoulder and pushed the power button until the computer shut down. Blake looked up at her in surprise and then in an understanding way stood up and moved away from the computer.

Nellie entered the kitchen. "I came back early. My sister needed to go to her daughter's house. What are you kid's doing with that computer in here?" She frowned. "The girls are helping me with a report. I thought we could all see it and then print it out in here. Is that ok with you?" He looked pleasantly at Nellie. She didn't seem to be suspicious. "Ok. Did you have breakfast?" They nodded. "Well, I'll just go to my room. I need to write some letters. See you kids later."

She started to turn and her hand accidently hit the side of the computer. "Ouch" she said putting her hand up to her mouth. The short loose sleeve of her blouse rode up on her arm. Dezza's eyes went like a magnet to the inside of Nellie's upper arm. An end of a tattoo was showing. It looked like a lower end of a lizard, two legs and a tail. "No" she thought. "That can't be a lizard." Nellie was oblivious to what was seen. She went out of the kitchen scolding herself for being so clumsy.

Dezza motioned to the twins to come outside with her. They followed her out the back door into the patio area. "We have to leave here" She whispered. "Why?" Courtneay whispered back. "Just trust me" she looked into their eyes. "Nellie?" Blake asked. Something deep inside of him knew there was something wrong with Nellie.   Dezza nodded her head "Yes". "Ok." he said in a whisper "I'll get my computer and go up and get packed.   You two get packed and then we will sit around this afternoon acting like we are just loafing around. We'll tell Nellie we're going to a movie or something, and then we'll leave." They all entered the kitchen and were helping Blake put up the computer when Nellie came back into the kitchen. "I thought you were going to work in here?" She asked.   "I decided to procrastinate." Blake put his arm around her shoulders.   I'll finish it tomorrow. I think I'll take a nap and then take these girls to a movie tonight."

Nellie looked him in the eye "Did you find out who this girl is?" He grinned and chuckled at the same time. "Yes. It seems that my buddy Carl asked Dezza to the formal Friday and he needed a place for her to stay."   "But, I thought she asked about some letters of your mother's?" Nellie asked trying to look nonchalant. Blake shrugged his shoulders. "I don't know." He acted like it was a nothing. "Really Nellie, you should be more careful who says they're our relative" he grinned at her in a childish sort of way. "Any Chinese person may say they're our sister and move in." Nellie acted relieved "That was pretty silly, wasn't it?   I can't believe we weren't more careful about letting her in." Nellie frowned at him. "Oh well" he laughed "All's well that ends well."

He left Nellie in the kitchen and went to his room.   Upstairs in Courtneay's room, the girls were quietly packing Courtneay's stuff. "We need to travel light" Dezza reminded her. "I hate to leave the house with Nellie." Courtneay whispered. "I know" Dezza whispered to her, "You'll just have to put it out of your mind." Just taking her essential makeup, and several changes of clothes and underwear, the girls made sure the room looked normal and put their backpacks in the closet. They made sure their letters were securely in them. "Tell me again what you saw on Nellie's arm?" Courtneay asked. "Remember what your mom said about the drawing of the lizard hanging?" Courtneay nodded "Yes"   "Well, I saw a lizard's tail.   I may be wrong Courtneay, but we can't take a chance." Silent tears started sliding down Courtneay's face. Dezza put her arms around her and held her tight. "Toughen up cousin. We can cry when the enemy is gone." She held Courtneay out away from her and looked her in the eyes. "I've had to."

There was a knock on the door. The girls held their breath. "Hey, you two, open up" Blake almost yelled. The door opened and Blake came in and closed the door and whispered. "I am going to keep Nellie busy while you two get our stuff in the car. Go by my room and get the two back packs by the door. "You have the letters?" They nodded yes.

Then in a loud voice, "We have to pick Carl up at seven. You two be ready."

With that he closed the door noisily and they could hear him running down the stairs in his usual way. As he entered the kitchen, Nellie was busy making a pie shell. "Pie?" he asked raising his eyebrows. "What kind?" "Your favorite" she smiled at him "mile high apple pie and I have American cheddar cheese for you to melt on it." Blake grabbed his stomach. "When? I can't wait" He made a mock gesture of love toward Nellie. "You are the best." Nellie laughed. She seemed to act relaxed as he acted the way he always did. "You are a silly boy. When are you going to be home tonight?" she asked "Maybe you can have some then." "With that pie waiting" he laughed "It'll be early. Probably not until 11 though, the movie won't get out until 10:30." "I'll leave it out for you." She frowned. "Be sure you put the dishes in the sink though. Ok?" "OK" he answered.

"Nellie?" he acted serious "I need to ask you something." Nellie jerked her head around in surprise "What?" she said carefully. "Well, I was just wondering what you thought about Mr. Anderson." "Mr. Anderson?" she responded "In what way?" "Have you known him a long time?" he asked her. "No" she answered "I met him when I applied for this job. He put the ad in the paper and interviewed me. What is bothering you about him?" "I probably shouldn't even be wondering, but I really don't know how much money we have. Altogether, I mean. I know the bills are paid and we seem to have plenty of spending money, but I think I should know what the total is. Don't you?" Nellie poured herself and Blake a cup of coffee and she motioned for him to sit down. "I think you are absolutely right Blake. You should know how much money you have. It seems you must have a lot of money, or he wouldn't have been able to hire me." She laughed "and I don't come cheap." Blake laughed too. "Really, how much do we pay you?" She shook her finger at him. "That's for you to find out." They both laughed. She seemed to be enjoying being his confidant and advisor. As they talked about the possibilities of finding out what he and Courtneay had, Nellie was not aware that the girls had loaded Blake's car with all the belongings they were taking with them. After they were sure they were not leaving anything they needed, they started taking showers and getting cleaned up and dressed for their movie night.

Blake and Nellie talked for about fifteen minutes and Blake excused himself to get cleaned up to go out. Nellie went back to making her pie and preparing other foods for future meals. As he left the kitchen, Blake stuck his head back in "Don't fix us anything. We are totally going to eat theatre food tonight." She stuck her thumb up okaying the decision.

"How do we look?" Dezza and Courtneay came rushing into the kitchen. "Very pretty, girls." Nellie complimented their attire. "Too pretty" She grimaced. "You girls be careful. Some boy will carry you off." They both acting in a giddy mood, hugged her "Thanks Nellie. And, for the pie Blake told us about. You're the best" Courtneay showed her affection. Nellie kind of frowned like maybe she was feeling affection and didn't want to.

"Let's go" Blake yelled from the front room. "Ok" Courtneay yelled back. "Bye Nellie" Dezza echoed "Bye Nellie." The girls left giggling and kidding Blake about his shirt.

As soon as they got in his car and were half a block away, they all looked at each other. "Whew" Blake whooped. "I am so hyped" Courtneay had climbed in the back seat to let Dezza be up front. She stuck her head between them "Now what?" "Well," Blake pulled out a handful of credit cards. "First, to the ATM machines. We need cash. A lot of cash. I want to draw out cash so that for some reason there is someone who can stop our credit cards. Do you have any cards Courtneay?" Courtneay dug in her purse then pulled out two credit cards.

This is for clothes and this is for food." Dezza chimed in "You guys are rich."

After stopping at their family bank's ATM, two convenience store ATMs and four other banks ATMs, Blake stopped at a service station, filled up with gas and the girls counted their money and divided it into three stacks. "We each will take care of a third" Blake told them, "Now we have to think of where to go."

Just then Blake's cell phone rang. They all looked a little pale. He looked to see who was calling. "It's our home phone." He gasped. "Why would Nellie be calling us?" "Don't answer" Dezza almost screamed. "What could it hurt?" Courtneay chimed in. "She knows we should be in a movie right now." Blake thought out loud. "She must know I would have my phone on buzz." "Maybe it's an emergency " Courtneay gave a thought. "But who could have an emergency that you two would care about?" Dezza asked. "Our aunt? Or , or Carl?" Courtneay looked at Blake. "Did you tell Carl not to call the house?" Blake shrugged his mouth. "Forgot that little detail. I'll call Carl." "What if he is at our house and with Nellie?" Courtneay looked scared.

"We're out of the house and on our way, no calling" Blake put his phone back in his shirt pocket. "I'll have to contact Carl later, if I ever can. Let's get out of town. California?" he asked. "No" Dezza shook her head "That is too easy. I think we should hide out somewhere and then research and then decide. What do you think Courtneay?" Including her in the decisions. Courtneay warmed toward Dezza. It was hard to believe they had only met. It seemed they had known each other forever. Courtneay thought maybe it was because they both had recently lost their mothers and especially since they were family. "I agree we should hide and try to figure this out. How about Santa Fe? My aunt lives there. She would help us." "I agree Santa Fe" Blake added, "But not with Sadie. That's the first place they will look, if they are looking." He made a face. "Wouldn't that be a laugh if that tattoo on Nellie was the bottom of an umbrella?" No one laughed or even smiled. The seriousness of the situation weighed severely heavy at that moment. "I vote for Santa Fe" Dezza broke the silence.   "Ok" Blake pulled into the traffic and headed the car toward the Freeway. "Santa Fe it is."

CHAPTER EIGHT

Wyoming Oct 14

Connie had just gathered the pie plates from the dining table and was about to get the Tanner's coats when the kids came down stairs. "Brie, get Jadin and Autumn's coats. They're on the sofa." She told her daughter as she and the other two entered the dining room.

"They're not going yet" Brie responded. "What?" her mother scowled at her. "Susan and Ron are ready to go home." "Well, we need to talk to all of you" Jadin looked over Brie's shoulder and addressed Connie. "Oh" Connie shrugged. The other adults had come back into the dining room from the living room. "What's going on?" Blane asked. "The kids want to talk to us." Connie answered.

Brie took her mother's hand and led her into the living room. "Could you all sit down please and let us talk to you?" Susan looked scared but kept silent. Ron led her to the couch and they sat down together. Connie went to her rocking chair as Blane sat in his recliner.

The three teens stood in front of them. "Shall I tell them?" Brie looked first at Jadin then at Autumn. "Go ahead" Jadin nodded his head. Autumn was nodding her head yes too. Brie took a deep breath. "Well, parents. We think we know why you two look alike" She looked first at her mother then at Susan. The parents didn't make a sound. "We know we are related." She continued. "How?" Ron spoke up. "Let's show them" Autumn put her hands on Brie's and Jadin's shoulders. "Ok?" They both looked at her, shrugged and said "Ok". "Come on" she pushed them gently toward the gold and green brocade curtains. They lined up in front of the curtains and disappeared with only their clothes showing. All four parents' mouths were as wide open as their eyes.

Connie and Susan instantly looked over at each other. Connie asked the question with her eyes and Susan nodded "yes". Connie got up and took Susan's hand and led her over to the curtain next to the kids. "Shall we?" she asked Susan. Susan laughed "Of course." They instantly disappeared with only their clothes showing. The men were frowning. Ron looked at Blane. "Do you do that?" "Not hardly!" Blane answered coarsely. "That damn curse. We knew there had to be more family out there, but didn't ever dream we would meet them. You?" He asked. Ron shook his head "No, I'm the spouse."

Susan and Connie came away from the drapes and their color returned. The children were still standing silently. Then Jadin came away from the window and changed back to normal. "We want to find the rest of our family." He announced. We want to go on the offense. We do not want to die and we do not want you to die. I didn't know until I got here that someone out there was out to kill our family. Our letters intimated some danger but Brie says her letters tell more. We need to read them and find out. Can we?"

Connie got up and went out of the room then returned with the stack of letters. "Here they are. Where does your family fit in? She asked Susan. Susan replied, "Our letters start with Hattie who was the daughter of James Johnston. Our Hattie was stolen by the Indians and sold to a trapper who married her. Her family must have thought she was dead. She wrote about her "gift" and thought, when she was little, she was a witch, but her husband told her she was not. She wrote the letter for her children and their children. So no one must know about Hattie or our line of the family. What about yours?" she asked Connie.

Connie put the stack of letters on the table. "You'd better read them. I have nine and my letter to Brie is the 10th. It all started with Elizabeth." The group gathered around the table. "I'll put on the coffee pot. It's going to be a late night. Go ahead and start reading them," as she left for the kitchen.

It was midnight when the last letter of Connie's was read and discussed. "We have to get to bed" Ron said as he picked up Susan's coat and handed it to her. "We can talk about this Tomorrow?" Everyone nodded agreement. As the Tanner's started to walk out the door, Brie spoke up. "I think we should meet early. I think maybe we are in danger. Like maybe right away." "Why do you say that?" Susan came over to her.

"Well, there is a new boy at school and my friend saw a tattoo on him. He didn't mean for Jed to see it, but he did. It's a picture of a lizard being hanged." She stopped and took a deep breath. No one made a sound. "Ok" Susan finally broke the silence. "Can you three come over to the ranch in the morning? I'll fix breakfast." Connie nodded "Yes, how early?" "I think we better do it early, how about six?" "We'll be there" Blane confirmed. The Tanner's got in their car and left for their ranch. No further discussions happened that night as they were all exhausted.

Morning light found Susan already ready to fix breakfast. She had the coffee on and potatoes were cooking in the large skillet. The ham and eggs were on plates ready to be cooked and the table was set. She had just poured seven glasses of orange juice when she heard the Benson's pickup drive up to the house. Everyone woke way earlier than their alarms had gone off. Once seated at the large ranch table, everyone ate like it was their last meal. No one talked other than "Please pass this" or "May I have that."

After Breakfast, they took their coffee into the living room. "Ok" Blane spoke first. "I have been up all night trying to figure this out. I agree with the kids. We need to go after whoever is after our families. If Brie could find information on you Susan, then they can find us; all of us. I don't want to hid my head in a hole and do nothing." "I agree." Ron stood up. "We need to make sure they don't find us. But how?" "How can we get away?" Connie asked Blane "All the stock, the fields and everything has to be taken care of." Silence reigned for a few minutes. "Joe Barnes will come out here and take care of everything. He has wanted to work for me for a long time. He needs work and I know I can trust him. He can bring his wife and kids and live at the house. I'll go find him this morning and get it arranged." He shrugged his shoulders then "But, where do we go?"

"With us" Ron said as he sat back down. "They don't know about our line yet. You could come to Bakersfield with us. We would have to make sure that no one here has our address because of this ranch. Could we count on this Joe to take care of the place and not know or tell whose it is?" Blane shook his head yes. "Connie" Blane took his wife's hands. "I know you probably think I should stay here and take care of the place and send you two, but I can't. I need to be with you. I need to protect you. Do you understand?" Connie put herself into his arms. "Yes" she whispered.

Adrenaline was flooding the total atmosphere of the old ranch house. Fear of the enemy that had invaded their hearts was quickly turning to anger. They had a unanimous resolve and that was to find the enemy and stop this family slaughter that had been going on for the many generations. Also, to find other members of the "Family" or "Clade" as Brie had called it.

"Brie, we have to change our cell phone numbers this morning." Connie told her daughter. Susan echoed that to her children. "We all will." Jadin coughed a little and then spoke up. "You know Dad," he addressed his father. "I think we should go somewhere now and then figure out all of this. This ranch is not safe. That kid at school obviously knows where the Benson Ranch is and might find out about our ranch. I think we need to go." "You're right son" Ron put his arm around Jadin. "We can take care of everything on line. I'll call my work and tell them I'm taking another week."

"Aren't we wasting time?" Autumn chimed in "I think I am little scared now Mom" Susan smiled at her daughter. "We all are sweetheart. We all are. Ok," she turned around "Connie let's pack up our stuff and then go to your house and get your things. We will only take what we need and make room in our car. The carrier on top is empty. I planned on buying out some antique shop somewhere." She smiled at her new found distant cousin.

As real as the phenomenon of the "gift" to the two women and three teens was, so was the reality of the eminent danger. They shut up the Tanner Ranch taking the sack of garbage with them to throw away at the Benson's dumpster. They made sure nothing was in it to indicate who had been staying there. As far as they knew, no one in town knew they were at the ranch except the Bensons and Jed. Brie convinced them that she needed to tell Jed that he was to tell no one about the Tanners or about her family. Especially the new guy. The Benson's felt certain that Jed could be careful, besides he didn't know their names or where they were from. Brie was sure that never came up.

Once at the Bensons, Connie directed what things could or could not be taken while Blane took their papers and made certain to take anything with the Tanner place mentioned on it.

After two hours of careful planning and packing, Blane locked up the house. Jadin and Autumn helped Brie feed the stock and do the morning chores of the ranch. Blane had called Joe and told him that his father was ill in Ohio and he was going up there to take care of him and his ranch and asked if Joe and his family could come and live there and take care of the place. He would pay him $1700 a month plus the house to live in and he would make sure the utilities got paid and the feed bills too. Joe could raise his own stock along with Blane's. Joe jumped at the opportunity as he had been out of work for three months and was out of rent monies. He had a wife and three children and this was a God-send for him. He promised to come over that day and start taking care of the animals and would move his family in before the end of the week.

That done, Blane looked around his ranch, said his private goodbyes then joined the group in the Tanner car. Luckily Blane had a covered six foot trailer and they were able to pack both families' things in it, leaving the Expedition El for just the seven people, of course, also their iPods, computers, cell phones and personal backpacks. There was ample room as the three teens took the middle seats and Connie and Blane were comfortable in the third row.

They had decided that instead of going to Arizona through Nevada, they would go down through Colorado and New Mexico. Connie said she had always wanted to stay at the Hawkins Bed and Breakfast in Santa Fe. She had read in a magazine about it and the pictures looks so inviting. She got on the phone and booked two suites; one for each family. One had two bedrooms and one had a large bedroom.

As they turned out of the town onto the freeway leading to Colorado, they passed a car going toward the high school. Brie recognized the new boy and ducked down before he could see her. "That's him" she whispered loudly   "Don't look." Everyone wanted to look but kept their eyes ahead.   Ron was driving, however, and he watched the boy go by without an indication that he even noticed the car. "He didn't notice us" He said.

Brie sat back up. "I forgot to call Jed. I'd better do it now." She pulled out her cell phone and punched in his number. "Jed? It's me. Where are you? Are you at school yet? Great. I have to talk to you a minute. Can you stop your car and listen to me? Do you see the new boy anywhere? No, good. Well, Jed, just listen ok?   Jed, I have to leave with my parents. We are going up to Ohio" she lied "to take care of my grandpa. He's really sick and we have to help him.   No, Joe, you know Joe? Well, he's going to take care of the place until we get back. I will call you when I get there. But there is something else. Jed, you can't tell anyone you know where I am at. And, you can't tell anyone about the other ranch we were taking care of. I can't explain now. But I will. Promise. Please don't tell that new boy anything about me. Promise? Thanks Buddy. Please just act like you don't know anything about me. Please. I knew I could count on you. Jed, I'm going to miss you." She choked back her tears. She knew Jed could tell she was about to cry. "Bye" she hung up and sobbed into her hands. Jadin put his arm around her and held her close. She relaxed in his arms. Autumn reached across Jadin and patted Brie's knee.

During the trip to Santa Fe, Blane and Ron took turns driving while the others slept so they wouldn't have to stay anywhere all night. Cell phones rang from time to time, but, they had decided not to answer the phones and in California they would get new phones. They would call who they needed to in the evening after figuring out what should be said and what should not be said. Since it was clear that the Tanner family was not known to the killers since they were from Hattie's line, Bakersfield seemed to be the logical place to go. Ron had a friend on the west side of the city that was looking for a ranch manager and was sure that he could get Blane the job and they could actually change their last names and Brie could finish school there.

As the car pulled into the Bed and Breakfast which was on the Eastern side of Santa Fe, Susan and Connie looked at each other and said "Yes" at about the same time. When the families got settled in their rooms, Ron called a local pizza parlor and soon the group was sitting in a beautiful gazebo that sat outside the facility.

It was a little chilly out but the owner had a nice cage-type patio fireplace burning in the middle that gave off enough heat to keep the party comfortable. The pizza was good and the hostess had cocoa and giant cookies for their dessert. "Maybe we should stay here for a couple of days and try to do some research" Jadin addressed the group, "and rest." Blane nodded agreement to Jadin's idea. "I need some time to think about all of this and I know you kids can use those computers to find out some stuff about our families." Connie and Susan liked the idea. "We definitely could do some window shopping and relax" Connie stretched out her legs and leaned back in the large patio chair she was sitting in.

"I have to go to sleep" Brie stretched. "I hope Joe took care of Chieftain. I know he misses me." "I already called Joe" Her dad said. "I told him we were in Ohio and he said that all the stock was taken care of. He is already moving his family in and Sandy and Meg will make sure the horses are exercised and groomed. Joe is a good rancher and I know your horse is ok." Her dad reassured Brie. "Thanks Dad" Brie got up and started up to their room. "Goodnight" she looked at the group. "Wait, I'll walk up with you." Autie got up and hurried toward her. "Me too" Jadin echoed and followed the girls as they walked toward the large house.

The grownups spent the next hour hashing out all the things they needed to do to protect their children and themselves. It seemed surreal sitting there for all of them, here in almost a moment in time, they found out they were in the same family and in danger. Connie told them she thought it was God's doing bringing them together to help each other. Susan agreed. Blane, who had just recently found out his wife and daughter were "gifted", was still feeling mad at the whole thing. "It is just like a nightmare or horror movie" he told Ron. "I still haven't got it into my brain yet and to have to leave the ranch is really a hard thing here." Ron told him he thought he might understand what he was feeling. He had known from the time he married Susan that she was a Chameleon, however, they did not know about the people trying to kill them. "Your family might have been safe if you hadn't found us" Connie brought up. "I am so sorry." She looked at Susan.

"You don't know that they don't know about us." She reassured Connie "We can't take a chance." 'Let's get some sleep" Ron took Susan's hand and the newly acquainted families went to their rooms to get much needed sleep.

Santa Fe, NM

Blake opened thier door at the Purple Crystal Motor Inn. "Just a minute" he told the pizza guy and reached into his pocket and pulled out a wad of bills. "How much?" he asked. "Thirty-two fifty" the teenage boy answered. Dezza reached around Blake and took the pizza boxes. Blake handed the boy two twenties and thanked him. The boy left. "I am so hungry" Courtneay opened the top box that Dezza had sat on the dresser.

Blake came over and moved his computer away from the pizza boxes. Then put two large pieces on a napkin and he stacked up three pillows on one of the beds and leaned against them. "It didn't take so long to get here, but I feel like I have been driving for hours." "Do you want the TV on?" Courtneay asked him. "No, not tonight" he told her after a few minutes of chewing. "I think we should get some sleep and make our plans tomorrow. If you two want too."

Dezza was eating stretched out on her back on the adjacent bed "I agree. We need to sleep then figure out what our next step is." "Me too" Courtneay reached for another slice of pizza.

Blake didn't think he would be able to go to sleep, but as soon as he got comfortable on his pillow he was out. The girls had taken their showers and were sharing the other bed. They whispered for a little while and then almost at the same time went to sleep.

The bathroom light hit Courtneay's eye and seemed to penetrate the lids. She squinted into the light. "Is it morning?" she asked "Can you believe it's already eight?" Dezza answered. "Sorry about the light, but I had to get up. Do you think I could open the curtain and let some light in?" "Sure. Blake won't wake up until he's ready, no matter how much light comes in, or noise."

Dezza pulled the curtains open and the soft sunlight flooded the room. "Look" She pointed out the window, "There's a Crater's. I haven't seen a Crater's since I went to Idaho to ski" "A what?" Courtneay put down her toothbrush and picked up her makeup bag. "Crater's" Dezza explained. "They make the best waffles."

"Waffles?" a muffled voice invaded their conversation as a shaggy head appeared from under the covers on the other bed. "Did I hear Waffles?"Blake stretched his long arms up into the air and picked up a pillow and tossed it at Dezza hitting her on the legs. "Hey" she picked up the pillow and threw it back at Blake, but, he ducked and the pillow hit the headboard with a bang.

It didn't take the trio too long to get ready to go have breakfast. They had taken the motel room for three nights so they could spend some time in the library and on Blake's computer doing research.

Inside Crater's, Courtneay had ordered her breakfast and excused herself to go to the bathroom when she saw a boy about their age with blonde hair, almost white hair and the bluest eyes. She drew in her breath. He was so good looking and buff. Her eyes followed him as he crossed the restaurant from the bathroom hallway. He was going to a large table with four adults and two teen girls. She noticed that he looked a little like the blonde girl. She was a classic California surfer looking girl with blue eyes and a tan Courtneay could kill for. The other teen was pretty too but a taller more exotic looking girl with chestnut hair pulled back at the nape of her neck. "She's got a face for a cowboy hat" she thought and then thought "Why did I think that?" Her attention back on what she was doing, she headed for the bathroom.

Jadin had seen Courtneay, too. He looked back over his shoulder at the pretty girl and tripped over Autumn's chair. "Hey. Watch out" Autumn cried.   "Sorry" he said sitting down and then looking back. "Pretty girl" Susan smiled at Jadin. He blushed then looked over at the other table and caught the eyes of Blake looking at him with a funny stare. Jadin looked down. His hand had turned the same color of the dark oak chair arms. The other hand had turned green as he had it resting on a menu.   Jadin stiffened his arms and the correct color returned. He looked back at the boy across the room but the boy was looking at a menu and didn't seem to be watching or noticing. Jadin got lost in his huge plate of pancakes and forgot the incident.

Blake, however, didn't forget. He did see the guy across the room turn colors when he tripped into the girl sitting there. He pretended not to notice and looked down at the menu and was deciding what to eat.

CHAPTER NINE

Baylor Larkey sat still on the porch swing. His feet planted firmly on the deck. His stomach was queasy, almost to the point of vomiting. "How can this be?" he suppressed a tear that tried to escape his eyes which were burning and even felt like they must be red. He had seen the tattoo on his dad's arm a million times but thought it had been there from some childhood prank as his Dad always told him "When you are older, I'll explain." "Explain" the word exploded in his head "Explain?" How could someone explain that his whole life was a lie?"

The door from the house opened and Janice Larkey stuck her head out "You alright Bay?" she said in a loud whisper. Baylor didn't respond. He didn't want to respond. He wished she would just go away and leave him alone. But she didn't. She came over and sat down beside him and tried to put her hand on his shoulder. He moved away. "Not now" he shook his head.

Silently, his mother got up and went back into the house. She knew he had to process this information he had just received. She walked across the dining room and frowned at the stack of letters. Her stomach was in a knot. She understood her husband's world and had accepted her role in it, but she did not like it. It seemed to go against everything she had learned growing up. Everything about Church and God and all, but when she met Warren Larkey and fell in love with him, what he told her seemed to make some kind of sense and she felt she would rather choose to believe him than to lose him.

When they had Baylor, she secretly hoped that Warren would not include their son in his secret world. She was sure that Warren could never find those people that he was looking for and he didn't really seem to be trying. He wasn't good on the internet and she had done all of his research for him being careful to not find any information that he sought.

She remembered how stern his father was. Warren's father had died in a bizarre plane crash the year before she had Baylor. She was hoping that this would end the "quest". But Warren seemed lately to be fretting over his "God given job" to finish his father's and their ancestor's vendetta against what they called the "Clade." She had read the copy of the Agreement that Joshua Wells had and all the notes that had been passed down from Warren's ancestors. She felt like she was in some kind of horror movie, but Warren was her moon and sun and she dismissed any feeling of wrongness in it all. She had stopped reading her Bible the first year they were married as it seem to sting her heart and make her wonder about Warren's views on things.

Over the years she had hardened her heart until she didn't feel either wrong or right in any situation and especially not this one. There were notes attached to the original copy of the agreement along with the one that Warren had started just last month for their son. Janice had wanted more children but she feared having more. She deliberately kept from getting pregnant even though Warren was insistent they keep trying to have more. Sometimes he was angry with her for not being able to have more children and in the heat of some arguments told her that he would just get someone else to have his children. He, however, had an image to keep in the community as he was the Minister of the Wellshausen Congregational diocese and she knew that this was as important to him as was his family "Quest."

Janice started to fix dinner. Warren had made their eighteen year old son read all the notes and the Agreement and then he explained to him what he had to do. What their family and other relatives always had done and this quest was important to God and that they had to carry it out.

Baylor sat quiet through the whole process careful not to make his father mad. He had spent his whole life trying not to make his father mad at him. Baylor saw two sides of his father. One a religious and pious cleric and the other side had a mean streak that he only seemed to take out on his wife and occasionally his son.

Most of the time, Warren Larkey was a fun loving father eager to go to his son's ball games and skate board meets. However, a cloud would seem to come over him every now and then. He expressed that he, Warren, had not been a good son, a good Larkey, a good Wells and that he would be punished by God if he didn't carry out his family's God given function.

Now Baylor knew what this function was. It was to kill. To kill all family members of the "Clade." He now knew what the "Clade" was. It was a family of Lizard people. A family of witches. His mind swirled around the word "Witches." He had seen all the movies about witches, good ones and bad ones, scary ones and funny ones. However, he had always known that they were not real. "Why hadn't he been told this at a younger age?" he had asked his father as he was reading the Agreement and notes. "You might have told someone" his father answered. "This task of ours can't be found out by the world. No one but our family knows the importance of this. The world is stupid. They all do not know the inner workings of God. But we do and now, you do." He had placed his hands on his son's shoulders "And you have to make an oath to fulfill our quest; to end this family of lizard witches. You have to swear before God and on the souls of your ancestors that you will do this. Understand?"

Baylor shook his head "no". Warren fumed. "Well, you had better get it into your head. This is your destiny. This is my destiny. We have no choice." He stomped out of the room.

Baylor went out to the swing where his mother had tried to talk to him. He heard his father slam the back door and get into their car and leave. He was glad he left. He needed to be alone and think about this. He needed at that moment to talk to Buddy. His friend he grew up with. Buddy lived just around the corner from their house. Buddy's house was a large yellow two story Victorian remodel. Baylor took out his cell phone and called Buddy's number. "Hey" he said as Buddy answered. "I need to talk to you, can I come over?" "Sorry" Buddy answered, "I have to go with my Dad to the hardware store. I'll be back in a couple of hours. I'll call you when I get back."

"Ok" Baylor hung up his phone and went into the house and passed silently into his room where he plopped face down on his bed. His arms hung off the side of the bed and his fingers touched the Bible that he had laid down on the floor after reading his Sunday School lesson the night before. He jerked back as if electricity had touched his finger. He peeked over the side of the bed and looked down at the Bible. "Are all the things in this book a lie?" he thought. The extreme shock on his mind of the news he had been given had worn him down, he turned over and was fast asleep.

Janice woke Baylor up for dinner. When he came in to the dining room, his father was at the table dishing up his plate like nothing had happened. Baylor took food and slowly ate some of the dinner. He felt like a robot. Actually, he was feeling no feelings and that felt good at this moment. Janice tried to talk about general things and lighten up the atmosphere, but Baylor's mind was far away, trying not to think about anything.

This brain nap didn't last. Warren finished his plate and took his coffee cup. "Come with me son" he ordered in a kindlier voice than he had earlier. Baylor got up and followed his father into the living room and sat across from his father's chair on their formal striped sofa. He hated that room. It was always the place where he got lectured to as he grew up. He knew he could expect a sermon and at least an hour of discussing his sins and what he was going to do about them. "Baylor" his father leaned forward and looked him in the eye. Baylor grimaced visibly. "Don't worry," Warren frowned "you're not getting a sermon. However, you are going to hear me out." Baylor nodded.

"Do you love me?" Warren asked his son. Baylor looked surprised at that question. His father had never mentioned "love". Never once had he heard his father say to him "I love you." Now, he was asking him if he loved him. Baylor kind of coughed "Of course" he answered. "I mean really love me Baylor; enough to, say, die for me?" Baylor felt his scalp crawl. "Die for you?" he asked. "Yes, son. I mean to literally die for me." Baylor was silent for a moment then "If that were the only way to keep you safe, yes, I would die for you." He looked hard in his father's eyes. He was starting to feel a strange emotion. He had never really thought about loving his father. He did love him and his heart was feeling fear and anxiety at this moment. "Why, what's wrong?" he asked his father. "Thank you Baylor" He father looked flushed. "I needed to hear that."

He got up and paced up and down in front of Baylor for a moment. "Baylor, you have heard all my sermons for all of your life. I preached the love of God and I have preached His wrath. Well, I have not preached his "Army" because most people would not understand. Most people live in a shell and don't know what is really going on in the world. They are like sheep that have no sense."

Baylor was seeing a new side of his father. 'What do you mean?" He asked in almost a yell. "Just listen" His father said and kept pacing as he talked. "Our forefathers were all ministers and all in this church. It has been our destiny to fulfill the role of pastor and to carry out our ancestor Joshua Wells' oath to God to clear the world of the "Clade". These people are from the Devil and they are witches and they can only do harm to people. They must be exterminated. And we have to do it."

Baylor stood up now "You mean we have to kill people?" His voice squeaked.

"Yes" his father got up close to his face. "Kill, exterminate, take-out, whatever you want to call it. They are not human, Baylor, they are lizards. They are Chameleon lizards. They change colors. They are evil. They just have to die."

Baylor sat back down. "You said there were more of our relatives? I didn't know we have relatives. I only know Grandpa Hollandswirth." "He's on your mother's side. He is not a "Wells". You are a Wells. I am a Wells. She is not a Wells." He was turning red in the face.

"What about Mom?" Baylor asked "What does she think about this?" "Your mother trusts what I have told her. She is completely with me on this matter, but her family does not know and never will. My relatives have stayed secretly in touch as this was the plan." "What do you mean "plan"? he asked.

"My sixth great Grandfather Joshua Wells made a plan and an oath for his children and their children to follow. This oath, the Agreement is to God and if broken the member that breaks it must hang himself or another member of the family will kill him." "How is this oath broken?" Baylor enquired. "You read it." His dad said smirking, "If a family member that has taken the Oath, and all members must take it, they actually break it by not taking it, and if they see a Clade member, they must kill that Clade member or the oath is broken. Not only if they see a Clade member, but if they do not search out the Clade, that is also breaking of the oath."

Warren sat down and looked at his son. Nothing was said for a few minutes. "What you are saying" Baylor frowned "is that I have to kill people, I mean, I first have to swear to kill people and then I have to find them and then I have to kill them. Right?" "Right" His father answered in almost a whisper "But, Baylor, they are not people. They are something from the spirit world. They are from the Devil and they are truly witches. They are not, let me say it again, they are not people."

"Ok," Baylor swallowed hard. "If I buy this whole thing, that they are not people, then you, you my father, want me to swear and to fulfill this oath. Right?"

"Yes son, I do."

Baylor looked at this man who he had revered. This man, who, though he never told him he loved him, Baylor loved. He was his father. He was the minister. He was the Church's authority. How could he not trust that what he was saying was true? This man had taught him not to steal, to love his fellow man and now he was asking him to join in a hunt and killing of some things not human, some things evil. Witches.

Baylor felt dizzy. Somehow, all of a sudden, it seemed to be something that might need to be done. He hadn't really thought about the evil ones, the Devil and his army, but he knew that

123

there was a real enemy.   Now, he was being called to do something about it.

Warren got up suddenly as he saw a glimmer of acceptance in his son's face. "You think about it. " He said. "Baylor, I have to fulfill my oath or I will have to die. I have got a lead on one of the Clade. My cousin Harold sent me a name and address. I must take out this Chameleon and right away or I will have not fulfilled my oath. My other failure to fulfill my oath is that if you do not take the oath, I will have failed"

"Harold?" Baylor repeated the name. "We have a cousin Harold?   Where?"

"It isn't important right now Baylor, only that you take the oath. We are going soon to meet with the rest of the family for your ceremony."

"I'll have a ceremony?" Baylor choked. "I have to take this oath in front of other people?"   "Yes, In front of the family of Joshua Wells."   Warren left the room throwing over his shoulder "Think about it. I have to know tonight. I'm leaving in the morning.   There are six members of our family left. Two my age and four yours, including us. We are all meeting tomorrow." With that he was gone.

Baylor went into the kitchen where his mother was putting the dishes in the dishwasher. "Where are those letters?" he asked. She pointed to the little desk beside the refrigerator.   As he picked them up he turned to his mother. "You understand this?" She nodded her head yes.   "You believe they need to be killed?"   She nodded again but with a sad look in her eyes.

 He took the stack of papers and went to his room. He laid them out on the bed and started to read them again. The first one was from Joshua Wells. It read:

> This is an Agreement between God and the family of Joshua Wells.

I, Joshua Wells, upon finding out that there are witches in this world that have only one aim and that is to serve their father the Devil and to kill human beings, do declare war on the "Clade". The "Clade" being persons in the family of one Nora Lansing Coup, as it was discovered that she did indeed leave a child and that child has left this vicinity. In knowing that this name is probably a fictitious name, we will endeavor to follow this witch's family from hereto forward and to make sure that her line of Chameleon witches are taken off the face of the earth for the glory of God.

Also, upon finding that the people of this world are stupid and ignorant of these things, it behooves me to make my family not only swear an oath of secrecy, but an oath to fulfill my quest. I have, of late, realized that the Bible that I have been preaching from is not translated properly and that I have the only true link to God and to translating the scriptures as he, through me, thinks fit and proper for a world of people with no capacity to think for themselves. It is my duty to protect them, as sheep from the slaughter of the evil Chameleon witches.

It has been so desperately laid on my heart that I will not accept any rebuttal from my children and if they do not see eye to eye with my Agreement, I will have them kill themselves and if they will not, then another member of the family must so do to rid our family of any unbelievers. I have instructed my sons on my purpose and only Wilson understands and will stand firm with me. My other son Barton has disgraced the family by refusing to adhere to my teachings. He has also refused to end his unprofitable life and has fled the county. I have instructed, in this agreement, for his death by hanging.

The Agreement herein shall include the notes of each family member from hereto forward to what extent they have followed these directions and to what extent they have fulfilled our quest.

This Agreement shall be passed down in continuum and if there are more family members, than copies of said Agreement shall be copied verbatim and the notes also in order to have this Agreement carried out by our family to the complete destruction of the Nora Lansing Coup's Chameleon witch family thus called "The Clade".

Our family will also carry out a death sentence on anyone who aids the Clade. This is the word of Joshua Wells, Messenger and only Confidante of God to be fulfilled through his progeny. The family who adheres to this Agreement will take on the Sign of the Agreement and have it drawn permanently on the under portion of their forearm."

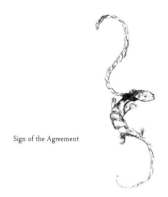

Sign of the Agreement

Dated April 2, 1806.

I set my name first on the Agreement and have left lines for my heirs to sign and agree.

There was a page titled Acceptance of Oath:

The High Reverend Joshua Wells, Minister in the Wellshausen Congregational Church signed this day April 2, 1806.

Each time a family member swore to the oath, they signed this page.

There was another page Roll of Extermination.

There Baylor read the following.

Exterminated:

I, Joshua Wells, High reverend and Confidante of God, put my hand to this note dated August 2, 1806. I have fulfilled my oath to exterminate the witch Nora Lansing Coup by hanging and burning her body. This one Nora Coup, I now know, through extracting the truth from Sara Waters, that the above Nora is Nora Marie Norris, daughter of Elizabeth Norris who was a professed Chameleon and therefore we know that she was a witch. She died in Colorado. This information came to us after a thorough interrogation of Sara Waters, who hid this known witch's daughter for all these years. Sara Waters has been hanged for selling her soul to the Devil by hiding a witch. We have discovered that Nora Norris' daughter Jewel married a trapper named James Johnston and they moved to Canada. I have set my oath, this day, that myself or one of the Wells family will find and exterminate this Jewel Johnston and her children if she has any and any that come after her.

Reverend Wilson Wells, Under Minister of the Wellshausen Congregational Church signed August 4, 1806

I have carried out the execution of my brother Barton Wells as he refuses to be a part of this Agreement and therefore is considered one of the enemy. He was hanged and burned on September 20, 1806.

"I, Wilson Wells, have carried out the execution of Jewel Johnston, daughter of Nora Marie Norris, known as Nora Lansing Coup. As I was unable to lure the witch away from her family to hang and burn her, I had to use an alternate method of destroying the witch. I put a poisonous snake in a burlap bag on her doorstep. She accepted the bait and was soon dead. I watched where her husband and son had buried her. I was seeking a way to destroy her son, but the two left and disappeared into the woods. I dug up the body of the witch and burned it. "

I, The High Reverend Winston Wells, Minister of the Wellshausen Congregational Church, have destroyed the Chameleon, James Johnston. I took a parish of the Church of the Wayland in a small settlement called O'Baren's Town. I used the name Reverend Paul Shimmer. After fulfilling this oath, I went on convocation to Montreal to put any suspicion off of myself. When I returned, James Johnston's daughter had married and moved away. No one in town seemed to know where she had gone. Johnston had another daughter, but everyone said she was most likely dead as she had disappeared at a very young age and they thought maybe the Indians took her.

I, Joel Wells, have exterminated the Clade witches, Viola Johnston Martinez and her daughter Mary Martinez Roll. As Viola Johnston Martinez sister Hattie was taken by the Indians, it is safe to assume that she is dead and I no longer need to pursue her extermination.

I, Rev. James Wells did exterminate the Chameleon witch Lilly Martinez Brown and Sarah

Martinez Barnes who gave her baby away to Madeline Straumberg.

I, Rev. Phillip Wells, did exterminate the witch Beth Roll Darnell. I also along with my sister Deaconess Patricia Wells Straman did hang and burn the bodies of Joshua and Jonathon Wells, our brothers who declined to be in agreement with our quest to get rid of the Chameleon. This we did in accordance with the will of our most Reverend Joshua Wells and with God as he has appointed Joshua Wells the all seeing prophet.

I, Deaconess Patricia Wells Straman, did, along with Phillip Wells, my brother, exterminate our brothers Joshua and Jonathan Wells, deserters to our cause and thus aiders to the Clade. I, also, did exterminate the Clade member and witch Willow Straumberg Ming, daughter of Sara Martinez Barnes.

I, Rev. Brown Wells have exterminated the Clade members Rudolph Brown and LuSong Ming.

I, Rev. Raymond Straman have exterminated the Clade witch Mercy Darnell Hart

I, Rev. Medford Wells have exterminated the Clade members Bill Brown and Judy Hart Webb.

I, Deaconess Clarise Wells Lackey have exterminated the Clade Chameleons Eric Ming and Crystal Hart Jenkins

Bill Straman died by own hand and in denial of Oath.

Tonya Straman died by own hand and in denial of Oath.

Mary Wells died in Child birth

I, Rev. Joe Wells, have effectively exterminated the Clade members Dawn Bell and Moonshadow Ming. I have also exterminated my cousins Josh Lackey and Lars Martell and my daughter Robin Soliere and her husband, all of which had denied the Agreement.

Robert Knott died by own hand in denial of Oath

I, Harold Knott, did exterminate the witch Windy Tollison and her husband by making their hot air balloon explode.

The testimony and records ended there with just the names of the Association that still had business to accomplish.

Jonas Straman has disappeared along with his two infant sons

Warren Lackey

Etienne Soliere

C.C. Martel

Dallas Knott

Baylor Lackey

Baylor shuddered when he saw his own name on the paper. And, that sign. He had seen that picture tattooed underneath his Dad's forearm. A scroll-type rope with the end a noose and a lizard's head in the noose and his body scrolled downward with its tail curved like the top of the rope. "That part of the ceremony?" he asked himself "This is insane." Baylor hit the wall with his fist. The sting felt good as it diminished the pain of thinking about the Agreement for a couple of minutes.

He had gone too far now to go back. He was beyond sick to his stomach. He was in another world; a world of shock. He seemed to be floating, not feeling anything. He had to understand what was going on and that meant he had to read it all again and this time take notice of everything.   "What about these other names. Names that had been listed but no notes, no exterminations. What about them?" His head ached.

Just then his door opened and his mother stepped into the room. "Baylor?" she asked. He didn't answer. "Baylor" she continued "I want to talk to you." She continued though he did not even look up. "I know this is a shock to you. I wish you could have learned about it years ago, but your dad said it was a safer secret if you didn't know until you were old enough to keep a secret." He looked up at her with fire in his eyes.

She continued "I did not agree with your father when I first learned of all this. But, I have come to understand and to accept it as truth."

"Truth?" he shouted. "What is truth, mother?" He looked up at this woman who he just saw in another light. He picked up his Bible. "Is this truth?" She nodded her head yes. "Well, then" he shoved it up at her. "It doesn't go along with what he said." Referring to his father.

"I know it doesn't seem to Honey, but….."

He interrupted. "Doesn't seem to?" He pressed his lips together in a hard line making his face very tight and his eyes bugged out. "I read this" he put the Bible on his lap. "I know it doesn't say anything about witches like lizards and that we have to wipe them out. At least not in the New Testament. This" he lifts up the Bible" says we don't war against flesh and blood" He looked at her and waited.

She didn't respond. Her mind was in a panic. She couldn't think of a thing to say to make her argument.   "Mom" he put his hand out to her. "What is going on?" She took his hand. "I'm sorry" she choked. "I am so sorry Baylor. I… I know it's…" She started to finish her sentence when the door opened and in walked Warren Lackey.

"Well?" he looked at his wife and then at Baylor. Janice had tears running down her face. "You" he looked hard at her. "Leave us alone and get a grip on yourself." His tone was one of those mean ones he used when he did not get total obedience from his family. Baylor felt the hairs on the back of his neck standing up. He felt anger and he wanted to get up and tell his father to lay off his mother, but he had learned over the years that that would make it worse for her. He kept quiet.

"Baylor" his father continued. "We are leaving at five in the morning. We are going to Sedona for the gathering of the Wells family." "Sedona, Arizona?" Baylor asked. "Yes, it will take us about nine hours." "Dad" Baylor stood up. "I don't think I want to go to this family thing. I don't understand what's going on and I am not sure I can agree with it." "Well" Warren said very slowly "If you want to die and you want me and your mother to be killed, then don't go. I can only tell you this one time. If we do not adhere to the quest of our family, we will die. We either have to kill ourselves or one of the other members of our family will kill us. We are either in compliance with the Will of Joshua Wells and God or we are not. If we are not, we have to die. That is just it." He stopped talking and stood very still.

Baylor sat still himself and didn't say anything but was thinking, then, asked "Couldn't we just hide somewhere?" he asked. "No, Baylor. The Agreement is the right thing to do. I have signed, I have accepted and I will carry out my part in this. I believe, Baylor, it is the right thing to do." Baylor knew then he was up against a rock and a hard place. Don't do it, they would all die. Do it, he would be a killer. He wanted his father to leave the room. He wanted to get down on his knees and ask God what to do. He wanted to stop thinking. But his father just stood there looking down at him. Then abruptly "We leave at five Baylor. Be ready." And he left the room. Baylor lay back in his bed and hugged his Bible unable to even pray, his head was too full. He finally fell into the arms of sleep.

Oct 15, 2009

It was a beautiful day in Sedona, Arizona and when Baylor stepped out of his father's car at the Los Palacio Lodge and stretched. He had not said a word to his father all day. His father didn't seem to care. He felt sorry for his mother, left back at home. She had seemed so sad. He felt that she did not believe his father was right. He knew his father had control over her all of his life and he didn't like the way she was treated.

He followed his father into the Lodge's office and waited while his father checked in, then followed him up to their room. When they had taken their bags in, his dad picked up the phone and dialed another room. "We're here" he announced into the phone. "Ok, six in room 219. Good, we need a bite to eat." He hung up the phone. "Hungry?" he looked at Baylor. They had not eaten since he munched on a few cookies his mother had handed him as he left. "Yeah" he nodded. Then his father picked up the phone and called for pizza delivery. Baylor turned on the TV and laid down on the bed. He certainly didn't want to think about this craziness. His father didn't push. He sat at the table with his notebook and seemed to be entranced in it. Baylor let his thoughts go to school. There was a girl he had been interested in. She was in his biology class. She was the perfect picture of what he thought a California surfer girl should look like. Her blond hair and blue eyes had him captivated the first time he saw her. He felt like she was interested in him too. He had caught her looking at him several times. It had taken his breath away. "What would she think of me now?" he thought and that thought made his stomach sick. He wished this could all go away and he were back home. "I'd call her. No, I'd.." his thoughts struggled against the fact of what was happening now. He kept an image in his mind of the girl, Autie, wishing he was there with her and not here.

CHAPTER TEN

--October 16 Santa Fe, NM

Richard reached over and tapped RuDee on the shoulder. "Hey, we're here." RuDee yawned and stretched. "Already?" she whispered. Sitting up, she looked around. "Ok, let's look for a hotel or motel or something. Something with internet." "Do you want to eat first, or get pizza?" he looked over to her. 'Pizza sounds good. I would like to stretch out on a bed." She pointed at a sign that showed an off ramp coming up. "Something Bed and Breakfast. That sounds good." Richard steered the car off the ramp and turned right looking for the B&B. RuDee beat him to it. "There it is." RuDee pointed "Just up there. See? Hawkins." Richard spotted it and turned in. "Let's check in." It was just minutes and they were in a lovely room with two queen beds and a large Jacuzzi tub. "I'm going in" RuDee squealed. "Ok" Richard smiled. "I'll order pizza. Maybe tonight we can go somewhere and get something more substantial."

Richard put his suitcase on the bed by the window and pulled out his computer and set it up on the table. It was nice to feel warm again. They had stayed in Pinetop, Arizona and it had snowed all three days they were there. Even the warm clothes they brought didn't seem to keep them warm. He and RuDee had poured over all their letters time and again to pick up clues. It didn't seem possible that the killers whoever they were could have known about RuDee's portion of their family. Other than maybe Martha Mason Radcliff had told someone the name of Victor Martinez. But the fact stood that someone had killed each of RuDee's ancestors that had the "gift".

There was a knock on the door. Richard looked through the peephole and saw a young man holding a pizza box and sack. Carefully he opened the door. "Pizza" the man announced, standing still. "How much?" Richard asked looking into his wallet. "Twenty two fifty." Richard pulled out some bills, put his wallet back in his pocket, took the box from the delivery boy with one hand and handed him the bills with the other. The boy handed him the sack, looked at the money and put it in his pocket with a "Hey, thanks Dude." He left smiling. Richard sat the box and sack on the little table and grinned thinking how happy he had made the delivery boy.

Richard had almost half of the pizza eaten before RuDee came out of the bathroom. She had on her Sponge Bob pj pants and a yellow tube top. Richard stared at her. "What?" she said in a cranky sort of way. "You're beautiful!" He blurted out, then got control of his self. "It must come from my side of the family." He grinned at her. "You'd better eat some pizza before I eat it all." She lit up "Pizza!. I need that" she said as she scooped up a big piece and put it on a napkin. "What's in here?" she peeked into the sack. "Yum" she picked out the box of bread sticks and a little container of sauce. "I love this stuff. Today, I am not counting calories. Nope, not one. I am having bread sticks with my pizza." Richard pulled out a bottle of soda for her and opened it. "I didn't get any ice, but it's cold." "Thanks" she said with her mouth full and reaching out for the bottle. "That Jacuzzi any good?" He asked. She nodded "Great! There's some bubble bath and oils, too, if you like them." "Bubble bath?" he winched "I don't think so." "Oh, come on" she smiled at him. "Try it, you'll like it." He didn't answer and went into the bathroom and shut the door.

RuDee, spotting Richard's computer on the table, sat down her food for a second and signed on to the internet, then stopped, her thoughts swirling. "I better not use my email." She tried to think of how the enemy might be tracking her emails. "Ok, first rule of this game. I'll hide from you and find you." She thought of how angry she was at the enemy. With the broadband access, she used a phony address, date of birth and phone number and soon had a new email address. She carefully went into her e-bank account and updated her account so that it would work through her new email address and no one could tell who she was paying. She felt confident that her bank account had enough safety so that she could use it to pay bills or pay for services on the net; services that might lead her to finding the enemy and for finding other family members.

Soon she had paid for several skip tracing companies. The ones that find people for you for a fee, but didn't try to use them. She logged into her account and put Victor Martinez Santa Fe New Mexico and hit enter. Ten entries out of eleven hundred possibilities showed on the screen. She grabbed her pizza and started eating as she scanned the entries trying to find anything that looked like an archive or old obituary. She now knew so much more by having heard Richard's letters. Victor had sisters and they would have had children. She knew they needed to look for clues, names, anything. She reached into her back pack and pulled out a zipper notebook and pen. She opened it up and arranged it neatly beside the computer hardly noticing the taste of the pizza she was eating as she worked. Then she had a wild thought and typed in the search line "Lizard Chameleon tattoo with hanging rope" She was getting excited as she scanned through the results. Tattoo parlors, lizard tattoos, Chameleon pictures, ropes, hanging ropes. Nothing that looked like the one depicted in the letters. She went back to the Victor Martinez search.

"Did you find anything" Richard's voice penetrated her concentration. Looking up, RuDee noticed his beautiful, big green eyes, dark black hair combed back against its nature, as some of the hairs found their way free and came down across his brow. His grin displayed large beautiful white teeth. "You must be the spitting image of Victor Martinez" she realized out loud. "No wonder my great Grandma was taken in." He blushed under the compliment. He pointed at the mirror over the dresser by where they were sitting. "Yes, cousin, we are a pretty family" he said with his chest pushed out, then he bent over a little and put his hands out into the air like claws "for lizards, that is." He raised his eyebrows and came at her. She stood up and pushed him towards the bed and as he was falling onto the bed he grabbed her and pulled her down with him. They convulsed into a fit of laughter then stopped abruptly as their eyes caught their reflection in the mirror, they were not there, only the multicolored bedspread and their clothes showed. Staying very still, they took in this moment, not like before when they were getting Richard's things out of his house. That time, it had been a scared lonely type of feeling when they saw they had turned colors, but this time, together, they both felt an elation, an empowerment, not a scared feeling but a proud communal, family feeling of unity. "Cool" Richard whispered. "Yeah" RuDee lay quietly in his arms for a second then jumped up very quickly. "Richard" she fairly shouted; tears streaming down her face. "We aren't the hunted anymore. We are the hunters. We are not alone. You and me, Cuz, You and me" She danced around the bed. Richard got up and joined her. They danced, without music, in a victory type dance. "Come on RuDee" Richard grabbed her hand, "Let's shake out some info from the net" and headed back to the computer.

...Just two doors away

Jadin, Autumn and Brie had spent the rest of the morning, after eating at Crater's, searching the internet for clues of family ties. Susan and Connie went shopping and returned with notebooks and pens. They had also bought the girls and themselves bikini bathing suits. They also had a small men's bathing suit for Jadin. All the suits were light colors. They had also bought some magic markers in various camouflage colors. They set the suits out and carefully drew soft lines and squiggles on the suits. "These ought to blend into most situations," Connie held up the last suit colored. "It looks good" Susan agreed.

The kids came over an inspected the suits. Jadin held up his. "Mom?" he looked at her with wide eyes in a question. "Extreme times must have extreme measures, Son" She patted his cheek. "Didn't ever think I would agree to nudity, did you?"

"Ugly" Autumn screwed up her face, then looked at her mom, "But, doable. I totally get it Mom." Susan laughed as she handed one to Brie who held hers up with two fingers like it was something stinky. Then she laughed and held it up against herself "I get it too."

Ron and Blane came in through the sliding glass doors from the patio. "What's going on?" Ron asked. The girls quickly put their suits behind their backs. "Nothing Dad" Autie smiled. Susan got up and came over to her husband. "Ron, we bought the kids and ourselves some slinky bikinis" she was holding up hers. He grinned at her then pretended to be gruff. "I don't think so." He acted like he was mad. Blane was taking all of this in. It seemed like a dream. "How" he thought "could this be happening? A few months ago, he had an ordinary ranch family and he was perfectly happy living a good life on the ranch. Now, he was watching his wife and daughter talking about wearing almost nothing so they could blend into the scenery." He shook his head, thinking "How am I going to protect them?" He turned to Jadin. "What did you find out on the computer?"

Jadin got a notebook from the table. "Here is some info we picked up. We put in Joshua Wells and 1700 to 1900 and found this guy. It seems there was a Reverend Joshua Wells in Ohio. He was a well known minister in the Wellshausen Congregational Church. It gives a little bit about him. He was elected Head Cleric over the Ohio Territory and was the Administer of Last Rites for prisoners that were to be hanged. He assisted the local law officials in dealing justice to the seventeen townships in the territory.   Then, we looked up a census and found he had two sons, Barton and Wilson. That's all we have so far. This guy is the one who hanged our Nora, according to our letters.   I was just about to pull some information about this certain church, but haven't found anything yet."

"Good work Jadin" he looked admiringly at the boy. Then he turned to the rest, "As much as I hate to think of showing off my wife and daughter's bodies, I think you all should practice hiding. I would also like to teach you some defense moves. I'd like to make it plain here today, that I don't know why your bodies turn colors, but I know it is not something that makes you evil or a witch. I just found out about this, but I feel that because of the lizard bite, your family's DNA got warped somehow. Anyway, I just wanted to tell all of you that though I have not been going to church for years since I was young, I have never stopped believing and I do pray. I do pray for my family. I don't know much, but what I do know is that we will have to call upon God to help us. It is plain in our face that we have an enemy and it means to exterminate us. Well, I also know that, if we go on the offensive, we can stop this enemy so they won't hurt anyone else. That's all I have to say, except I don't know what to do to help other than to stay on guard and watch."

A tear rolled down Connie's face. She was sorry she hadn't told him many years ago. She reached out and patted his hand. "Thank you" she whispered. Ron walked over and offered his hand "We'll figure it out together" Blane took his hand in a firm handshake both feeling the bond of being the two protectors of this family.

"Ok" Susan got a hold of the moment. "Tonight, we five" she pointed to the kids and Connie and herself "are going out and we are going to practice." "Yes" Jadin pulled his hand down in a mini gesture showing his pleasure in the adventure. Both girls looked at him with frowns on their faces. With that, Jadin went back to the computer and the girls stood around him as they tried to find out about their enemy. Susan announced that the adults were going out and would bring back lunch for the kids and the four grownups left.

That was in room three, over in room five, Richard and RuDee were also on the computer searching out census, death, marriage records and any other thing that crossed their minds about the people that might be trying to kill them. They too had put in Joshua Wells and had found out about the church and some of Rev. Wells' bio. RuDee had her notebook and had quite a lot of information already about her family and some on the fifth great Grandfather that never knew he had other children. Victor Martinez' family had been her goal and now that she was with Richard all sorts of questions were answered for her.

The afternoon seemed endless and the information seemed too little for all their efforts and thoughts. RuDee took a nap about mid day, but Richard kept right on searching. He had found Victor's mother Viola and then found her two daughters Sarah and Mary. The records of a census for Sarah showed her married to a Barnes, but a further census didn't show any children. Mary, however, was married to a John Roll and they had a child; Beth. Putting all this information down in a spread sheet that RuDee had created was like working a great jigsaw puzzle. A piece here, a piece there, fitting one together while a few were out in the middle of the puzzle not connected to anything.

He knew he had to keep going on it. He now not only feared for his life but for RuDee's. He looked over at her sleeping on the bed. It seemed impossible that he had only known her a few days. They interacted like they knew each other forever and it was like they were brother and sister. He did think she was beautiful, but the idea of her being a relative kept him from letting his feelings go in a boyfriend girlfriend type of realm.

Richard thought of how his mother had always turned to God. They went to a big church downtown Flagstaff when he was growing up. He had not gone to church after he got out of high school and went to college, but now wished he could go into that big sanctuary on a Sunday. He remembered how safe it felt being there, there in God's place.

He wondered about the people after them. "How" he thought "could they possibly get so mixed up as to think they were witches?" He couldn't fathom a person who would say they are God's and then kill someone. "Maybe" he mused "they were just wearing religious type clothing to fool everyone." He turned to his search and typed in Connie Benson. One search result was a blurb about a Connie Benson who won a blue ribbon at a fair for her rhubarb pie. In the article from a local newspaper, it also told that a Brie Benson had won the barrel racing competition. Another search result told of a Blane Benson, a veterinarian, who was running for city council.

As he scanned all this information and wrote down certain facts that might prove important, his mind wandered back to Flagstaff and his mother. He wanted to find out about her body; if the Police Department had released it for burial. He had not called his good friend yet to close up his house. Maybe he would do that tomorrow and try to find out what was happening there. It made him queasy to think about her body lying there all alone. He put his head down for a minute and stifled the tears that wanted to get out. He tightened up all of his muscles and drew in a deep breath and started working again.

It was almost six when RuDee woke. She softly went up behind Richard and put her hands on his shoulders. "Find anything?" she asked in a whisper. "Yeah, but nothing seems to fit yet. I put it all on your spread sheet."

RuDee picked up the paper and smiled. "You found a lot of stuff. That's incredible. I'll bet you're hungry. I am." She urged. Richard turned off the computer. "Yes, I am starved, and not for pizza or junk, but for a steak and baked potato." "Great" She chirped "give me five minutes and I'll be ready."

Not far from the Bed and Breakfast, in the Purple Crystal Motor Inn, another computer had been very busy. Courtneay and Blake took turns with Dezza looking up information and had also, like Richard, found information about Connie Benson. Dezza had already found information on Mary Martinez Roll, her fourth great Aunt. And researching the census and other records had found Beth and Mercy. Blake found information about the twins; Judy, their grandmother, and Crystal, her sister and now they had information on Connie who would be about their mother's age.

"I feel like we're spinning our wheels" Blake put his hands up in the air. "I need some air. Can we please go eat? It's been a long time since breakfast." As he said that, a thought entered his mind. "I can't believe I forgot" he looked at the girls, "But this morning at Crater's, I saw someone turn colors." Both of the girl's eyes got big and their mouths dropped open. "What?" Dezza said trying to take in what he had just said. "You saw someone turn and you didn't tell us?" Blake shrugged his shoulders "I can't believe I forgot it." "Well?" Courtneay raised her voice a little. "What did you see?" "I saw a guy turn the color of the table cloth and the menu. It was the guy who was walking back from the table and he was looking at you. You were just going into the bathroom and he had just come out of the men's room." Courtneay's eyes brightened. "I remember him" she squealed. "He was so cute, Dezza, blonde, like a surfer." Blake continued "He was turned looking at you and

he ran smack into a chair at his table. His hand turned the color of the table cloth and the menu. He didn't see that I saw."
Dezza, taking all this in, jumped up "We have to find him." She demanded. "How?" Courtneay asked, not really expecting an answer. The thought of finding someone in this city was just stupid. "I don't know" Dezza quipped, "but we have to try. Maybe if we go to where kids hang out, we'll spot him. Besides, we have to eat, don't we?" she sat down on the bed and picked up her tennis shoes and started to put them on. "Let's go eat then walk around the shops, maybe we'll spot him." Blake and Courtneay both made a b-line for their shoes. They were hungry and the thought of being outside in the night in a new city was exciting. "Let's eat at the Cattle Drover place we saw. I'd sure like a real meal." Blake suggested. "Sounds good to me" Courtneay agreed. Dezza nodded her head also in agreement.

The Cattle Drover was only two blocks away from their hotel and it felt good to be walking in the cold crisp air. When they entered the restaurant, they saw that there was a little bit of a wait and the hostess gave Blake a beeper to hold. They found enough room at the end of the long bench in the foyer to sit down together to wait.

Dezza slowly and carefully scanned the room, looking at all the people. She had been on the defensive for a long time and she always liked to know who was around her. Several old couples were sitting together and at a cocktail table having a soda was an extremely good looking couple. The boy was about 19 or 20, tall dark hair, green eyes that seemed almost luminous and a smile full of large white teeth. He looked white, but also could be Hispanic. She then assessed the girl, obviously a small Black girl with pristine features. Her short hair cut gave her stylish curls opportunity to dance around her face showing off startling green eyes not unlike the boy's. He had combed his hair back straight, but some strands had come loose and floated across his brow.

Dezza watched for a moment but then the couple's beeper went off and they followed the hostess into the darkened doorway of the main dining room. It was less than a minute and their beeper went off. They followed another hostess into the dark inner sanctum. The tables were enclosed in rough lumber to resemble corrals. The boards were thick, but, you could see parts of the parties setting on either side through the gaps.

Dezza noticed they were right next to the couple that went in before them. She poked Courtneay. "Look" she nodded her head toward the other table. Courtneay carefully moved until she could see the couple. "He's cute" she whispered leaning close to Dezza. The girls grinned at each other. Blake leaned over a bit and frowned. "Just a guy" he observed "But she's a knock out." He talked slowly as if he were talking about the weather. Their waitress appeared and took their order.

RuDee had just received her salad, when she noticed a pair of eyes looking at her through the boards. When she looked back, the girl on the other side of the boards quickly looked away. She leaned over to Richard and whispered "I think we're being watched." Her face turned away from the suspicious table. Richard didn't look right away but when his dinner came and the waiter was setting down the plates, he leaned back and looked over between the boards. He saw an exquisite Oriental girl glancing at him. She saw him look at her and put her eyes down and smiled. When the waiter left, he leaned over a bit and told RuDee. "She is looking" he said with a self satisfied smile. RuDee caught the inference. "Oh" she said "I guess girls are always looking at you?" He just kept grinning. The girl was cute and he would have liked to make some kind of contact if the circumstances had been different. He turned his attention to his steak and potato. This was the first time in days that he enjoyed his food. RuDee, too, was enjoying her food. She had ordered the grilled salmon and was savoring every bite.

Dezza was trying to concentrate on her food, but she felt like a magnet was pulling her eyes in the direction of the two at the other table. She had ordered a filet mignon and was busy cutting it up in little pieces when her fork slipped and skidded across her plate causing a piece of the steak to become airborne. It flew over the middle board and landed 'ker-Plunk"

143

right on Richard's shoe. Startled he looked down at the piece of meat sitting on the top of his foot and then looked up to see the surprised and panicked look of the girl at the next table.

There was silence for a minute while all five people wrapped their minds around what had just happened. Then as if someone had uncorked a bottle of Champaign, all five started laughing at the same time.

Dezza stood up and came around the side of the boards "I am so sorry" She exclaimed trying not to laugh. "It's ok" Richard himself was unable to stop laughing. "Do you want it back?" He almost choked. "I don't think so" Dezza smiled at him "Do you want me to take it off of your shoe?" "I got it" Richard had scooped up the piece of meat in a napkin and laid it on the table. "No harm."   Dezza started to turn around and go back to her table. "Wait" Richard called out. "Are you guys locals?" RuDee looked alarmed. Dezza saw her look of concern. "No, we're just visiting. What about you two?" RuDee stood up "I'm RuDee and this is Richard. We're on vacation too."   "Hi" Dezza responded. "I'm Dezza and I'm here with my friends." She turned to go "Again, I'm sorry."

She walked back around the board that separated the table and her arm was too close and she scraped it on the rough edged of the corral board. "Ouch" She winched and grabbed her arm. RuDee looked up when she heard Dezza and her eyes went right to Dezza's arm that had suddenly taken on the color of the board so much so that RuDee could not see the arm, just the board and the starting of her blouse. Richard saw it at the same time and drew a big breath and stood up. RuDee jumped up too.

"Are you alright?" She asked Dezza.   "Yes" She answered holding her arm. Then she looked down and saw her arm the color of the board and looked up to see the two staring at her arm.   Blake and Courtneay had also stood up to see if she were ok.   Blake also saw RuDee looking at Dezza's arm. "You turned colors" Richard blurted out. RuDee came closer "Yes Dezza, you did turn colors."   She then whispered "Are you chameleon?"

Dezza looked scared and Blake came to her rescue. He put his arm on her shoulder and answered RuDee. "Yes" he said with a straight face and a deep frown, "We are Chameleon. How did you know to call her that?" RuDee put her hand out to the board and it suddenly disappeared. "Oh?" Dezza smiled a crazy smile wobbling her head twice. "I guess that's why." The five stood silently and then Courtneay took charge "You know we shouldn't stand around here. Why don't you two join us at our table. Bring your plates. OK?" Quickly Blake and Dezza helped RuDee and Richard bring their plates and utensils over to their table. Richard then retrieved their drinks.

The group sat in silence again until Richard broke the ice "Do you by some miracle, have letters?" Courtneay answered. "Yes, we do. Whose letters do you have?" RuDee responded. "Richard has all the way up to Elizabeth and I have only five. What about you?" This time, Dezza answered "I have ten and Blake and Courtneay have ten. Why in the world are you two here. Now. At this place?"

RuDee quickly stood up and looked around the restaurant. "We might better do this somewhere else. Would you come to our room?" "Yes" Blake said "Let's finish our meal and then go. I think we need to get out of here. Who knows who else is in here." They all nodded and concentrated on eating their food, shyly looking up now and then at each other. The air seemed alive with electricity and a strange unearthly atmosphere.

Blake took both tickets from the waiter when he came back and Richard pulled out some bills for a tip. They didn't even pass the usual niceties like "Thank you" or "I'll get the tip." It still seemed like such a dream.

As they walked up the hill toward the Bed and Breakfast, RuDee, Dezza and Courtneay walked up front and the guys walked behind them. It was getting chilly and Dezza shivered. Richard noticed and told her that they were almost there and the room would be warm.

As they turned into the courtyard of the B&B, they noticed that the garden lights were out. Richard thought it was odd and took the lead so they could follow him. There was a sliver of light coming from the street light about 300 feet from where they were. As they started to turn into the hallway, Dezza jumped. "What?" she blurted. She stood stock still. The others followed suit and didn't move.

"Dezza!" Courtneay shouted in a whisper. "Something moved over there." They all looked hard at the brick wall that surrounded the little garden area. "I saw something just now move" Richard put his arms out in front of the girls. "Get back" he ordered them. They stepped back and got closer together. RuDee suddenly ran forward and grabbed the brick wall. "Hey" a male voice yelped. "What are you doing?" RuDee pulled the brick wall toward them, however as it came out from the wall, they could see that it was a boy about their age not wearing anything but a small swimming suit and he was the color of the bricks. As he got closer, he turned back to a normal human color. As they stood looking at this boy,

"It's you!" Courtneay shouted, recognizing him. "We saw you at Crater's." Just then four other figures came out from the bricks and turned into people. Blake almost fell backwards and Dezza gasped for air. "Whoa" she said in a very low voice. "How many of you are there?"

An older lady whose color was just coming back to normal held out her hand "I'm Connie and this is Susan and these three are our children. I am sorry if we startled you. Who are you?" She asked much like any mother who was demanding facts and now. Richard stepped forward. "I'm Richard, but should we be standing out here?" "No, of course not" Susan spoke up "Please come into our room. We will explain what you just saw. Please. We won't hurt you. Our husbands are in there and I think they should be in on this. OK?" The group that had just came from the restaurant walked slowly with a little apprehension. But they followed Susan, Connie and the other skimpily clad people into the big room at the end of the courtyard.

CHAPTER ELEVEN

--Sedona same day.

Baylor hung back as his father knocked on the door of the room where they were going to meet with their relatives. He had not even known he had relatives until Yesterday. The door opened and a girl with dark brown hair pulled back into a low ponytail, wearing a large oversized sweater and dark rimmed glasses invited them in. Once inside the room, Baylor could see that there were, besides his father, an older man and two boys his own age along with the girl that answered the door. "Warren." A tall gaunt looking man with a purple scar, going through his left eyebrow, held out his hand to Baylor's dad. "Harold." Warren responded. The men shook hands. "This is my son Baylor." Warren pulled Baylor up even with him.   Harold pointed to a short stocky boy with very red hair and a multitude of freckles, that you could see only between the tapestry of tattoos that lined his right arm, the right side of his neck and down on the left side of his face about an inch. "This is my son Dallas" Dallas nodded his head at them. Harold continued "Baylor, this is your cousin Etienne." He nodded toward a tall boy with light brown hair that was cut in an older man's haircut, very Ivy League. He was sporting a clean shaven face and seemed to be very clean unlike Dallas' scruffy appearance. "And" Harold reached over and took the hand of the girl who had opened the door "This is C.C. your other cousin."   C.C. nodded to him and then went and sat down on the couch and tucked her feet up under her.   Harold gestured to them all to sit down.   They sat on the couch and the few chairs that were in the middle of the suite.

Harold, Warren's fourth removed cousin, took charge. "As you know, we are here to induct Baylor into the Well's Agreement." He turned to Baylor "Baylor, we all have taken the oath to the Agreement and have been marked with the special symbol of such.   Dallas has been in agreement for four years now and is coming close to finding a member of the Clade" He then nodded to C.C.   "C.C., too, has been on the search for the Clade and will be filling us in on what she has found. Etienne

147

just got back from Wyoming, where he came close to eradicating a Chameleon witch. Actually, two of them. A mother and daughter, Connie and Brianna. However, they suddenly disappeared. He does have some resources to find them and I am sure he will be back on their trail in no time." He looked at Warren. "Warren, do you have anything to report before we go on?" Warren squirmed a bit in his seat. "Well," He stuttered "I do have a lead about a descendent of Victor Martinez and a lady named Luz. I have found some evidence of a Bob Swann living in Idaho. I am planning a trip up there soon and will exterminate this Chameleon." Baylor felt a wave of nausea flood over his being. He looked at his father, usually a hard, totally in-charge domineering person, acting like a cringing, scared predator. His mind suddenly saw a closeness of his father to an image of a hyena.

Just then C.C. pulled out a notebook and held up her hand as if she were in a classroom. Harold nodded to her to speak. "I found a strange entry in a published journal of a Mr. Milton Sparick, a teacher in an elementary school in Seattle, Washington. The journal was a compilation of essays written by 5th grade students about their ancestors. I'd like to read one of them." She looked around the room for assurance. Everyone was looking with interest. She continued "It is written by Mildred Douglass, age eleven. It reads 'My ancestors by Milly Douglass. My great great Grandfather's last name was Bonne. He was French and was a trapper in Canada where he hunted beavers for their skins which he sold to the fur traders. His wife, who was my great great Grandmother was stolen by the Indians when she was just my age, eleven, and was rescued by my great great Grandfather who bought her and kept her safe and when she grew up, he married her. We don't know much about her except that she had a twin sister named Viola who she never saw again in her life time. They shared a family secret that now I share. A secret family secret. That I cannot tell in this essay. My other ancestors were not so interesting as great great Grandma Hattie was.'"

C.C. smiled "And now I have actually traced this line of Chameleons, that were lost, to Mildred's daughter, Charlene Jones married to a Wills, who lives in Colorado. I am leaving for

Colorado as soon as this meeting is over." C.C. stood up "I am going to make up for what my father and his mother could not do." An evil sneer crept over her face. Baylor's stomach tightened as he watched this somewhat dowdy person lighten up and seem to come alive with the announcement of her evil intent. His head started to hurt. There was no escape. He knew and felt it in his being that this girl could and probably would kill him and his family if he didn't become a part of this hideous plot.

He got up and told his dad "Got'ta go" and headed for the bathroom. When he came out, the group was looking up at him. They had waited to continue. He sat back down, his mind swimming. "Dallas?" Harold looked at his son. "What do you have?" Dallas stood up and put his squatty hands on his non-existent hips. "I am staying up at Flagstaff for the time being. I have one of our Deacons watching for Richard Bell. Etienne gave me this lead. Uncle Joe took care of Richard's mother and we are sure he will come back up there to take care of his mother's funeral services. And, when he does." Dallas made an obscene gesture of slicing his own throat and pulling his hand up sharply like he was being hanged." Baylor felt the evil that exuded from Dallas. His eyes seemed bug-eyed and his grin was almost as evil looking as C.C.'s had been. Harold jerked his attention back. "I have also leads to give out today. However, that will come as we all leave here. Right now, we want to have Baylor join us in our God given quest.

Baylor looked over at the door wanting so bad to jump up and run. His father must have sensed it because he laid his hand on Baylor's leg bringing his attention back to the group. "Baylor, please come up here" Harold gestured for him to come and stand with him. Baylor slowly got up and stood by his uncle. He tried to pray but nothing came to his mind. His thoughts kept coming back to the savagery of the group in the killings that they had done and that their own parents had been killed because they did not participate. He sent up an unheard moan in God's direction. Then, as clear a bell, the thought came to him. "It's just words. I don't have to do anything."

So with his uncle leading him, he said yes to all the questions he was asked and then sat in a chair and yielded his arm to Dallas who adeptly poked what seemed to be a million little holes filled with ink into the underside of Baylor's forearm producing a picture that any seasoned tattoo artist would have been proud of. There it was; a rope with a noose and in the noose the head and neck of a chameleon with its body curling down like the rope curled up. It stung sharply and Etienne who sat silent through all of this walked over and took, from a small bag on the sink, a bottle and some cotton swabs. "Here" he took Baylor's arm and gently patted on something cool and the stinging instantly went away. "Keep this stuff on it from time to time and you won't get infected." Baylor said thanks with his eyes and seemed to sense some sort of a compassionate look from Etienne.

Harold quickly concluded the meeting with the handing out of new information on the Clade family members and the information that they had found as they tried to track down every living Chameleon and wipe them out. He also handed everyone a cell phone. "These are only to be used to keep us in touch with each other and for calling in one of us if you need help." He said they would get a call about the next meeting. Then he added "Oh, yes. These phones have a GPS tracking devise and I" He grinned a silly grin that maybe you would see on a Devil's face "Have the control." He shook hands with Baylor and Warren and he and Dallas were gone. Etienne asked if they would all like to go to dinner and C.C. said no, she had to go and she left. Warren accepted the invite and he and Baylor followed Etienne across the street to the Red Dirt Café.

After a pasta supreme and salad bar, Warren excused himself saying he was going to bed so they could leave very early in the morning. Baylor told his father he would be back at the room shortly.

Baylor and Etienne shared small talk for a while, then Baylor asked point blank "What do you think of all this?" Etienne raised his eyebrows in surprise of the question. All this? He returned. "Yeah" Baylor pushed "All this Chameleon stuff and actually killing them."

Etienne stared hard at Baylor for a moment then slowly answered, "My parents died from rejecting the Agreement" he looked down and continued "I made a choice to live. And that choice consists of becoming a part of the Agreement. I don't like it, but it is there and our heritage. I don't want to kill, but I plan to see if the persons are really lizards or can really turn colors before I do anything. That is confidential" He squinted his eyes as he took a chance on Baylor by saying this and Baylor knew it.

"I guess we are both in the same boat. I can't be the reason my parents are killed, now can I?" Baylor felt some comfort and safety in Etienne. It was a mutual feeling for the both of them. "I don't think I could ever talk to C.C. or Dallas. I really think they totally believe in killing the Clade, and enjoying it." Etienne shared his feelings. Baylor shook his head in agreement to the statement about their cousins. "Yeah" he said "I saw something in both their eyes that told me they enjoy this quest. What are you going to do now?"

Etienne shared with Baylor his stay in Wyoming and how he started school there and was getting close to meeting this Brie and her mother Connie; Clade members, and when they disappeared, he felt a relief. "I thought about maybe pushing for information from her boy friend, but instead, I just left town. "So, I called Harold and went to stay with him until this meeting. Harold is a true Wells, totally in agreement with the Agreement. I am very careful what I say around him."

Baylor shook his head in a discouraging way "Yeah, I think my Dad is scared of him and my Dad isn't scared of anything. Speaking of which, I'd better go. Maybe we could meet up again?" "Sure" Etienne smiled "You have my cell number. If you are ever in trouble or need me, just call." With that the boys shook hands and Baylor went back to his room.

Just a block away, C.C. was repacking her suitcase. It was a large suitcase with a three inch secret compartment that took a certain turn of a small lock mechanism to open. C.C. unpacked its contents on her bed; one small revolver and a box of bullets, one thin nylon rope, matches, duct tape and an assortment of wicked knives rolled up in canvas. Gingerly and lovingly, C.C. patted each item as if they were precious to her. Then she neatly repacked them, shut the secret panel and repacked her clothes. Then she got on her computer and printed out a map to Colorado on the printer that was provided in her room. Taking her hair out of the bun she had it in, she shook it free and let it fall around her shoulders. She threw the glasses that she was wearing in the pouch of her suitcase and sat down to put on her makeup. When she was through, there was a definite contrast between the plain somewhat dowdy girl the others had seen and the beautifully made up almost movie star like, young lady.

She slipped into some tight jeans and a tight fitting v-neck sweater and pushed up the sleeves. Donning high heel stilettos, she finished putting her luggage together and rolled the two suitcases out to her car where she deposited them in the trunk. Lighting a cigarette, she climbed into her 1969 apple red Camaro, peeled rubber out of the parking lot and headed for the outskirts of Sedona and Highway 17.

As she looked into the rear view mirror of the town she was leaving, she felt the excitement of the hunt and hungered to get to Colorado and find her prey.

C.C., abused by her parents, had secretly enjoyed watching as a Wells family member put both her father and mother to death. She had turned them in for not following through with their part in the Agreement. They had planned to, but she made up a story and soon her parents were targets. She seemed to feel an exhilaration and being taken in by Harold and Dallas and found she liked their thinking. Their cruelty matched her own and soon she was with them wholeheartedly in the quest to chase down the Clade. She and Dallas spent hours on the computer trying to find links to Elizabeth's family. When she was sixteen, C.C. was given a ceremony and she made her oath and received her tattoo. She was soon sharing Dallas' affinity and almost an addiction to tattoos. All of hers were where no one could see them unless she wore a tank top and short shorts.

She was thinking of Baylor as she passed Flagstaff, wondering if he was sincere about the Agreement or not. She had a passing thought that if he wasn't, she would be the one to take him out.   After Flagstaff, she turned her stereo up loud and sped off across eastern Arizona.

Dallas was dropped off in Flagstaff and Harold was already crossing over into California by the time Baylor got to sleep. Harold was relieved when he left Dallas and was now himself driving. Dallas drove way to fast to suit him. However, Harold never told Dallas what to do. He had trained him from a little boy to want and to accept the Agreement and once he knew that Dallas was all for it, he let him pretty much do as he pleased.   He gave Dallas all the computer equipment he wanted for this quest and even though he was the minister of his congregation, he allowed Dallas the tattooing.   He explained to the people of the church that it was a trade off to keep Dallas off drugs. His congregation took whatever he told them as Gospel.   However, he did suspect that Dallas was indulging in some sort of chemical experimentation.   He was headed home so that he could get Sunday's services in order.

As Baylor fell asleep that night, he wondered at what kind of congregation was at Dallas and Harold's church. He was just about to fall asleep when he felt the urge to get down on his knees and pray as he used to when he was very small, but it didn't seem appropriate as his father was in the same room and it seemed like such a ludicrous thing to do to pray in the same room with a man that intended to kill someone else and was expecting him to kill someone also.   Baylor suppressed the urge and looked up in his thoughts trying to form some sort of prayer.   Nothing came but a silent "help" from his heart directed at Heaven.

--back in Santa Fe

Room 3 of the Bed and Breakfast came alive as Connie led the group of people into the now getting crowded room. Ron and Blane stood up and stepped back as their wives, in bathing suits, no less, came in with five new people plus their three who also were still in "almost nothing" bathing suits.

No more than they had all crowded in and the door shut, Dezza took charge at the amazement of their new found Chameleons. This small little Oriental girl all of a sudden was asking questions like a large army Captain. "Ok" She said loudly, "Who are you people?" she was looking directly at Ron. Connie stepped between her and Ron, however and looked this little girl in the eyes, "As soon as we know who you are missy." She took on a mother tone "Then we will tell you who we are." Richard put his hand up in the air like a traffic cop. "My name is Richard Bell and this is RuDee" he pulled RuDee up to him "We are Chameleon and we are cousins. We just met Courtneay and Blake and Dezza here and they, too, turn colors." Everyone stood in silence. He continued "I take it that you are Chameleon from what we witnessed outside. And, I don't think we have to fear each other, because the enemy" He gestured with big arm movements "thinks that turning colors is bad, so they wouldn't or couldn't do it, Right?" He was sounding excited and his voice was higher than usual. Blane moved closer to Richard. "It's ok Richard." He pulled Connie up by him. "This is Connie, my wife. She is Chameleon as is our daughter here, Brie. Do you kids have letters?" "Yes" Richard shook his head. "Do you?" Connie shook her head yes. Susan nodded too. "Let's all sit down for a minute and sort this out" Ron interjected and started to put chairs and the little sofa into a circle.

Susan and Connie had put on a robe and Brie, Autumn and Jadin had put on their clothes. Ron had the circle completed and said "Some of us can sit on the floor." Dezza, Courtneay and Blake sat down on the floor in a line in front of the chairs. Susan sat with Autumn and Jadin and Ron stood behind them. RuDee and Richard sat down on the floor on the other side of the circle and Brie, her Mother and Dad took the chairs behind them.

"Let's introduce ourselves and tell a little about us so we can get some sense of this" Dezza spoke up again looking at RuDee.

RuDee took the hint. "I'll start. I am RuDee Swann, and I am of the line of Victor Martinez, son of Viola Johnston Martinez.

I'm in the illegitimate line, or limb." Then, she pointed to the top of her head "As you see, I am somewhat different than you all." A small chuckle wave went around the room. It was such an incredible moment as again each person had to grasp the concept of yet another happening in their lives because of a lizard bite. She continued "I have five letters."

She poked Richard. "Yes," he responded "I am Richard Bell and I, too, am from Victor Martinez" he looked over at RuDee and gave her a little push, "The legitimate line." He said in an arrogant tone of voice. She gave him a hard push back. "I have ten letters" He told them "From the beginning."

After a moment Dezza spoke, "I'm Dezza Ming and like RuDee, I look somewhat different from all of you white people, however, being half, I fit in right?" she looked around the room.

"You would fit in half or not" Brianna spoke up. "I am so glad you all are here."

Dezza smiled at this lovely girl "Thanks, I'm glad too. Anyway, I do have ten letters, also. I am from the line of Sarah Martinez and also, like RuDee, of another illegitimate limb of this family tree. I have some relatives to find someday that are not Chameleon. They are my great great Grandfather that fathered Sarah's baby. My parents have been killed by the "enemy". After searching, I found Courtneay and Blake and thus, we three are here."

She looked at Courtneay. "Hi" Courtneay said shyly "I'm Courtneay Tollison and" she pointed at Blake "This is Blake, my twin brother. We just lost our parents this year and probably would be dead now if Dezza hadn't found us. She saw a tattoo on our housekeeper and figured that she was one of the people who are out to kill us. So we ran and here we are. We came here to figure out what to do next."

Blake motioned to Brie who was sitting across from him. "I'm Brie; Brianna Benson. My Mother, here, is Connie. She and I are Chameleon. That's my Dad Blane, he's clean." Several chuckles broke loose from the group. "We have ten letters including my Mom's. We just came from Wyoming where we discovered the Tanner's and now we are on our way to the Tanner's house in Bakersfield and decided to stop here to throw any one off our track. There was a new boy in my school that had the hanging lizard tattoo and we are sure he was one of the enemy. We are staying here to do some research, also."

She looked over at Jadin. "I'm Jadin Tanner and this is Autumn, my twin sister. That's our mom and Dad, Susan and Ron and we are from Bakersfield. Mom, Autie and I are Chameleon. Dad's not. We think that no one knows about us because we are from a line that the family didn't know about. Our ancestor Hattie Johnston was stolen by the Indians and we are sure everyone thought she died. But, we can't be sure and we are now on the offensive."

The stories were out and everyone sat silent for a few minutes. Then Dezza stood up. "If it's alright" she looked around the room "Could we please share our letters and our research? I don't think this meeting just happened. I, even though I don't go to church, like I should, I think it is Providence that we all came together like this and it has to be for our ending this blood coup from the "Well's family".

"I think you are right Dezza" Susan spoke finally "But, we all need to get some sleep. Why don't we all go to bed and in the morning, I will arrange for some sort of room somewhere where we can all sit around a big table, maybe at Crater's. I'll bet they have a large room for big parties. We can eat breakfast while we are sharing our letters. Would that be alright with everyone?"

Richard wanted to speak up and tell them he thought they should do it now and be prepared quicker, but noticed that most shook their heads in the affirmative.

It was a tiring evening, a mind boggling evening, like an evening out of "Twilight Zone". However, Courtneay did speak up "I think that all the rest of you should get your stuff and move in here with us, in this room." "Great idea" Connie took over "I'm sure we can all make room. I don't like to see any of you get out of our sights."

It was agreed and the eight teens went to the Purple Crystal and then to Richard and RuDee's room and brought back all of their stuff. Connie laughed as the kids left "Well, I don't believe that modesty or convention can be worried about at this point." Susan put her arm around her new found cousin. "Nope, Cuz, we will have to relax and turn our thoughts to more important things like keeping our children alive and ourselves." The parents kept the two room suite where Ron and Susan had one room and Connie and Blane the other.

The other suite was a large one room with two king sized beds and make-down couch. It also had a small roll-away cot in the closet. Dezza and Courtneay shared one bed. Brie and Autumn took the other bed while RuDee grabbed the little cot. Richard insisted that Blake and Jadin take the couch bed and he took the some extra blankets and made a pallet between one bed and almost under RuDee's cot.

Before going to their separate rooms, the grownups agreed that they would have to come up with a plan in the morning, not just to read the letters, but then what to do with this group of Chameleons that had suddenly come into their arena of care.

"I counted ten Chameleons." Ron handed Blane a beer he had pulled from the mini-fridge. "Do you drink beer?" "Occasionally," Blane reached for the brew "And I think this is an occasion. However, I don't drink much around Brie. She knows I have a beer now and then, but it just seems appropriate not to." "Me, too" Ron responded, "I do keep a few in the back of the fridge when the temperatures are over 110 or when something major is happening. Like this." He was feeling a warm kinship with this new found friend. They had a lot in common. He grinned at the thought that they both were married to lizards. He raised his beer can "To our lizards." "Blane responded "Here, here."

Susan and Connie were having hot cocoa and sitting closely together on the couch. They too had found someone in common. They found family and it was such an overwhelmingly comfortable feeling having each other and even the kids that had just come into their lives. "I think reinforcements have come in" Susan told Connie. Connie grinned "Yes, I am thrilled about all these kids. I wonder if there are more out there somewhere. Safety in number, I always say." She and Susan both had a glad heart feeling as they watched their husbands seem to bond in a friendship and a common thought of protecting these people.

Over in the other room

"I still can't believe that hot water is still going." Dezza mused as yet another one of them took a long shower and emerged from the one bathroom they were sharing. "I know" Brie agreed "At home, my hot water runs out in exactly ten minutes. I was in there at least twenty."

When everyone had bathed and brushed their teeth, the last one out of the bathroom was Blake. "Did you have hot water?" Dezza asked him. "Yeah, lots. Feels good to be clean."

They all laid in their various places facing each other. Richard spoke first "I think, like Dezza, that the prayers of our ancestors are being heard. I still can't believe we're all here and that we all came to Santa Fe at the exact same time. My Mom warned me to get ready, to find the enemy before it found me. She thought I should find our family and band together. And, well, here we all are. We need to get serious about how we would handle the enemy if they come around. He told them how he and RuDee stripped down and hid as they got his stuff out of his house. Jadin chimed in "Yeah, that's why you found us outside, we were practicing. I agree with you. We have to get ready."

Brie threw a pillow and hit Jadin in the head. "I'll show you my colors, if you'll show me yours." She said cockily. Jadin picked up the pillow and jumped up and on top of Brie and held the pillow about an inch from her face. "Now what are you going to do?" he teased. She immediately turned over and scooted out from under him. "I'm going to get you before you get me." And with that she jumped right on top of his back flattening him to the bed. "Good job" Dezza squealed.   Everyone started laughing.

"Let's hide" Courtneay tucked her top up to make it into a bra like top and took off her long pjs. Now only wearing her skimpy panties and top, she jumped up and flattened herself against the curtains. She disappeared.   It was contagious; everyone stripped and assumed positions against a wall, a bed, the curtains, the door, the floor and the dresser. The room looked empty.   As each Chameleon looked over the room not seeing anyone a new sense of community swept over them like a wave of security, courage and family. Lips on the wall opened sowing teeth as Autumn made a statement and not to any of them.   "Lord, intensify our colors and teach us to use the abilities you gave us." She heard one "Amen." However, she could not tell who said it. Autie had gone to church all her life but hadn't really thought about prayer since all of this happened.   It was so confusing; she seemed to put her thoughts about God on the back burner as she explored this new realm that she had entered. Tonight, however, her belief and faith washed in like a tidal wave as she seemed to understand that this meeting was for their benefit and safety and that only God could have arranged it.

Out of the corner of the room an arm came out and turned a fleshy color, "Let's practice un-coloring then coloring as fast as we can. Let's race." It was Richard. The room took on a gallery of sights as each appeared and disappeared sometimes one at a time and sometimes two or three would come out, un-color and recolor. Blake seemed to win in the speed of it, however, Courtneay's colors were more vivid and close to the color of whatever she was near.   Dezza stood everyone in a row. "Wave" she shouted. One at a time and in synchronization followed the other out away from the wall and then back causing it to look like the wall was doing the "wave." They were watching in the mirror across the room and the girls started giggling. Soon they were all laughing and doing funny antics. Finally, Jadin ordered "Stop" he shouted. "We need signals, commands or something to let us know when to duck." He jumped back against the wall and colored "See?"   What if I don't see the enemy and you do. And you say hide but that is not a good word to use. We need a plan." Blake answered him "Good idea, but I think that we should get some sleep. We can't cram it all in one night." They all agreed and put back on their pjs and laid down. Dezza said sweetly "Nite Blake" "Nite Dezza" he replied, mimicking her. Then it started "Nite Courttteenneee", Nite Reechard", "Nite Rude Deee", "Nite John boy.." They all went to sleep with an incredible peaceful feeling; like when your mother has locked the front door, tucked you in and turned off the lights. They weren't alone in their dilemma anymore.

CHAPTER TWELVE

C.C. pulled her car in behind the Wal-Mart store where the trucks park and turned off her headlights. She had started to nod off as she came close to Santa Fe, realizing she needed to sleep and now. She pulled a blanket she had in the car around her and lowered the driver's seat back until it lay against the back seat. As she yawned and stretched getting in a comfortable position to go to sleep, she leaned over and pulled a large hunter-type knife out from beneath the back of the passenger side and laid it across her chest. Pulling her left arm up past her head so she could lean on it against the door her eyes went to her tattoo and she smiled her incredibly insane smile and drifted off into sleep.

Dallas had reached Flagstaff much earlier and had a meeting with Chad Ringle who had been watching Richard's house, right there across the street from it.

Chad, a deacon of the church in San Francisco where Dallas' father was the minister, had joined the secret inner circle of deacons that had sworn to help their pastor fulfill the Agreement. He had driven out with Dallas to assist him. He informed Dallas that no one had come or left the residence and he thought they had better contact Richard's college and see if he had gone back to school.

Dallas walked around the house and tried to look in. Carefully he crept to the edge of the house and carefully worked his way around the house looking in the windows where the curtains were not pulled. "Nothing" he shook his head at Chad. He tried the back door and then the garage door. They were both locked. "Well" He shook his head, "He isn't there."

"I have to get back home Dallas" Chad told him. "My wife is about ready to have her baby." Dallas frowned, but addressed Chad "Ok, but be on alert, just in case I call you. You'll have to take the train. I can't go back just yet." Chad nodded that he understood and got his pack out of the car. "The train station isn't far from here, I'll walk. Good luck." "Thanks" Dallas smiled, but it was anything but sincere. Chad felt a shiver go up his back as he left and walked away from Dallas. He always felt afraid in Dallas' presence. Like he was in some kind of danger and that danger would come from Dallas.

Dallas went down to the police station and went to the man at the front desk. "Excuse me?" he politely asked, "I'm looking for my cousin Richard Bell." He waited. The man just kept looking at him. Then, "I don't know a Richard Bell." Dallas turned red. He didn't like when people did not answer him quickly and to his satisfaction. "You know" He frowned "The guy whose mother was killed." "Oh, him" the policeman smiled. "I haven't the faintest idea where the kid is." "Well" Dallas squinted his eyes at the man. "Did his mother have a funeral?" "No." The policeman wasn't smiling this time. "Excuse me, I have work to do." he looked down at his paper with an air that let Dallas know the conversation was over. Dallas fumed out of the station. As he walked out the door, the policeman was watching him with a frown. He turned to the man sitting behind him. "Something funny about that boy. I don't believe he was Richard Bell's cousin at all." The other man just shook his head.

Dallas walked a few blocks in the brisk air trying to calm down. He was incensed at the policeman. He couldn't handle anyone standing up to him or ignoring him. "He'll be sorry." He mentally threatened the man. He left to go home and figure out what his next step would be. Getting back in his car, he slammed the door and peeled rubber down the street toward the freeway which he entered going west toward California. He planned on driving all night and getting to San Francisco in time for church.

--October 16th Santa Fe, NM

Susan woke with a start. "Mother" she whispered into the air. Her mind went to the fact that the enemy could find them and, if so, then they could find her mother. She knew she had to do something. Looking at the clock, she wished it was later so she could call her. Quietly she slipped into the bathroom and put on her makeup. Her stomach hurt, waiting to get in touch with her mom. "Please" she directed up to God.   After getting dressed she curled up in a big arm chair with a notebook and pen and started writing down all the things that she and the group needed to do. First on the list was "Call Mom." Then she tried to put in order what things she thought they should do to confront the enemy and to hide from the enemy. The second was to decide where the group would go. She put next to that "Bakersfield" with a little question mark beside it. Her thoughts went to her house. It surely couldn't house all these kids. They would have to think of some alternatives. They all needed to get back to school, enemy or no. After two pages of notes on what needed to be done, she snuggled down in the chair and dropped her head to the side of the plush soft wing and slipped back into sleep.

"Susan" a gentle hand shook her shoulder. Susan opened her eyes to see Ron bending over her with a look of concern. "Hi" she grinned up at him. "I guess I fell back to sleep here." "I guess" he tousled her hair. "Get up and let's get these kids some breakfast" "What time is it" she asked. "Eight thirty" fell across her ears causing her to jump straight up. "Eight thirty?" She ran over to the phone. "I have to call Mother."   Ron nodded his head.

Not far away

C.C. had wakened also at four am, Eager to be on with her hunt, she drove to a local service station and bought a large coffee and two snickers bars. As she headed north toward Colorado, she flipped on her radio and turned up the sound so that the bass booms shook the whole car and the tweeters screamed through the air. If any older people were in the car they would have felt like it was vibrating to pieces. "I'm coming to get you Charlene!" she yelled in a creepy and sarcastic tone of voice.

After eating the candy bars, she pulled a cigarette out of its pack and stuck it in her mouth, but didn't light it. Rolling it around in her teeth, she grinned at herself in the rear view mirror. She felt wicked and she reveled in that feeling. She was elated and felt like she was on an African Safari.

C.C. thought about Etienne. She had had such a crush on him. Right off the bat, when she met him, she thought of ways to be near him. She pretended she just wanted to be friends, but her insides actually burned like a giant fire was in her. She wanted so much more. She had wanted to get intimate with him, that is, until Reed came into her life.

She pulled down the sun visor and there staring back at her was a picture of Etienne and one of Reed, both pictures she had very sneakily took with her phone's camera. "Wish you were here, sweetheart" she blew a kiss to Reed's picture. She had daydreamed of the two of them on a hunt with her for the "Clade".

Etienne had never paid much attention to her however, and C.C. chose to believe it was because they were related. She figured once she convinced him that they were only distant relatives as they shared fourth great Grandparents, he would look at her in a new way. He was still on her mind even though she suddenly was in total love with Reed. She took her hands off the wheel and waved them frantically in the air to the head banging music and sang loudly "Reed, Etienne, Reed, I love you, kill, kill, kill, I love you, I love you, kill, kill, kill." only putting her hands back on the wheel when the wheels hit the safety bumps on the side of the road.

It was one o'clock when she pulled off the freeway and into the business district of Colorado Springs. It had started to snow and the road looked like white snakes dancing across the freeway. Pulling into a motel, she grabbed her suitcase and ran inside to the office. Once she had her suitcase inside room 17, she set up her computer and logged on to Maps4U. She had found an address of a Charlene Wills. 1220 Alvarado Drive. "Ha" she exhaled heavily "That is just around the corner" she smiled. "Well, Charlene, I've got'cha now. But first, I'm going to eat. Can't wipe you out on an empty stomach" she said loudly as if her prey were right there in the room with her.

Picking up the phone she ordered a bacon cheese burger and fries, a cherry coke and two fried cherry pies from room service. While waiting for the food, she took a shower and washed her hair. It was like a bull fighter's ritual to her, getting ready for the kill. "Toreador. Lover and conqueror. You are a hero, Toreador." she sang softly as she gazed at herself in the mirror as she dried her hair. She had just finished her makeup when her lunch arrived.

She turned on the TV. and sat back against the headboard to eat. The weather was calling for two feet of snow. "Snow, snow snow" she mimicked and grinned at the TV. "Snow, snow, blood on snow." She saw herself in the mirror and was pleased with what she saw, not noticing how wicked her features were as she contemplated the evil deed she was about to do.

Back in Santa Fe, Susan called her mother in Colorado Springs. "Mom?" Susan asked the voice at the other end of the line. "Yes, Susan?" her mom answered surprised to hear her daughter's voice. "I thought you were in Wyoming. Are you home?" "No, we're not. We're in Santa Fe" "Santa Fe? What are you doing there?" her mother asked. "Mom, I have to tell you something." There was silence. Charlene sat down in the chair near the phone, expecting some bad news. "The children?" She whispered. "The kids are alright. We are too. It's not that. Can you just listen for a minute?" "Sure, honey. I'm sitting down, now calm down and tell me." Her heart was pounding. She had never heard Susan's voice like that before. "Mom, we have found more Chameleons." "Wha...?" Her mom started to say. "Shhh, just listen" There was silence. "Mom we found great grandma Hattie's sister Viola's descendants. Mom, there are ten of us, eleven counting you." Susan paused expecting her mother to say something, but there was silence.

"Mom, all of the other's except my children and Brianna have lost all of their parents and Grandparents all the way back to a Nora. Nora's mother was bit by a Chameleon and became the first one. Mom, I mean, they were all killed by the family who are trying to kill all of the Chameleon people. They haven't known about our family, I don't think, but now with the new technology I know they are going to find us. We have banded together and are going to make sure these people do not kill any one again. Are you still there?" she asked the phone. "Yes, honey, I'm here" her mother answered in a stronger way than Susan had expected her to do. She actually thought her mother would freak out.

"Go on Susan" Charlene said in a strangely powerful way. Susan continued "We have found out that a Joshua Wells had our ancestor Nora hanged and burned for being a witch. It was her mother Elizabeth that started all this when she was bit by a Chameleon lizard. Each time someone died, there had been a person around with a cleric collar and some had words written on walls that said "die witch" and a drawing of a lizard being hanged appeared on a wall or sidewalk.

I wish I had time to tell you everything, and I will, but not now. Mom, you have to leave your home, right now. You have to get to us. We all have to stay together. We've even put on bikinis and practiced concealing ourselves. Can you imagine? Me in a bikini? Not pretty." She halfway chuckled, then in a serious sounding voice. "Can you get what you need and get out of there?" Silence again. "Mom?" "I'm thinking Susan, just a minute. Just hang on."

There was silence for at least three minutes. "Susan, I am going to pack and get in my car and go to a motel. It's snowing really hard here and I can't get on the freeway. I will call you when I get in a room. Ok?" Susan breathed a sigh of relief . She thought she would get an argument. "Oh, Mom, I feel so much better. I woke up this morning so worried about you. Please hurry, I know I am probably being too careful, but I can't help it. I need you. I love you. Please hurry" "Okay Susan, now let's get off the phone so I can get it together. I'll call you later. Bye" Before Susan could say good bye, her mother had hung up.

Charlene walked through her house looking at all of her treasures and sighed sadly knowing that she would be leaving them here. Then she packed two suitcases being sure to take

166

her letters, pictures and important papers. She quickly looked through all the papers she was leaving and pulled out anything that had Susan's name or address. These she put in the suitcase. After she had the car packed, she made sure the thermostat was on 45 degrees and all the lights and water faucets were securely off. She started to leave then went back to her desk and took out a piece of paper and a pen. She wrote note to a pretend maid. "Dear Milly, Please clean the baseboards this week and dust the ceiling fans. I will be back next Thursday. If you need me please call me at my brother's in Minnesota. You have his number. Please don't over water the African violet. Thank you, Charlene." "There, that ought to confuse someone" she thought. She got into her car and raised the garage door, the snow was coming down heavily now, but her driveway was still ok.

She pulled out onto Alvarado and then turned down the street and noticed the Arms Hotel. "Who would dream, it's so close to home." She pulled in and went into the office and registered. Putting her card into room 19's lock, she pushed the door open, picked back up her suitcases and entered the room. Looking out the window, she stood on tiptoes trying to see her house from there as it was just around the corner. She hadn't eaten lunch and was starting to get weak. After deciding to go to the hotel's restaurant, she washed her hands, picked up her purse and opened her door. As she stepped out into the hall, she almost ran into a very pretty young girl who had just come out of the room next door. Both women stepped back and said "Sorry" at the same time and then, they both headed for the front lobby, Charlene turned right into the restaurant and the other woman turned left to exit the building. Charlene thought how nicely dressed the girl was and how she looked just like she had stepped out of a bandbox. "Must have a date" she thought.

There were only two other people in the restaurant and she got her lunch in a hurry. Then she left to go back and rest.

C.C. walked through the blowing snow up to the door step of Charlene's house. She rang the bell, waited, and then rang it again. She made an ugly face. "Hello" she called out then again "Hello!" very loudly. Nothing. She waded through several inches of snow to peek into the front window. The blinds were down, but there was a space between the last two slats that she could actually see into the room. The house looked empty. "Maybe she is out shopping" she thought, trying to think if she should hang around in her car for while to see if Charlene would come back. She couldn't understand an old lady out in this weather. After an hour of waiting in the car, turning it off, getting cold, turning it on again to get warm, she thought she had better go back to the hotel and plan this for later, when the snow let up. The snow was getting deep and her car was a rear wheel drive. It slid a little but did make it into the parking space.

Once in her room, she paced like a caged animal hungry for meat. Then she remembered the heated indoor pool. "That" she brightened up "Is just what I need, a good swim." Pulling out some short shorts and a sports bra, she changed and grabbed a towel, draped it around her shoulders and headed for the pool.

The only other person in the pool area was an older lady sitting on a chaise lounge reading a book. It was the lady she almost ran over in the hall earlier. She nodded a greeting. The lady nodded back and continued her reading. C.C. dove in the pool with such gracefulness, Charlene couldn't help but admire this young woman's form and her body was almost perfect. She wondered how Autumn was. She missed living closer to Susan and her children. She went back to her reading.

C.C. continued to swim laps for about thirty minutes then she swam to the side where her towel was and laid her hands on her arms on the side of the pool. Charlene had decided to go back to her room and stood up to leave. "Excuse Me" the young lady called to her. "Yes?" she answered looking down at the girl in the pool. "Would you mind handing me that towel? I don't want to get out without it." C.C. pointed to the towel that was draped over a nearby chair. "Sure" Charlene grabbed the towel and walked over to the side of the pool. As she carefully sat it down beside the edge, the girl reached for the towel. Charlene's eyes went straight to the top of the girl's underarm.

A tattoo stood out boldly on the girl's fair skin. It was a tattoo of a lizard hanging in a rope noose. Charlene's eyes got big. C.C. saw the alarm in the lady's face. "Sorry" she said as she pulled her arm down. "Stupid, huh?" she shrugged her shoulders. "Oh, I'm sorry" Charlene got a hold of herself. "I just am not used to how everyone is getting tattoos these days" she smiled at the girl "That is an unusual one, isn't it? I really don't know about these things." "Yeah" C.C. got out and wrapped the towel around her. "I was just a kid when I got it. What are you going to do?" she laughed shrugging her shoulders, "Can't take it off now." "Well, have a nice day." Charlene said and turned to go, C.C. caught up. "I'll walk with you" When they got to Charlene's door, C.C. looked at her. "Are you on vacation?" Charlene opened her mouth and started to tell her why she was at the motel, then thought better about it. "Yes" she lied "I didn't want to drive in the snow. I'm from Steam Boat Springs and I'm going to be at my daughter's house in Kansas but I guess I'll be staying here until the roads are clear. What about you?" C.C. lied too. "I'm here to see my boyfriend's mother. He's going to take me over to her house later tonight. He is spending some time with his father, their divorced, for a few hours. Well, here you are. Nice talking to you."

Charlene turned to her door "Bye now, yes it was nice to talking to you and good luck" "Luck?" C.C.'s eyes got wide. "Yes, Good Luck with your in-laws." "Oh, yeah. Thanks."

When the door was shut and locked, Charlene sat down quickly in the chair and looked for her cell phone. She assessed the room. The girl was right next door but their bathrooms were not adjacent. That gave Charlene comfort. She would call Susan from the bathroom. She heard the TV in the girl's room come on and it was a little loud as all young people seemed to have it. She turned her's on, too, to a news channel and a little louder than she liked to have it. Then she went into the bathroom.

Oct 15th morning Santa Fe

It took an hour for Ron and Blane to find a place for the group to have breakfast in a conference room. They had run onto a convention center hotel across from the local community

169

college and convinced the manager to let them have a room for a "traveling college class". The restaurant next to the hotel, agreed to cater the breakfast. Ron had convinced Blane that money didn't matter anymore, if they had to spend to do what they needed to do to keep these kids safe, then so be it.

When they came back to the B&B, They found that everyone had packed up their stuff and put them in their cars. Susan told them that they, Susan, Connie and the kids, thought that if the boy had found them in Wyoming, then he might find them here and they should keep moving until they get to Bakersfield. As they caravanned over to the conference room, each in the car that brought them there, Autumn turned to her mother. "Did Grandma call you back yet?" Susan frowned "No, but she said she was going to a hotel. If she doesn't call me by noon, I will call her cell. I know she doesn't like to use it except for emergencies." "I'd jump right to emergencies on this one." Brie spoke up. "Me, too" Jadin agreed. Brie poked him in the ribs and he turned and pinched her arm. "Ouch" she cried "You beast".

Ron looked at them through the rear view mirror and smiled. Brie was a beautiful girl, tall and strong. He could see how Jadin was evidently attracted to her. "Want me to reach back there and smack him Brie?" he offered. Brie blushed aware someone had seen her carrying on with Jadin. "No, that's alright." She looked at Jadin "I think I can handle him." "And she can" her father's rough voice sounded from the back seat. "Hey" Jadin leaned over hard against her "Handle me? Can you?" Autie pushed back from the other side of Brie. "Stop, you two, I'm being crushed." Everyone laughed, except Autie that is.

The restaurant was expensive but the breakfast was well worth it. There was a huge buffet set up in the room and soon everyone had a plate piled high with eggs, bacon, biscuits, fried potatoes, sausages, ham and toast. They then had another one with pancakes and a bowl of fresh fruit. Everyone had coffee and a glass of juice. "I could get used to eating like this" Richard spoke up. "Ditto" RuDee chimed in making everyone laugh to think that this tiny little girl could eat that much.

RuDee warmed under their friendly kidding. She had been alone so long and this new family was making her feel so much a part of them. She still gravitated toward Richard. They had become instant friends and now she had all these cousins and the grownups treated her as if she were raised by them.

She helped herself to two more pancakes. Jadin reached across the table and forked off the top one. "Yours looks better than mine." She pretended to try to stab his hand with her fork. "Go ahead, Cuz" She laughed "You need to put on some weight." "Hey" Jadin held up his arm in a muscle "Don't you be slamming on me." He winked at her.

Jadin, too, was secretly enjoying all of this. Even though he fully realized their danger, and he had dozens of friends in school, there was something special about being in this "family." He really liked Brie's Dad Blane. He also liked the fact that his Dad liked him. He hadn't ever seen his Dad talk much to other men. He had friends, but he mostly just hung out at home and if he did go fishing or hunting, it was with the family. He was proud how his Dad made Blane feel comfortable about leaving his ranch and joining them. He kept looking at Brie's mother Connie since she looked so much like his mother. "Weird" he thought as he, like all the others, tried to digest this whole realm they were thrust into. And to think that all these years he wasn't afraid of anyone and now it was a reality that there was a group of people who were out to kill all of them. He felt himself getting angry at these people. Jadin was friendly with everyone, however, he had a resolve within himself that would not back down from anyone or thing. He knew they had to go after the enemy as well as hide from them. He felt the hairs on his neck bristle, thinking about these people.

"Jadin" Brie, sitting next to him put her hand on his arm. She looked into his eyes and then down at his arm. He looked too. He had turned as green as the napkin that lay on his lap. "Oops" he grinned at her. "I was just thinking about those people out there. We have to get them first." Brie nodded her head, her eyes looked sad. She agreed with him, but also, she had felt a sort of jealousy when he teased RuDee.

The morning went quickly as Susan introduced her check list of things they would need to do, things they would actually need and where they might live. Their discussion ensued with everyone feeling free to put in their ideas. Courtneay took the list from Susan and told her that she would be the secretary. Susan told her "I knew I liked you." Courtneay smiled. She had been taking notes since she was small and loved to make lists and organize, taking over this task made her feel like she was contributing. Dezza suggested that they make a list of their assets since there were ten of them, "that is twelve, with the non-lizards" she said with a flair. "Most of us do not have parents, but we do have assets that we really need to take care of and share, of course." Courtneay looked over at Blake "Blake, we have assets, right?" "Yes" he answered looking at Ron, "We have a house and money, I think. I took out a lot of money from the checking accounts, but I do have a lawyer and I know we have money. I just don't know how to get it and we don't know if that person is still at our house or not. We'll really have to be careful about it." There was a silence for a minute then Ron addressed the issue. "We'll have to be very clever how we find out about everything. But, I do think we have the mental resources here to not only be sleuths and find the enemy, but "smoozers", manipulators and find out about all of our properties, etc, etc, etc." he ended like Yule Brenner had done in "The King and I." The women laughed, but the teens just looked at him. Obviously they didn't watch the oldies movies.

Susan looked at the clock on the wall wondering about her mother. It was already One and she hadn't called yet. The group had agreed on many things and the most immediate was that they would get gas and all head for Bakersfield. That seemed to be the safest place at this point as they didn't know if the enemy had found any of the Tanner's branch of the family tree. They did know that as of right now, Susan's mother was safe and if they had gone down into the family tree she would have come first, in the enemy's findings.

Blake stepped outside the building as the group was just milling around. They had stopped planning and were going to leave at Two. He felt suffocated. At school, Blake had a lot of friends

172

and he was involved in all the activities he could cram into in a day. Being on each sports team as the seasons permitted, he kept in good shape. He was feeling the need to exercise. It seemed he had been sitting forever. He looked around trying to see if there was a place he could run. Just then, Ron came out "You alright Blake?" he said gently. "Yeah" Blake turned toward him. "I just need to run or swim or lift weights. I feel like my body is in a box." "Well," Ron looked down the street. "We're not leaving for an hour "Why don't you run? Say, in a four block square. It looks like a pretty quiet neighborhood" He looked into Blake's eyes "Please just four blocks. Go twice or three times, but stay in that four blocks so we can find you if we have to. OK?" Blake nodded affirmative. He felt elated. "Thanks Ron." And with that he was off. Ron was amazed at the kids speed. He was already down one block in what seemed like the next second. "Wow" he thought out loud "That kid is fast!" "What?" Susan asked as she came out and found him looking down the street. "Blake needed to run, so I told him to take off." Susan looked worried "Susan, we have to let them be normal. Anyway, he is staying in a four block square if we need him." Susan held up both hands in a surrender type gesture and turned to go back in. "Wait" Ron caught up with her. He pulled her into his arms. "You alright with everything?"

Susan had tears running down her cheeks "Can we keep them safe Ron? I am so scared. I am going to call mother right now. I hope she's alright."

At that very moment Susan's phone rang. "Hello" she answered "Mom? Yes. It's me. Are you at a motel?" Susan stood listening as Ron watched her. "Slow down Mom, I'm trying to understand. Can you talk louder?" She looked at Ron frowning "Susan" her mother whispered loudly "I have to talk quietly. Can you hear me now?" "Yes, I can, go ahead." Susan held her hand over her phone at her ear so she could hear better. "I went to the pool to read and there was a girl who is staying next door to me. She had a tattoo of a hanging lizard on the inside of her upper arm." Susan gasped. Charlene went on. "She said she was here to meet her boyfriend's family." Susan cut in "Mom, listen. You have to get out of there and away from that girl. That is the sign that the people, who want to kill all of us, have on their arm. Is there any way you can leave there?" "It's snowing too hard, but I think it is supposed to let up tonight. I thought I might call Mike. Maybe he could help me." Susan had met Mike a man friend of her mother's and had liked him, "That is a good idea Mom, Can you call him?" "Susan, I made sure there was nothing at home to connect me to you. I took all my papers, pictures and letters. I'm pretty sure I got everything. If Mike comes to get me, I'll have to take my car away from here somehow." "Mom, please be careful." There was silence then "Sweetheart" her mother said gently "I'll do the best I can. If something does happen just know I love you. But I am strong Susan and I am, if I don't say so myself, a pretty good Chameleon" she laughed. "I have to go now and make a plan. I'll call you when I feel I am hidden and safe. Love you Susan" and she hung up. Susan stood there looking at the phone. She told Ron what was happening and they went into the rest of the group.

1 pm   Colorado Springs Oct 16

Charlene had just hung up when she heard the door next to hers close. She hurried to the peep hole just in time to see the girl go by and toward the exit.   Hurriedly she called Mike. "Mike" she said excitedly "I need your help."   "What Charlene?" he asked.   Charlene had confided in Mike as they had been close for a lot of years. She told him about the girl and how she needed to sneak her car out and to get away from there. "Ok" He agreed "Go now while she is gone. Drive to the A&W and park at their back door by the big dumpster. No one can see it from there and I think the snow doesn't pile up there as much. I'll be right there and we can move your stuff out of your car. Hurry!" He urged.

Charlene put herself in high gear, making sure she had not left anything in her room and took her suitcases to the car. She noticed that the space beside her car was empty. She quickly got in and drove up Carson Street and turned left along Mission Blvd for four blocks, then turned right and went two blocks, left for two blocks then left again for two blocks. Then she turned on Cicero Street and entered the alleyway behind the A & W. There, she pulled her car up tight between the large dumpster and the store. Within seconds, Mike had pulled up behind her and was waiting by her door when she got out. "Hurry" she said "I am so scared." They put all of her things in Mike's trunk and made a thorough sweep of her car making sure nothing was in it. Mike reached in and took the pack of papers out of the glove compartment. "She doesn't need to know anything else about you."

Mike was a retired Detective. He had been on the Colorado Springs Police Force for forty years. He had been skeptical of Charlene's phenomenon but when she showed him her colors, he was amazed and cool about it. Then when she told him about Susan's call and that there was someone out to kill them, he started to worry about her. Charlene locked her car and took the keys. When they had pulled the car onto the street, Mike went back and with his car's window scraper and his feet, he made marks in his tire tracks from her car to the street. "That ought to confuse her" He said as he got in the car." Mike drove up and down the main streets of the town to completely hide their trail then he headed north and out into the country where he lived. By the time they got Charlene's things into his house the snow had covered even the tracks that led to the garage.

Meanwhile, over at Charlene's house, C.C. had walked around the house several times peeking in all the windows where she could. Finally, sure that Charlene wasn't home and wasn't coming home, she took a wire from the lining of her jacket front and slid it in and under the door's lock. The lock popped open. She put her tool back into the hem of her Jacket front. Once inside she shivered. It was cold in there. No one had been home for a while she guessed. She started to look around and in drawers. She couldn't find any papers and it seemed odd that there were no pictures of anyone sitting around. Even Harold had family pictures around and he didn't even like his family.

After she had thoroughly searched the house, she went into the garage and opened drawers and doors; nothing. She was fuming. She hated when someone got the best of her. "She knew I was coming." She thought bitterly. Her hatred grew toward the Clade member she was out to exterminate. "I'll get you Charlene" she screamed up into the air."

She stormed out of the house slamming the door so hard it didn't shut but hit and bounced and stayed open. She got into her car and drove very slowly to the street. Her car slipped several times and threatened to stop altogether. She worked with it going up a little and back this way a little then this way until she finally maneuvered onto the street where she turned and got in line right after a big snow grater. She followed it up the street and it turned off just as she entered the hotel parking lot. It had been shoveled, but there was already another four inches of fresh powder. She was glad when she pulled into her parking stall. The car that had been next to her was gone. "Now, I wonder where an old lady would be going in the snow." She thought. "I wonder."

As she entered the building she crossed over to the desk. "Has the lady in 19 checked out yet? She smiled sweetly at the young man. Taken in by her beauty, he actually forgot what she had just asked. "I'm sorry" he stammered."What?" She repeated herself still smiling at him as if he were the last man on the planet. "Let me look?" He started to look in to the computer. "No" he said "She's still here. I mean, she hasn't checked out." He looked at her "Are you two together?" he asked. "Oh, no" she laughed, "We just met at the pool and she was such a sweet old lady. We became friends quickly. You know." The boy nodded still smiling. "Thank you" she said and turned away. "You're welcome" he stammered. She headed to her room.

As she passed Charlene's door she stopped and knocked. No answer. Back in her room, she paced; wondering how to get into that room next door. She went out on her patio and tried to see into Charlene's patio door. The curtains were open. She climbed over the rail and looked in. There was no sign of anyone or their things in that room. "She's gone" She was surprised that anyone could get out today. Putting back on her coat, she went to the parking lot and followed the tire marks into the street, but had to come back as the snow grater had come by just ahead of her and there were no tracks to be seen.

C.C. was furious. "That's you Charlene!" she screamed and kicked the snow. "OOOOh!" her face turned contorted and ugly. Her appearance looked demon like as her eyebrows seemed to take on a devilish pointed arch. Her eyes looked dark and hollow.

She stormed back through the lobby, but when she reached her room she stood still in front of her door and composed herself, turned around looking like any normal pretty girl and went back to the front desk. "You know?" she cooed at the young man. He blushed. "Yes?" he responded. "I am so worried about my little friend. She is rather old and I am so afraid she tried to drive out in this mess. Could you see where she is from?" The boy didn't hesitate doing whatever this goddess asked him. "Huh" he grunted. "She lives right here" he frowned "That's funny. She lives right around the corner." "You're kidding" C.C. faked a girlish giggle. "What do you know. I wonder why she was here." "But, she hasn't checked out" the boy said. C.C. made her eyes get very wide and innocent looking. "I'm still worried about her. Could you give me a ring if she comes through here?" He nodded yes. "Great." She turned and went back to her room.

It was getting dark early and Charlene was settled into Mike's big overstuffed chair by his roaring fireplace. She thought of how many times he had asked her to come and live here with him. She did love his house. It was a sprawling ranch house and he had such nice furnishings. Mike handed her a hot steaming cup of coffee. "Thanks" she took the cup. "I'm sorry Mike." "Why?" he sat down on the rocker beside her. "You can't help it. I get so mad just thinking that there is actually people out there that want to kill someone because they have some kind of difference. Hell, no one thinks there are witches nowadays." His gruff voice emphasized his disgust with the situation. "I would like to go over there and confront her." "Oh No Mike" Charlene sat forward "Please don't." "Well" he looked deep into her eyes "I just might. That is after I know you're safe." He patted her knee "That's not today Charlene.

177

He winked at her. "Now, tell me what your daughter said. And, I think you ought to call her, don't you?"

Charlene sat her coffee down and got up to get her purse. When she had it she sat back down and dug to find her phone. Her face drained white. "Mike" She whispered a scream. "I left my cell phone in the hotel bathroom." He stared at her dumbfounded. "I remember" she said "I called you, then I put the phone down, went to the bathroom and then put my stuff together. I have to go back. I have to get it."

"Yes" he nodded in agreement. "We'll have to take my snowmobile. It'll take us longer, but I think it is better than taking a chance on being stuck in the snow." "Let's go now Mike," Charlene was getting antsy. "I have to change first, though" She announced and headed for the bedroom where he put her suitcases. "What?" he started to question her, but changed his mind.

"I'll get the "Mo" and put gas in it." He put on his parka hanging by the door and went outside. In the bedroom, Charlene pulled out a thermal jumpsuit, took off her clothes and slipped herself into the suit. Then she put on her down parka and slipped on a pair of swim shoes that were very low cut. She slipped into her oversized rubber boots and pulled her hair back into a low ponytail. Charlene had been a Chameleon for many years and she had practiced using her traits.

Mike pulled the snowmobile around to the back on the motel and he and Charlene entered with her key through the back door. She told him to wait, slipped out of her parka and jumpsuit and blended into the walls of the hotel hallway. Mike squinted to try to see her, but he couldn't. He thought he saw a wavy wall but squinted again and couldn't be sure.

Charlene moved stealthily down the hall and was just about to put her key into the door when C.C.'s door opened and C.C. came out in rather a hurry. Charlene stood stalk still. C.C. frowned as she went by seemingly sensing something but not able to wrap her mind around it. She continued on to the front desk. Charlene waited until C.C. was half way across the room, then slid her card into the lock and quickly entered the room careful to close the door quietly.

There it was, her phone, on the back of the toilet. She grabbed it and headed for the door. She could hear someone talking outside and she peeked out the hole. There was C.C. and the desk clerk. C.C. was exclaiming that she was sure that something was wrong with the lady in this room.

Then she saw Mike bustle down the hall acting drunk. "Hey," he slurred "Hey, I don't know where my key is." The clerk turned from what he was doing and went to address Mike. C.C. frowned and stood there with her hands on her hips. "Sir" the clerk tried to maneuver Mike into the lobby. Mike stood still looking hard at C.C. "Who is that?" he said to the clerk "Why, she's purrdy." He wavered. "Come on Sir, let's find your room." C.C. looked disgusted and turned and went into her room.

Charlene heard the door shut and she quickly and quietly opened her door and scurried down the hall. At the back door, she slipped into the jumpsuit, donned the parka and the boots and went out the door. She stood beside the garbage cans hiding from the windows.

Soon Mike had managed to go out the front door like a drunk then disappear around the hotel and start up the snowmobile. Charlene jumped on and the two sped down the street and into the night. Charlene started to giggle like a young girl. "Mike, you were so great." She squeezed her arms tighter around his waist." " I still think I should have taken her out." He yelled into the cold night air."

The drunk being gone, the clerk went and knocked on C.C.'s door. When she opened it, he told her that he could open the room now. They looked in Charlene's room and there was nothing there. C.C. stood at the door for a moment feeling that something strange was happening. Her eyes narrowed as she looked hard at the walls thinking "Are you there Charlene?"

"Mom?" Susan yelled into the phone. "I thought something happened." Charlene told her daughter what had transpired. "I'm going to stay with Mike until you all get settled then we are coming out there" Charlene announced "Oh and by the way. Mike and I are getting married." After Susan's reaction and oohs and aahs, Charlene put Mike on the phone. "Hi, Daughter to be. I just want you to know that I am going to protect your mother and the two of us are going to help find those people." Charlene got back on the phone." Where are you?" she asked her daughter. "We've left Santa Fe and we're caravanning to Bakersfield. We are going to drive straight through. We have a lot of drivers. I'll call you when I get home. I love you Mom." "Ditto Baby" her mother responded "Night dear."

CHAPTER THIRTEEN

October 18th Bakersfield

Baylor hadn't come out his room the whole of the day after they got home. His mother had knocked on his door to tell him when a meal was ready, but he said he was sleepy and would eat later. He did sleep some, but mostly caught up on his school work. He had maintained an A average and just realized he was putting his grades in jeopardy getting entangled in this Chameleon mess. "I have a life" he glowered as he looked down at the tattoo on the inside of his arm. He felt himself getting mad all over again for having to be initiated into the Agreement. He was anxious for tomorrow to come so he could go to school and just be normal. He could forget about his father, about his new found cousins and he sure didn't want to think about Harold. His Dad had some papers he had gotten from Harold about Clade members he supposed. His dad didn't mention them to him; just said that he should get back to school and they would talk later. "Great" he thought "a reprieve."   He thought about Etienne. He liked this cousin. He felt that Etienne and he were on the same wave length concerning the lizard people. He knew Etienne had gone to San Francisco to regroup and try to find out more about this Connie and Brianna.

Baylor was out of the house before his mother came down to fix breakfast. He didn't want to talk to her. He was feeling a strange bitter feeling toward her. He couldn't understand how his mother, as mild manner as she was, could condone killing of any kind. He just didn't want to see her face. It sickened him to even think about her being a willing participant in this craziness.   He took his car today. Usually, he walked, but today for some reason he decided to take his car. It was a classic and he had gotten it when he turned seventeen. It was a shiny black 1965 Mustang with red leather interior. It had been his Grandfather Joe's on his mother's side. Baylor and his Grandpa had been very close. He spent a lot of Saturday afternoons with him out in a boat on Lake Isabella fishing and along the Kern River. "Maybe" he thought wishfully and on the brighter side "Maybe I'll see Autie today," But when it was science lab, she was not there. He wondered if she were sick. He hoped to see her and invite her to the Winter Formal. It was only three weeks away. He wanted to get lost in this academic life and forget he even had a home life. After gym class, Baylor had an hour to kill before English. He decided to go to the Burger Hut for a root beer. On the way, he stopped at convenience store and bought a package of peanuts. At the Hut, the waitress brought him a big frosty mug. He quickly deposited the peanuts into the foamy glass. The root beer tasted good. It made him feel almost normal again. Suddenly the passenger side door came open and in slid a pair of Levis topped by a blue tee shirt and a face underneath a meticulous Mohawk haircut. "Where have you been?"

"Man.. Buddy!" Baylor jerked around. "You scared me to death." "Sorry!... I have looked all over for you Bay." Buddy relaxed into the seat. "I had to go with my dad to visit an uncle in Arizona." Baylor said. "Oh, is he sick or something?" "No, just visiting him. So, are you going to the formal?" Baylor changed the subject. "I doubt it, the only girl I would go with is Jilla and she probably already has a date. I don't think her mother likes me."

"I'll make a pact with you" Baylor laughed. "I'll get up enough nerve to ask Audie, if you'll ask Jilla. OK?" "Ha" Buddy cut his eyes at Baylor. "That's a deal. I'm safe then, cause I don't think you'll ask her. I don't even think she dates." "We'll see" Baylor backed out of the parking lot and headed back to school.

Pulling into the Samford Inn, four dirty vehicles packed full of people and suitcases parked near the office. Ron alone got out went into the office "Hi. Can I help you?" The young girl at the front desk greeted him. "Yes" I would like two rooms that have a king bed and do you have suites?" "Yes" she nodded, "How many people in each suite?" Ron counted in his head. "Five in one and three in the other. Are they close together?" "I think I can arrange that" the girl was into the computer.

"Here, we have Suite 12 and 14. They do have a connecting door, if you would like it unlocked. We also have a suite right across the hall with two bedrooms and two baths. Would you like that instead of the two rooms? I can give the suite to you at the same price as the two rooms."   "Yes" Ron agreed and pulled his credit card out.

Collecting the information and the keys Ron headed back outside and motioned for everyone to park around the side of the hotel away from the street side.

After getting out, everyone followed Ron up two flights of outside stairs and into a doorway that led to the hallway. He handed a key to Richard and one to RuDee. "There, he announced "Boys with Richard and girls with RuDee."

With that he opened the suite across the hall and turned to Blane. "Pick a room for you and Connie."   Connie had already passed him and was in one of the bedrooms. Susan opened the other bedroom door and went over and checked out the window and then the bathroom. "This is nice" she said. "Let's let the kids bring up the bags and we'll all get cleaned up and go have dinner.

It was only four in the afternoon, but they hadn't eaten since breakfast.   "I'd like to go check on our house" Susan whined up to Ron." "I know. Tomorrow, we'll do it." He encouraged her.

After everyone had cleaned up, they came into the grownups' room. Ron had taken leadership and everyone was in agreement that he should. He carefully included Blane as much as possible. "Ok, gang, here's how it's going to go."

He sat down on the sofa and the kids dropped to the floor in front of him. Dezza dropped herself on Richard's lap. "Hey" he yelped "You're heavier than you look." She laughed and scooted off. "Sorry, you looked just like a chair." That broke the ice and everyone laughed.

Ron smiled and continued. "Blane and I are going to go out and get his job set up. Then, we are going to decide exactly how we are going to live. I mean who with who. Or is it whom with whom?" Susan pushed his arm. "I think the kids should get into a school as soon as possible." "I agree" Connie spoke up. "They will." Blane helped Ron. "Let's do first things first. All of you can stay here until I have that job pinned down, then we will get on with where. OK?" Everyone nodded.

Ron continued. "Do any of you need money?" All heads shook no. "Ok" he continued, "Divide up, better yet, I'll divide you up. Dezza, you go with RuDee and Autumn. Richard, you go with Blake and Jadin. Brie, you go with Courtneay. We are going to have to be careful to switch off with everyone. Susan and I are ordering our meal right here in this room. So, that's leaves you Blane to go out with your wife." Jadin and Autumn gave everyone an idea of what was out there and they all went their separate ways to eat.

Autumn, RuDee and Dezza walked to the Mall that was just a block from the hotel. "I love the food court." Autie said. RuDee and Dezza agreed that was a safe place to be. "We can shop, too. Dezza's eyes sparkled. "I am so in the mood for something new to wear." RuDee just whooped "Woo Hoo…Shop!"

They separated and rejoined at a table in the middle of the court. RuDee had opted for pizza, Dezza had a large rice bowl full of orange spice chicken and Autie had a huge plate of nachos.

They had just started eating and Autie had a mouthful of chips when two tall boys loomed over their table. Autie looked and put a napkin to her full mouth. "Baylor?" she almost choked. She swallowed "What are you guys doing? Hi Buddy" she looked over to the other boy."

"Autie, my love." Buddy made a bowing gesture. "You have not been in school for a long time?" He announced holding his hands up in question.

"I'm back." She said as if it were nothing. "Church mission." She looked at the girls then back to the boys. "Baylor and Buddy, this is RuDee and Dezza. RuDee is moving here from Houston and Dezza is new from Wisconsin. They are in our church group" she informed them.

"Wow" Buddy was looking intently at Dezza. "From where?" Dezza smiled her dazzling heart breaker smile. "Cheese country. Wisconsin. What school do you two go to?" Baylor had a hard time taking his eyes off Autie, but he turned to Dezza. "Same as Autie" he answered her. "Buddy does too." "And you" Buddy pulled up a chair close to Dezza. She got up and pulled her chair a little ways from his. "I'll be running into you, I guess" She smiled at the boy. "RuDee's in college.

She looked at Buddy "And what church do you go to?" She asked. Buddy almost fell out of his chair "Church?" he yelped. "I haven't found one of those yet, maybe I'll go to yours." He started to move his chair closer to her, but she held up her hand protesting the move and he sat still.

"What about you?" RuDee asked Baylor. "What?" Baylor looked into her incredible green eyes. She stared back into his. "Church?" "Uummm" he looked down and then back at her "It's across town, actually, my dad's the minister." "Really?" Autie swallowed hard "I didn't know your dad was a preacher." "Well, I don't talk about it much." He enlightened her. "Oh" She said quietly.

RuDee persisted "And that would be what church?"

"The Wellshausen Congregational Church" He said rather softly. RuDee's face stayed straight and unmoved. A contrast to her heart leaping to her throat. "Where did I hear that church name?" She thought to herself.

Audi finished her last bite. "We've really got to hurry" she told the girls, "my Mom will be furious if I'm late again." She lied. Both of the other girls got up. Autie looked at Baylor "I'll see you Monday in school." She had always liked Baylor, but she had not started dating yet and didn't see the since of thinking about him. But there he was and paying attention to her.

She smiled to herself. "Wonder what he would think if I turned the color of this table." She almost giggled out loud with the prospect of seeing someone freak out over her gift. "Ok, see you" Baylor got up and turned to the other girls "See you, too." They both nodded and the three girls turned together and headed down the mall. Baylor was about to go the other way, when Buddy shoved him. "You going to ask her or not?" he held up both hands. Baylor started to say no then he thought about his dad and got angry. "Yeah, I am" He took off running after Autie.

"Hey, Autie wait up." Autumn turned, saw him coming and stopped in her tracks. "Could I talk to you?" he asked pointing over to the doorway of the toy store. She moved over with him by a table full of fuzzy stuffed animals that kept doing backward flips. She stood there looking up at him. He cleared his throat and then quickly blurted out "Want to go to the Formal with me?" He just stared at her face. Autie blushed, she certainly didn't expect that. She started to explain her parent might not let her and then she changed her mind. "Yes, I would love to go with you." She looked up in to a smiling and blushing Baylor. "Good…. Ok, then, Well, I'll talk to you more about it Monday, OK?" She shook her head yes.

Baylor turned on heel and was gone. She turned back and walked over to the other girls. "What?" Dezza asked. "He asked me to the Formal." She shrugged her shoulders in a euphoric way. "Cool" RuDee smiled at her. "Now, that is what I call getting back into normal living. Your folks going to let you go?" Autie's face turned into a frown. She pressed her lips together hard. "I hope so."

Suddenly Dezza squealed. "Look at that blouse!" She grabbed Autie's arm, "Come on. Let's shop." The girls entered the large doorway of Gramet's Groove, the clothes store where all the teens and young people shopped or at least wanted to be able to afford to shop there.

Baylor walked into a dark quiet house. "Mom?" he asked the emptiness. No answer came from the cool interior. He looked all over the house, but no one was home. He wondered if his parents were at the church as they sometimes took over the janitor duties in times when they were in between volunteers that cleaned the church.

He built a huge sandwich and closed himself in his room sitting in a corner of the room in his special overstuffed chair that had belonged to his Grandpa. He must have nodded off, for when he opened his eyes he noticed it was dark out. He got up and opened his door. The house was still dark and quiet. He walked to the kitchen and turned on the light. Nothing had moved. His cheese wrappers were still on the sink where he made his sandwich. He went and looked into the garage, his mothers little antique turquoise Nash rambler was sitting in its place. But his father's SUV was gone. He went in the living room and turned on the television to pass the time. A movie came on he had wanted to watch so he got a bag of cookies and a large glass of milk and settled down to watch. He pushed the pause button and using the house phone called the church phone. No answer.

The group at the Samford Inn gathered in the parents' common room that evening. Susan and Connie had brought in a lot of food. The men had been busy. Blane took a soda and some chips "I'd like to hear about your day." He gestured to the whole group.

"Autie got a date for the formal." RuDee laughed. "Autie?" Susan frowned at her. "Baylor, that guy I have been telling you about." She looked scared. "He and another boy Buddy were at the mall." Fear shot through Susan's heart. Connie was conscious of her feeling and put her hand on Susan's arm. "It's ok" She whispered. "Life as normal, remember?"

"OK" Susan shook her head yes.

"What else in these few hours since we got here?" Ron started in an exaggerated voice. Courtneay laughed "Well, I didn't get a date, but I would like to go to a dance, and Brie and I saw a lot of cute boys." Then she blushed. She was normally a very private person, but now, under the circumstances, she was losing her shyness. Brie looked at her with a perturbed look "We bought some clothes and had some pizza. That's all. No interaction with the opposite sex." She cut her eyes over at her Dad's and grinned at him "However, there is a hope of cute boys." Blane shook his head and smiled at his daughter. "We'll see" he gave her that I'm in charge here look.

RuDee turned to Richard "I guess you guys went girl shopping?" She was glaring at him. "Me?" he pointed to his chest. "What would I be doing looking at girls? He grinned at her. "Lot of blondes though here in Bakersfield" he teased.

Blane stood up. "OK, ok. Let's get down to business." He filled his cup up and turned toward the group. Here's how we are going to do it." The group got quiet. "I took a job as ranch foreman with a friend of Ron's. Its eight miles from town. It's a large cattle/grape operation. The main house is huge. The owner lives in Colorado and only comes to the ranch twice a year to go over the books and order whatever is needed. I told him I had a large family with some adopted kids. He never even asked how many or anything.

"Therefore," He stretched and yawned, showing his tiredness. "We, between us," he pointed around the room, "have two houses; the ranch and the Tanner's. Ron and Susan and Me and Connie want to invite you, Richard, Dezza, RuDee, Courtneay and Blake to be our children, our grown children, that is. We have decided that the only way all of you Chameleons will survive is in numbers and us, Ron and me, the non-chameleons." He drew N O N in the air. "accept the responsibility of being your fathers."

He looked around at each person's eyes. There was more than one mouth hanging open and eyes of disbelief. "I know you are all mostly grown up and have been out on your own. But you don't have to be anymore. We want to know if this is acceptable to all of you. If it isn't then we will find another way. There was silence in the room.

Ron stood up not waiting for anyone to speak. "We will consider the two houses as one. My kids, of course, will stay at our house. It will be an adjustment for all of you. We thought that since we have three bedrooms, we could hold some of us and at the ranch house there is three, but different sizes.

We will have to have a story to tell the world why we have so many of us." Autie held up her hand "I told Baylor that RuDee and Dezza were new comers to town and were in our church group.

We'll have to get our story straight then and get them to the youth pastor of our church here to get them started. Meanwhile, let's look at who goes where.

First, Susan and I will live here with Jadin and Richard in one bedroom, Autie and RuDee in the other.

In the ranch House, of course Connie and Blane, then, Brie, Dezza and Courtneay in the one bunkhouse type bedroom off the back of the house, Blake, you will have the small attic type bedroom. We'll tell everyone that Richard and RuDee are our foster children."

He looked at Autie "You'll just have to adjust that story you told that boy. I doubt if he would remember anything anyway. Boys usually don't when they are out to ask a girl on a date." "Ha Ha" she made a face at her dad, then "Ok, I can do that."

Connie stood up and put her hand on her husband's shoulder. You all are going to give up some privacy. But, Susan and I have resolved that you will all keep your individuality. You kids who have been on your own will not be under constraints that we have had on our children. We don't believe that we need to re-raise you. And as for our own, my one and her two, well, we both decided with our husbands that we are taking hands off and letting our three be grownup just like you all. How does that sound?" She threw out to the group and sat down.

There was a few minutes of silence, then RuDee got up and went over and hugged Connie and then turned to Susan and hugged her. She had tears coming down her face. "I think my parents would be very happy for me. I have been so alone and I feel like you love me. I feel a part of this "Clade". I promise to be respectful of your ways of life and feelings and I take responsibility along with everyone else to protect each other and to help each one of us to have a normal life, as much as we can" She sat down, but then held up her hand" Oh, I can cook too." Everyone laughed. Richard put his arm around her shoulders and without getting up. "I ditto RuDee's sentiments exactly. I didn't even get to bury my mother." He looked down then up. "Now I have two more. I like that."

Dezza stood up this time. "I fully agree with everything you all have said; and, I would like to get started soon. It has been a very long time since I have had a bed I could call mine and a closet or drawer. I want to be normal again, too." Blake reached over and squeezed her hand "Me too." He looked at Blane. "Didn't you say that you knew someone who can get our money and property together secretly?" Blane nodded.

Then, Susan said rather loudly. "This is enough for tonight. We are all going to go over to our house and everyone can help us get set up, then we will all go out to the ranch and get things set up there. This is going to be an intense weekend, getting groceries and everything else we need. You up to it?" She asked the group. Then as if their minds were totally in sync, all of the teenagers went and stood by the drapes, linked arms and turned the same color and pattern as the drapes. Ron looked at Blane "I guess that means yes."

CHAPTER FOURTEEN

C.C. hung her feet over the pier at Pismo Beach in California. She had left Colorado fuming as she had just missed finding the Chameleon, Charlene. She called her cousin Harold and told him she was going to Pismo for a few days. C.C. had just started a relationship with Reed in San Francisco five months earlier.

He was everything she dreamed of, tall, good looking, blonde hair and blue eyes and that special California tan. A real surfer slash college preppie look.   They had dated for two months and then he left and moved to Pismo where his folks owned an ocean side hotel. He was supposed to be going to college in the bay area for Hotel Management but couldn't seem to keep himself on course and was usually not in class.

He dated C.C but was not very attentive to her. She found herself doing something she had never done and that was to chase a boy. Usually, the guys were all over her trying to date her. That is except Etienne, but then he was another study and even as she went after Reed, she thought a lot about being close to Etienne. She became obsessed with getting Reed to like her. Then she had to go off on this "lizard chase". She loved the hunt but she was at all times still antsy to get back and try to get close to Reed Loudin.

She booked herself into the Loudin Lodge a very rugged looking lodge on the edge of the Pacific Ocean. She had left a message at the front desk for Reed to contact her on her cell phone. She then went down to the pier downtown Pismo to relax. She was mulling over the whole Colorado trip when her phone rang. "Hello?" she answered in a false sweetness. "Reed" she said with enthusiasm. "Guess where I am?... Oh, well, could we get together tonight? Ok, well, how about breakfast?.. Great, I'll meet you in the lobby, at 7, ok? Ok. See you then."

She hung up and hit her fist on the plank of the pier. She was furious at him, but that soon dripped away from her as she started to look forward to tomorrow morning's meeting. She fantasized that he would find out what she was doing and that he would whole heartedly support and join her in the quest.

Unsuccessful in finding out any information about Charlene's family, C.C. turned her research direction to the family of Sarah Martinez that lead her Uncle Joe Wells to Moonshadow, Dezza's mother. Joe Wells had been surprised by a neighbor when he had shot Moonshadow and fled the scene without getting any information on her daughter. Dezza had disappeared by the time that Joe was able to start more research on the family.

C.C. went to her room and opened a bottle of champagne she had bought in town. She raided the mini bar of its cookies and candy. C.C. was in the habit of celebrating her successes before they happened. Making a toast to herself in the mirror, she congratulated herself for capturing the heart of the most wonderful man in the world and soon to be hunting partner.

Morning broke with C.C. out on her deck watching the ocean as the sun peeked over the mountains and made a million sparkling lights on the waves as the light invaded the water. She had been dressed for two hours waiting impatiently for seven to get there. Only five more minutes. She paced back and forth like a caged lioness.

Finally, it was seven. She went through the door, down the elevator and into the lobby. There he was, looking just like she hoped he would. He smiled at her but not on a grand scale. She pushed the thought that he wasn't really glad she was there out of her head. "Hi" she went up and gave him a hug.

He gently patted her shoulder once. He gestured toward the open doors of the dining room. "Let's go eat." He followed her and pulled her chair out for her at a table. "What are you doing here?" he asked. "Looking for you, of course." She smiled her sweetest most innocent smile. "Is that ok with you?"

"Sure, but" he hesitated. "I'm seeing someone here." C.C.'s face started to drop and she corrected it with sheer determination. "Oh" was all she could get out. "I'm sorry you came all this way C.C., but" He shrugged his shoulders. "That's about it. I've found a girl that has captured my heart." He looked at her like she was ten years old. The rage started to mount in her very being. "How dare you!" she thought at him. She had to manually make herself breathe. "Got to get out of here!" She screamed silently to herself.

She stood up. "Wait," he reached for her hand. "Can't we be friends?" He stood up too. She looked up into his eyes. He strained his eyes looking into hers, thinking "Could that be a true sight?" He felt like he was seeing evil itself. Her eyes almost glowed with anger.

"Of course" she literally hissed as she turned and stormed out of the restaurant and headed for the elevator with Reed standing in the middle of the room.

It took her all of five minutes to throw her things together and she was on the freeway headed north within the next ten. "You're dead Charlene" she threw her anger over Reed into the air toward her escaped prey. Then she added "And you spawn of Moonshadow, I'm coming for you." And she laughed hysterically as her car flew along the coastal freeway.

"How did your trip to Pismo go?" Dallas welcomed C.C. into the house. Piercing eyes hot with hate answered his question. He pierced his lips and shook his head "Sorry." He followed her up the stairs and was going to follow her into her room but almost got a door in the face. He stood outside her closed door for a moment then went back down stairs and entered the den where his father was at his desk mulling over papers. "I guess something got her tail in a knot." "Humm?" His father asked without looking up. "Oh, you mean C.C.?" He looked up "She's always in a snit" he laughed.

Just then C.C. entered the den. "I am not" she threw at him. "I am just angry tonight, that's all. That Chameleon got away from me, but she won't again, nor will Moonshadow's brat." Harold looked up at her. "I take it your romantic adventure didn't happen?" She shook her head. "But, it will. Right now he is just confused. He is the one, you know." She looked deep into Harold's eyes "I feel it to the bottom of my being."

His grin was devilish at the thought of how deep and low her being did go. She was the one who really wanted to go after the Clade and destroy them. Dallas was in sympathy with the Agreement, but he was lazy. Harold looked at his son in disgust. Such a wimp, he was. Talked a good fight, but didn't seem to carry out anything to completion. He could count on C.C. He looked admiringly at this girl. "So, now what are you two going to do? Go back to school?"

"School?" C.C. looked intently at her cousin, "I don't think so. I have a quest, you know. After they're dead, then I'll do something, that is after I find out just how I am going to fit into Reed's life.

I am going to spend some intense time in that temple-like church over in Sacramento in their genealogy library. I will spend whatever time and money I need to find Moonshadow's child, if she had one, and I suspect she did, they all do, you know, spawn like fish. Then I will find where Charlene went if I have to tear apart that town she lived in. Someone will know."

She fairly danced around the room as she talked about her plans.

Dallas liked C.C and would have liked to get personally close to her, but there was something about her that made shivers go up his spine. He definitely was afraid of her. As children, they pulled wings off of grasshoppers together and loved to torture any animal that was unlucky enough to get in their path, but all the while he knew deep in his insides, that she wouldn't hesitate to do the same to him.

Harold's voice penetrated his thoughts "Dallas, I suggest that you go with C.C and maybe the two of you together can find out more information. C.C. frowned but didn't say anything. She didn't mind having Dallas around. He was easy to boss around and an excellent gopher always ready to run her errands and bring her things. She knew he was afraid of her and she used that to her advantage.

"Great" she smiled at Dallas "We're buds, right?" Dallas forced a smile back at her. He would have rather stayed right there in San Francisco and played computer games. He also wanted some more tattoos and that was time consuming. He'd have to wait now. "When are we going?" he squinted at C.C. "Oh, how about tomorrow?" He nodded yes and turned and left the room. C.C. put her arms around Harold. "Cuz, I should so like to kill a lizard." She twirled his hair around her finger. "Wish me luck." She leaned close and slowly kissed his cheek. "Luck C.C." Harold stood up. "Don't let J.W. down C.C." with that he left with C.C. standing in the middle of the room.

Reed Loudin looked sadly as C.C. exited the restaurant at his family's Lodge. He had really liked C.C. for a month of their relationship. But as she got more anxious to be intimate with him, something made him shy away from the closeness. He had thought she was stunning and desirable, but as her true personality started to show, he noticed cruelness in her thinking. She always would add "just kidding" when she would say something hateful or harmful about someone, but deep down he believed she really had a mean streak.

Once when they were cuddling and kissing, C.C. decided to get bold. She pulled her sweater over her head and with only her tank top on, she leaned against him. Reed at first was excited, then his eyes saw her tattoo. His stomach lurched. He was repelled. Holding her at arm's length, he told her "I am not ready for this yet C.C. I am not a person that takes sex lightly. I like you a lot, but it's not going to be a casual thing with me." She looked at him in disbelief. At first she was mad then she realized that this man was special.

"Sorry" She grabbed her sweater. Her face was beet red. "I thought you wanted me." She said in a sweet almost coy way. "I do" Reed looked deep into her eyes. "I couldn't think of a sweeter thing, but it's too soon to know if this feeling between us is something that will last a life time or not, and I'm just not willing to full around with my life that way. You do understand?"

She calmed herself. "Of, course, I think we should wait too. I have to go somewhere for a family reunion maybe when I get back we could go somewhere together and really get to know each other." Reed just nodded and smiled at her, feeling both a repulsion of her and a desire for her. "Good" he thought "We will have some space from each other."

Now, she was here and he had found someone that he really liked, not just desired. Nicole was young and innocent and had a sweet disposition, unlike the cruel nature that peeked out from C.C.'s make up. He was glad she stormed out, then he didn't have to feel guilty he made her mad.

Nicole had invited him to go for the Christmas holidays to Bakersfield to be with her family. He asked his mother Sandy if she would be ok at Christmas without him and she told him that she and Lee would have lots of friends to spend their time with and to "Go, have fun". Sandy Dorsey Loudin had been a single mother to Reed and spent her life just taking care of him. Then when Reed was ten, she married Lee Loudin, owner of the Loudin Lodge on the Coast. They had met in the beauty shop where Sandy worked. Lee had a thick head of dark curly hair and started to come to Sandy to get his hair cut. Soon they were dating and then married.

Sandy had kept contact with Reed's father, a man, who also had been a customer when she had lived in Flagstaff, Arizona. His name was Bill Brown, he was thirty years her senior but they seemed to be instantly attracted. Bill was a widower and had a daughter her age. When Sandy found out she was pregnant, she told Bill that she was going to keep the baby and he could be as much of a father as he wanted to be. He told her that he was too old to be married again and couldn't handle this.

Bill didn't see the baby but did make sure a check was sent to her once a month. When Reed was five, Sandy received a special envelope with a key to a safety deposit box. The instructions were to give the key and access to the box to Reed when he was sixteen. She put the key away for safe keeping.

Then, when Reed was ten, she heard that Bill had been killed. At that time, she was dating Lee and put all this out of her mind as Lee had included Reed into his life like a real son. He even adopted Lee and made him a Loudin. Reed was so thrilled to have a father. He never asked or thought about his real father.

That is until he was fifteen and was out with his friends on jet skis in the bay just in front of their hotel. One of his buddies, Jake, had made a teasing run at him and Reed jerked the wheel to turn away then over corrected and went sailing through the air and landed in the sea with his face in a huge clump of sea weed. His head became entangled and when his friends had jumped in to help him out of it, they couldn't see him in the kelp. Suddenly, Trisha saw his foot and hung on. It was such a scary time that no one really noticed that he had turned the color and pattern of the sea weed. Trisha saw it, but as she pulled him toward her, his skin reclaimed its proper color and her mind didn't grasp what was really happening. She just thought he was coming out from the midst of the great sea wad. Reed saw it though as he threshed around trying to get a hold of something and get loose of those tentacle like arms that were pulling him down. He saw himself fade into the mess.

Even after they pulled him up onto a jet ski, he kept looking at his arms and legs expecting them to go all green and gooey looking again. After this experience, he finally told his mother that he needed to know something about his ancestry. "Why?" she asked like it were nothing. "I might need the medical information of my real father. You know; blood type and all. Like what diseases he and his family had and all." "You father is dead, I told you that and I don't know his family or how to find out." She stared at her son wishing she had more to tell him, then "Wait a minute." She went to her jewelry box and came back with the key. "He did leave you something. Maybe a letter. I don't know. It's in the Flagstaff Bank. It was supposed to be yours next year, but I guess it's okay to give it to you now." Reed stared at the key. "This is insane" he frowned at his mother. "I can't believe you didn't look into it and see what it was or said." "I know" she shook her head, "but, I was busy falling in love with Lee" she smiled. "Go call the Bank and see if they will mail it to you." she gently shoved his big shoulders "Let me know if you want me too." She sweetly released him from having to share this adventure with her. "Thanks Mom" he told her with a hug.

CHAPTER FIFTEEN

The rural streets of Bakersfield were decorated with Christmas bows. Cheerful lights seemed to be in every window, doorway or roof top of the country homes around the ranch.

Brie thought it strange that there would be no snow for Christmas. "I want snow" she whined to her mother as she went through the back door with her mucker boots on. She was always first out in the morning to help her Dad with feeding the stock. Courtneay and Blake scrambled each morning to beat her, but getting up that early wasn't something they were adjusting to quickly. Dezza didn't even bother. She fit right in helping Connie in the kitchen. She loved to cook and Connie loved to let her.

There were so many things to do for this new large family. Everyone pitched in. Had it been a regular life for each person involved, it would have been more relaxed and different. But every teen and the four parents knew that their very lives depended on their working together and being disciplined.

Twice a week, the "family" got together and the Chameleons went off into different places to practice and hone their skills at becoming invisible. Sometimes, they divided up and played hide and seek or kick the can. Sometimes they, as a whole unit, crept into town at different times of day and night and blended in so well that no one saw them or even thought there might be people there the same color as the walls, fences and other scenery.

On Thursdays, RuDee taught the group the martial arts that she had become so adept at. Even Connie and Susan worked hard at acquiring these skills. Charlene and Mike had moved to the city and she joined in their exercises except for the

200

martial art stuff. She said she would just hide and let someone else younger break their bones. They all loved her. She was spunky for an old lady. And they admired how she could completely disappear before they could. RuDee still insisted she learn how to get out of the grasp of someone, so Charlene complied and soon was very good at making her attacker lose grip on her and she could disappear fast.

Mike, Ron and Blane the three "non-lizards" as they called themselves successfully maneuvered Richard, Courtneay and Blake's assets into a trust fund that had all been directed to a lawyer friend of Ron's in Los Angeles. This friend was trustworthy and kept all the information about the monies secret. Dezza and RuDee had smaller bank accounts and they had their money wired to this attorney who in turn wired it into bank accounts set up in Bakersfield in their names and Ron's name. They had full access, however, to as much money as they wanted. Richard, Courtneay and Blake had property which the lawyer secured the physical custody of the houses and set them up with realtors in their respective towns to be rented out. The monies went through the Lawyer and for anyone looking; it was a dead end street. They had done their job well. Each person had his or her own bank account.

It looked like the Clade members, to the world they knew, had just dissolved into thin air. Blane made a general account for the up keep of the homes and each person put in their percentage of the monies needed to run the households. In the Tanner household, Ron paid for four-sixth of the household costs, Richard and RuDee each paid one-sixth. The same principal applied in the ranch house with the others.

They all wished they could contact their old friends, but knew that might be a deadly thing to do. Susan and Connie decided that each house would decorate for Christmas but they would have their Christmas Eve and morning together. Connie would host the Christmas Eve party where they would all open one present and then everyone would go to Susan's for the morning festivities.

Everyone had started going to the church that the Tanner family had always attended. It was a very large church with a teen and young adult group that they blended into very well and the minister didn't wear a cleric's collar. It was easy in such a big group to do all the activities and yet no one really considered that they were all together.

It was the night of the winter formal. Baylor was nervous. He had rented his tux and bought some flowers for Autumn. His parents had been very secretive and distant since he got back from Sedona and he was glad they weren't really talking to him. They even stayed away from home for a few days at a time. He felt like he could lead a normal life if they would leave him alone. He dreaded every time he saw them that they might start talking about the Agreement. They didn't even seem to want to know about his plans for the dance.

He had gotten up enough nerve to ask for money for the tux and for renting a limo. He was going to share the rent with Buddy, and Autumn's brother. His dad just pulled out a wad of bills and peeled off five hundred dollars and gave it to him. He didn't speak. Baylor stared down at the money thinking how unusual it was that there was that much cash around their house. He, however, didn't question that gift horse and hurriedly got the limo rented and his tux. Autumn had told him she was wearing lavender with black trim and when he was at the florists he ordered a black orchid wrist corsage. His tux was black with lavender cummerbund.

As he was about to go out the front door both his mother and father came into the room "Baylor" his father said in a serious tone. Baylor turned. "Baylor" his father continued "We want you to have fun tonight and enjoy this moment in time when you are young and can be carefree. However, we must tell you that there are new things happening you need to be aware of."

Baylor laid down the keys on the entrance table "And that is?" he asked feeling himself get mad at this intrusion. He had finally gotten rid of the sick stomach and was looking forward to the evening. "C.C. has found another Chameleon. Charlene who she tried to find in Colorado has been located. She is here, in Bakersfield. C.C. has found her and has left San Francisco to join us here. We are to help her find this person and her family."

Warren looked at his wife then back at his son "You know what that means, don't you?"   Baylor looked a long time into his father's eyes, experiencing the cold darkness that seemed to excrete evil. "Yeah" he shook his head yes, just wanting to get out of there. "Ok" His father patted his shoulder "Go to the dance. We'll talk in the morning. Dallas and Etienne will be here too. Harold will come later." Baylor took his escape and once outside the shut door, he breathed in the night air and exhaled any thought of what was going on and what had been said on the other side of that door.

Everyone had gathered to get ready at the Tanner house and there was an electrical excitement that ran through the house. Richard had asked RuDee if she would go to the dance with him. Being college students, Autumn had gotten permission for them to go.   Jadin had asked Cindra Jennings months ago when school had first started. He would have liked to take Dezza, but knew he had already committed himself. Cindra was a nice girl and he thought a lot of her. The girls had gone off the prior week with Courtneay, Dezza and Brie, all of which had quickly gotten dates, to the mall to get their formals. They all had a multitude of boys chasing them. The phone at the ranch house was constantly ringing. Courtneay had accepted a date with Justin Pivott, their minister's son, Dezza had been asked by several guys at school, but she really didn't like them and when Blake told them at the dinner table that he didn't know of a girl at the school he would like to ask. Dezza spoke up "Well, since you can't find someone better than me, why not me?" The house rocked with laughter. Blake turned red and in a bold and completely Blake manner, he stood up and told her "Dezza, I thought you would never ask." He bowed "I accept your invitation." He sat down "Oh, I think I am wearing a blue shirt" he looked at her and winked "For flowers, you know." Dezza picked up a dinner roll and threw it at him and just grinned. She couldn't even think about another boy since she had met him.

The rest of the family looked on in awe of this revelation that was so obvious and in front of their noses. Blane had helped over the awkwardness of the moment. "How about you Brie? You have a date?" Brie nodded "But, I don't think you're going to like it." She made a face at her father. "How is that?" he frowned at her. "Well, I don't know. I mean I don't know him." Everyone's eyes widened as they turned to her. "And how did this happen?" her mother spoke up. "My lab partner Savannah's brother. He goes to UC Davis and he's coming home that weekend. Savannah has a date and her sister Nicole is coming in from the coast with her boy friend, so they needed a date for Steven." She shrugged her shoulders. "So, I said I would do it. That's all. Really." She looked around the table and everyone stayed quite.

Connie stood up "Ok, let's get the table cleared" then she looked at Brie, "I think that is nice Brie."

The evening was at a perfect temperature. The large silver Hummer limo pulled up in front of the Tanner residence. Soon Buddy, his date Jilla and Baylor were standing at the door. Ron ushered them into the living room. At about the same time, the door bell rang again. This time it was a group of five to pick up Brie. The living room was getting crowded as more came in. Justin Picket was right behind them. Susan and Connie came in with their cameras and had each couple stand for pictures in front of the decorated mantel. Susan smiled as she thought how handsome Autie's date was. "A preacher's son" she said half under her breath. Brie stood by Steven, but she had a hard time not looking at Savannah's sister's boyfriend Reed. He was blonde but was built like Richard and had some of his features and mannerisms. She wasn't the only one that noticed. RuDee noticed his eyes, even though blue, had the same intensity and shape of Richard's. He also had a beautiful set of teeth that almost mirrored Richards. Soon the group all had their pictures taken with their respective dates and were off in two limousines and one Camaro convertible. Ron, Susan, Connie and Blane sat in the Tanner's kitchen sipping coffee.

Courtneay and her date waited, in front of the gymnasium for the rest to exit their limos. From the street to the doorway, there were thousands of red, blue and green lights made into a high tunnel. Candy canes by the hundreds were hung all over the inside of the tunnel and large balls of mistletoe, each graced with a large red velvet bow, hung from the ceiling of the tunnel every five feet.

Inside the double doors, the walkway was covered with an inch of man-made snow and on one side a large white deer made of twinkle lights stood moving his head up and down. On the other side was a white sleigh where each couple in turn sat and had their picture taken.

As the troupe finished their pictures, they entered into the main part of the gym. The room looked like a giant skating rink with trees decorated with white flocking and white twinkle lights sitting among the white tables that were circling the rink-like dance floor. There were solid white snowmen for centerpieces. In the middle of the giant dance floor was a slowly revolving band stand that resembled a hill of snow painted solid white with silver sparkles all over it and the band was dressed in white with sparkly silver collars to blend into the scenery. You had to squint to see there were people up there playing. Even their instruments were camouflaged with white and shiny silver. In the middle of the band stand was a winding glittery white road that led to a two-seated solid white throne.

Jadin had arranged with his friend Jaime, head of the decorating committee, to have his group sit together. The tables each held ten and their tables were next to each other.

The evening was magical, the band's music made every one want to dance. Courtneay and Justin were the first out of their seats and onto the dance floor. The group marveled at how well the couple danced together.

Baylor was so happy to be there with Autumn and to be a part of this group of happy people, normal people. It was so pleasant to be a teenager and not a killer. He pushed what his father had told him completely out of his head. He certainly didn't want to think of those things. He loved people and he cared about all of his classmates, especially Autie. He had wanted to date her for the last two years but knew she wasn't allowed to date. He loved how she was so nice to everyone. She always had the prettiest smile on her face. She wasn't stuck up and he was proud to be her date this night, well aware that almost every other boy in the school wanted to be her date.

Across town

Warren answered the doorbell and found C.C. and Dallas standing there. "Come in." He ushered the two into the living

206

room. "Etienne is already here. He's upstairs. He'll be down in a minute." He enlightened them. "Where's Baylor?" C.C. asked looking around. "At a dance. He'll be here later." "A dance?" C.C. looked perturbed. "Yeah" Warren explained. "He had these plans for a long time."

C.C. shrugged her shoulders and walked into the kitchen. "Can I get a drink?" she threw over her shoulder. Warren followed her and told her to make herself at home. "My wife has fixed you a bed upstairs. Dallas, you'll have to sleep on the couch. "No" C.C. interrupted "We have a hotel. We'll come back in the morning. When we are all together."

Etienne came down and greeted everyone. C.C. just nodded to him, then told the room "I'm going now" she frowned. "I'm tired." With that she and Dallas left the house. Etienne returned to Baylor's room and went to bed.

Janice had been listening quietly from the dining room. She had what felt like a giant thumb in her back. She knew she was siding with the wrong people. She had tried to pray for days, since she found out that the people her husband and son must kill might live close by. Warren had been gradually getting more and more hateful and mean to her. It was all she could do just to sit through one of his sermons; sermons of God's love and she knew he did not have that love. She had gradually allowed herself to rethink what their life had been like. And now, her son was involved. She shuddered when he showed her that tattoo that he had to get. She didn't let him see that dismay and hurt that she really felt. Tonight she felt like she was at her wit's end. She saw C.C. storm out and knew that the girl was evil.

Janice went out into her back yard and sat down on her porch swing. She was afraid Warren might come out and look for her. Looking up She whispered "Will you hear me?" tears were falling down her face. "Can I talk to you God?" She silently slipped down on her knees with her face in her hands on the seat of the swing. Pouring out her heart to God, she wept and told him she was sorry she had been a part of something she knew was wrong. She had told Him how sorry she was and how she wanted to do right. She asked for his help.

Just then she heard the back door open "Janice" a too familiar voice penetrated the air. "Are you out here?" She sat very still and quiet, she was in the shadow of the building there on the porch. Warren didn't waste his time waiting for her to answer, he went back in and shut the door. She got up and sat on the swing and sniffled trying to stop crying. "Do with me whatever you see fit" She told God. She went in and proceeded to go up to her bedroom.

Back at the ball

The song was slow and Autie was in Baylor's arms. He looked so handsome in his tux. For this moment, she had totally forgotten her dilemma. Dancing with him made her feel special. Normal. Finally, she was able to date and with the boy of her dreams. She did not want the song to end. But it did end and they sat back down.

The principal took the microphone "It's time to announce the Queen of the Winter Formal. The Queen is elected by the Senior boys and tonight, it is my pleasure to announce that Autumn Tanner has been chosen as Queen. Autumn, please come up here." Autumn sat stock still. "Did I hear that right?" She thought. "No." She stayed still. Dezza was sitting to her left. "Autie" she whispered loudly. "That's you." She looked at Dezza in disbelief. Baylor took her elbow "Come on Autie, you're the Queen"

Autie allowed herself to be escorted up to the band stand where the band members made an extravagant ushering of her up to the throne. Then they made Baylor go up and sit on the other side of the throne. "We have Autumn Tanner, our Queen and her escort Baylor Lackey. Give them a hand." The crowd went ballistic with clapping, wolf whistles and stomping of feet.

Autie felt she were in a surreal world. It wasn't possible she could be Queen. But, here she was and everyone seemed so happy about it. She looked over the crowd. There was Jadin grinning up at her. She hooked her eyes to his. He winked at her and put a thumb up. Then she looked at all of her cousins. They were all smiling and laughing. "I guess I'll feel something about this later." She thought.

She looked over at Baylor. He was looking down at her hand. Her eyes followed the path his eyes. Her arm was the color of her wrist corsage, black. She tightened her arm and it looked like an arm again. Baylor squinted and when he looked back she looked normal. He looked around to see if a light had cast a shadow on her arm.

Autumn knew he saw her turn black so she took her hand and slid it into his. Baylor immediately forgot what he saw as he felt the warm soft hand curl itself into the protection of his much bigger hand. That was the feeling he liked. That hand just fit in his. There was so much electricity between them at that moment it might have lit up the room if they were plugged into a circuit. Autie had to concentrate on breathing; the warmth of his body seemed to go over her like a coat.

There in the midst of hundreds of people, all of which were looking at them, Autumn and Baylor felt what every couple in love feel at the first touch. They were there, but they were somewhere else at the same time. Somewhere very far away and very much alone. They weren't alone, however, and two other pairs of eyes saw Autie's hand go black. One was RuDee and the other was Reed.

It was after two in the morning when the troupe entered the Tanner home. The laughter and joking was enough to gladden any heart. Susan had a their dinning room table filled with all sort of food. She and Connie took special care to decorate and make it seem like a feast.

Baylor was having such a good time, he beamed beside Autie. He kept taking her hand at every opportunity. He liked her brother, too, and now he was with her family and friends. He felt like he was in another world. He loved it. "Can people really be this nice" he thought.

Blane announced that the evening was over. Autie walked Baylor to the Limo where Buddy and his date were already sitting. They had come out earlier to be alone. Autie tried to pull her hand out of his, but Baylor didn't want to let go. He didn't want to leave her, not now, not ever. "I don't want to leave you" he whispered in her ear. "Me, too." she whispered back and leaned into his arms. "Shall we just get in the limo and go to Canada? Just run away from everyone?" He took her other hand. "I would you know." Autie wrinkled up her nose at him. "We'd get maybe to Oildale, then my Dad would have a full police escort bringing us back" she smiled at him. "It's a nice thought though."

The other limo had left. Autie finally did pull her hand free. "Thanks Baylor, I had wonderful time. I've got to go in." Baylor relented "Ok, I'll call you tomorrow, OK?" Autie shook her head yes. She started to turn to go into the house when Baylor put his hands on her shoulders and turning her shoulders toward him, he bent down and gently and tenderly kissed her lips. Autie's heart pounded like a kettle drum. He bowed and got into the limo. Autie floated into the house.

Justin had managed to give Courtneay a kiss under the mistletoe and she, too, like Autie, was floating on air. She waited watching his Camaro disappear down the street before she came in.

All the dates had gone, leaving only the "family." Gathering in the living room, Ron addressed the group. "How did it go?" "Great" Dezza smiled "It was so much fun and especially when Autie got to be Queen. It was like our family ruled." RuDee turned to Autie. "Did you turn?" "What?" Jadin and Richard said at the same time. "I think I saw Autie turn when she got Queen" RuDee said looking at Autie. Autie turned red "I did" she admitted. "My arm turned black like these flowers."

"Did Baylor see it?" Courtneay asked. "I think so, but I don't think he realized what he saw. I put my hand in his and he didn't mention it." Autie recalled out loud.

"Autie" Connie stood up "I think we had better practice harder. All of us. We have to master this." Everyone sat silently but nodded in unison. Autie looked down at the floor. "It's okay Autie" Dezza came over and took her hand. "If I had got to be a queen, I would have turned royal blue and never came out of it." That made everyone laugh. Autie felt better. "Ok, gang" Blane spoke up "Let's go home and get some sleep."

Everyone belonging to the ranch got up and headed for the door. "Night everyone" Susan bid the group farewell. A smattering of goodnights echoed around the room and then they were gone and the Tanner household went to bed.

Baylor slipped into his bedroom around four-thirty in the morning. After laying his tux on the arm chair he climbed into bed and was asleep before he could even think about the awfulness of being home, much less the fact that Etienne was sleeping in his other bed.

CHAPTER SIXTEEN

Morning threw sunlight across Baylor's face causing him to wake much sooner than his body wanted to. Stretching, he rolled over and his eyes caught sight of a movement in the other bed. He stared at the lump in the other bed and sat straight up. Then he remembered that his father said that Etienne and the others were coming. The bump turned over and there was Etienne's face peeking out from the covers. He was still asleep. Baylor, even though he liked Etienne, felt sick again. He got up and found his Levis, "Cinderfella is back at the castle" he thought bitterly.

Leaving the bedroom, he quietly went downstairs. He didn't want to wake anyone and surely didn't want to talk to anyone, especially his father. The kitchen light was on. Janice had already started the coffee and was frying bacon. "Hungry?" she asked him in her sweet voice. He shook his head no. "I ate late last night." "Where?" she looked at him He looked annoyed "Over at the Tanners." .

"Oh" she responded and turned to watch the pan.

Baylor was on his second cup of coffee when there was a knock on the front door. He, with cup in hand, pulled open the door to find C.C. standing there looking totally different from the nerdy girl he had met in Sedona. She was actually quite beautiful. And it was not hard to believe that she knew it, too. She came through without waiting to be asked. Right behind her Dallas nodded to Baylor and followed C.C. in. "Where's your Dad?" C.C. asked. Baylor just shrugged his shoulders.

Janice appeared in the hallway and invited them all to come into the kitchen. She motioned everyone to sit down. Etienne was just coming downstairs. He didn't say anything just nodded and sat down at the table. Baylor sat down by Etienne while C.C. and Dallas sat at the opposite side of the table. "My Dad will be here this afternoon" Dallas informed the group. "He says we have to work fast." C.C.'s grin was large and evil as she held up her coffee cup for Janice to fill up again. Janice poured the coffee, but if looks could kill, C.C. would be dead. Janice had put up with the incredible theology of her husband for years and now it was like she had been shut in a dark room and was suddenly let out into the light.

This C.C., this cousin, reeked of evil. And here she was holding her cup up like Janice was her personal slave. C.C. saw the look but dismissed it as she had always thought of Janice as a little doormat type wife and certainly nothing for anyone to give thought to, unless they needed a cup of coffee. Turning to her breakfast, C.C. didn't give Janice another thought. Janice, however, did give C.C. another thought. She even recoiled inside watching C.C. touch the food she had cooked.

Baylor sat watching as everyone ate. Warren had come in and taken his seat at the head of the table, even though it was obvious to everyone that C.C. was in control, that is, until Harold got there.

After C.C. had eaten her fill and held up her cup for Janice to refill, she took control of the group. "I have found the Clade" she said rather smugly. "I have tracked the Chameleon Charlene to her family right here, right under your very nose Warren." Warren shrugged his mouth and then his shoulders. Dallas kept silent.

"When Harold gets here this afternoon, we will make a plan and take her and her whole family out." She gestured up in the air with her coffee spoon. "How did you find her?" Warren asked. Dallas sat up straight and was going to answer him when C.C. cut him down with a look. She turned to Warren. "I went back to Colorado Springs and" she nodded toward Dallas, giving him a little credit "we asked questions of everyone in the immediate area of her home, the beauty shops, grocery stores, churches and we found out that she had a boyfriend." She looked at Dallas "Dallas pretended to be an insurance agent claiming that his client owed her money and found out where they went. And that was here. The neighbor wasn't hard to fool either, she told me the name of her daughter and grandkids. She has two."

There was a silence around the table. "And?" Warren held up his hands in a question. "Who are they?" Baylor was trying not to listen to the discussion and was thinking about leaving the kitchen but was afraid to draw attention to himself. He had noticed how his mother was acting. It was a weird thing, but he felt like he could feel her anger over all of this. He suddenly had a new respect for his mother. Maybe she didn't buy into this Agreement business.

He stood up and was just about to turn and slip out into the hallway when he heard C.C. answer his Dad's question. "Her name is now Charlene Cox and her daughter's name is Susan Tanner" He stopped dead in his tracks. He couldn't believe his ears. Then she said it again only worse. "Tanner. Her daughter's name is Susan and the kids are Autumn and Jadin."

The room seemed to rock around Baylor's head. His stomach didn't feel sick anymore, just completely up in his throat. He put his hand on the door frame to steady himself. "No" he said to himself. "Not Autie" Suddenly, his mind went to last night when he saw her arm go black. "No" he shook his head.

"Baylor?" his mother put her hand on his shoulder and leaned very close. "Is that your Autie?" He turned and silently looked deep into his mother's eyes. Then he thought of his Dad, wondering if he remembered who he went to the dance with. He looked at his father's eyes. There was no change. No sudden recognition of names. He felt a little relieved.

"Anyway," C.C. continued, "We have to find where they live here and then we need to make a plan of attack" Janice, who didn't know what to do a little earlier suddenly found herself feeling like a warrior. "This cannot happen" she thought to herself. She knew her son liked this girl. She knew her son would do the right thing. Then she looked at her husband and for the first time in their marriage wasn't afraid of him. She saw a shriveled up soul sitting there and he suddenly looked ugly and disgusting to her.

"Warren" she came over to her husband "I need some money." He looked up at her and didn't move. "I need to send Baylor to get a few things for me. I plan to bar-b-que when Harold gets here." That seemed to sound reasonable to Warren and he took out his wallet and handed it to her. She took out several bills and handed it back.

"Baylor" she called over her shoulder as she walked into the den, "I need you to help me make a list." He followed his mother into the other room. She had never asked him to do any shopping. His adrenaline started run a notch faster. C.C. and Dallas didn't even pay any attention. C.C. was busy making notes and Dallas was sitting nodding off as if he had not got enough sleep. Etienne, however, had been totally quiet and had just observed the happenings. He had seen the faces and the expressions and had felt the sudden electricity that seemed to flow between the mother and the son. His eyes followed Baylor and his mother out of the room.

In the den, Janice pulled a note pad out of the desk and said rather loudly, "Baylor, I am going to need these things right away so I can get started on the bar b q. I think we'll eat at 6." Baylor watched as his mother was writing, it wasn't a list. When she was through, she put the money in his hand along with the list. "Go now" she said "I need this stuff right away."

215

Baylor took the car keys off the hook and headed for the door. He got in his car and drove off down the street toward the freeway lane.

Once on the freeway, he pulled off at the next exit and pulled in to a gas station. There he read the letter.

> "Baylor, I can't go along with this anymore. You must warn the Tanners. You must get out of here and never come back. Your father is wrong. He will kill them and maybe you. Maybe me. Don't come back to this house. Either help the Tanners, or, leave town and make a life for yourself. Don't worry about me. I love you and am glad I can finally be a mother like I should be. Your father is wrong. His family members are killers. Don't let them find you, Mom.

Baylor sat for a long time with his head on the steering wheel. Fear for his mother swept over him. He wanted to go back and take her out of there too, but something stopped him. She wanted him to save the Tanners, she didn't believe as his dad did.

He headed his car toward the Tanners, but noticed that all their cars were gone. He remembered them talking about the ranch out on Rosedale Hwy and headed that way. He called Autie's cell. "Hey" he said "I was wondering, can I come and talk to you?" There was silence. ""I'm not at home" she answered "Yeah I know. You said you were going to the ranch today. I thought I heard. Can I come out there?" "Just a minute." Autie asked her Dad if Baylor could come out to the ranch. They had gathered there to practice their hiding and martial arts. "My Dad says maybe you could come over to our house tonight." "Autie" Baylor almost shouted, "Could I talk to your Dad?" Autie handed her phone to her surprised father. "Yes?" Her Dad put into the phone.

"Mr. Tanner, this is Baylor" "Yes Baylor?" his voice was still steady. "Mr. Tanner, could I please come out there and talk to you?" His voice sounded urgent. "Baylor" there is a deli at the corner of Rosedale and Fern. Meet me there. I'll be there in 5 minutes." Ron hung up. "I'm going to meet Baylor he told the group. He seems to be having some sort of problem. Want to go with me?" he addressed Blane. Blane nodded and they got in Ron's car and left without another word.

Autie stood standing in the middle of the room. "Baylor" she said to the eyes that were all watching her. "I don't know what's going on." RuDee captured the room "Ok, let's start over. Charlene, could you show Court that move after you have rolled over under your attacker how you were able to raise you knee into his groin?"

"There he is" Blane pointed as they pulled into the Daily Deli parking lot. Ron pulled his car up next to Baylor's. Baylor looked as white as a sheet. He didn't move; his hands were fixed to the wheel.

Ron opened the driver door. "Baylor, come over here with us, we'll sit at that table under the tree." Baylor got out and followed the men over and sat down. Ron put his hand on Baylor's shoulder "What is it Buddy?" he said in a kindly fatherly way. Blane sat across from him and reached out and put his hand in front of Baylor in a friendship manner that didn't expect him to take his hand. It was just there for comfort. "We are here to help you Baylor" Blane looked deep in to the troubled eyes of this youth.

Baylor couldn't find his voice. He just looked at these men, not knowing where to start. "We can't help you unless you tell us." Ron sat down beside Baylor. Baylor was wearing a long sleeved shirt unbuttoned and over a muscle type tee shirt. He leaned back and slipped off the shirt and turned his arm so they could see the inside of it.

There in front of their eyes was a tattoo of a lizard being hanged. The world seemed to reel around them. It was like they had slipped into a B-rated movie or maybe even onto another planet.

Ron took Baylor's arm in his hand and pulled the image closer to him. "Is this what I think it is?" he asked Baylor. Baylor choked a little "What do you think it is?" he asked turning red. "I think it is a lizard, maybe a Chameleon lizard being hanged. Is that what it is Baylor?" Ron's eyes had become like little slits. "Yes" Baylor said very slowly and quietly and then looked at the men one at a time "Are you Chameleon?"

Anger had welled up in Blane "Listen kid" he said rather meanly "Do you want to tell us what is going on?" Then it came out like a flood. Baylor's months of frustration, anger and fear came bubbling out to these men who were much more like father figures than his dad had ever been. He told them about finding out his family had been killing the Clade members since the very first and that he was expected to kill and that his father, the minister, did not really believe the Bible like it was supposed to be, but he was in agreement with the Agreement of Joshua Wells. He told them about the meeting in Sedona about his horrible cousins. That is two; he knew were bad, but wasn't sure about the other and his older cousin Harold. He told them how he was afraid for his mother's safety because she had gone against his father for the first time that he could ever remember. It was obvious that Baylor was in a sticky situation.

Ron finally put his hand once more on Baylor's shoulder and calmed him down. "It's ok Baylor. It's going to be ok. You are coming with us out to the ranch. You can leave your car here. Is there a way you can get a message to your mother and so she can pretend that she doesn't know what happened to you?" Baylor shook his head no. "She's not allowed to use the phone unless my father is there." "Well, we will just have to take the

218

chance. It looks like we might have time to make a plan before this Harold gets to town. Are you with us?" Baylor shook his head yes. Blane handed him his shirt to put back on. "Let's go" he told Ron, "we don't want to waste any more time."

Back at Baylor's house, C.C. had gone into the living room and put her feet up on the coffee table and got on her computer. Dallas went out on the porch and was playing his video games. Etienne went back up to Baylor's room to lie down. He was pondering whether or not to try to talk to Janice.

Janice was busying herself like she always did preparing food. She did not look suspect as she was always in the kitchen preparing for Warren. Warren liked and expected things made from scratch. Janice started to make his favorite cake and turned on the radio very low to the golden oldie station. This again was what she always did.

There was a peace in her heart that covered the fear she felt for her son. She secretly hoped he had kept going in his car and would end up in New York or somewhere and never come back, but she knew her son and knew he would go to help his girlfriend. "How ironic" she thought, "my son saving the enemy?" She smiled to herself then straightened out her face. She had never had reason to smile for at least 20 years. As she beat the cake mix, her thoughts turned to her mother and dad and the way they were and what they had taught her. It was like years of barnacles coming off of her skin. She felt clean.

"Is Baylor back yet?" Warren stuck his head into the kitchen Janice shook her head no. "And, I need that oil he's bringing," she threw back at him. It had been two hours since Baylor had left. "Now" she dreamed "If somehow, I could just disappear" she made a smirkey face. ""Guess not" she shrugged to herself.

At the ranch, Ron relayed the happenings to the group. They all sat in complete silence as he told them everything that Baylor had said. Baylor sat there with his elbows on his knees and his head in his hand. "Can I see it" RuDee finally asked when Ron had stopped talking. Baylor looked up at her for a long time then he silently removed his shirt and stuck out his arm.

They were all on their feet in an instance examining the tattoo. "Cool" Jaden whispered "I mean cool, but bad." He looked sheepishly at the group. Dezza knelt down in front of Baylor "This is an awful brave thing to do Baylor. This isn't a trick is it?" Baylor bit his lip, a tear escaped and came careening down his cheek. "No Dezza, no trick."

Autie came and sat beside him. "Baylor, do you realize what exactly is happening here?" He shook his head no. She addressed the group. "We need to tell Baylor the whole story. So he knows that we are not evil. That we are not witches."

Connie stood up. "I'll tell him." and with that, Connie in her wonderfully soft and compelling voice relayed the story of Elizabeth and gave him a recap of all the letters and how the remaining cousins found each other and that that was not just a happening. She told him she thought it was from God that they found each other. Just like she believed it was from the God that Baylor knew and had loved all these years that he was freed from the people of the Agreement and how his mother had sacrificed herself to get him out of harms-way and to keep him from having to do something he knew was wrong.

Baylor sobbed like a baby and instantly Blake, Richard and Jadin positioned themselves around him in a show of unity and acceptance. Courtneay handed him a hanky and extended her hand to him. He took it.

Charlene and Mike were silent bystanders while all the stories were being told, then Mike told them that they had better get their plan laid.

Charlene spoke up "We have to rescue Baylor's mother. She cannot be left with them. Once they find out he is really gone, I know she will be in danger. Isn't that right Baylor?"   Baylor nodded yes.

"We have not been practicing for nothing." Courtneay leaned back into the couch and turned its colors. Baylor's eyes got big as he watched for the second time the phenomenon happen. He felt light headed. He had been told they were witches and now it looked like they were, however, he really did not believe in any such thing and now that he knew that it was from a bite, he believed them. He relaxed.

RuDee saw his face contorting and laughed. "I think we need to give him a real shock and show him how we can control our GIFT." She emphasized "gift". "Don't be offended Baylor."

Autie got up went over to the rough wood paneling and pulled off her top and jeans. She was gone. Baylor had a hard time swallowing. Blane put his hand on Baylor's shoulder "Take it from a non-lizard, it's spooky. But not evil."   Baylor gave him a weak smile.

"Baylor" Mike addressed the confused person sitting there "Buy us some time. OK?"   "How?" He looked up at this large military looking person. "Call your Dad and tell him you are at the lake with friends and ask if Harold has gotten there yet. When he starts yelling, act dumb. Ok?"   Baylor took out his cell.

"Dad?" Baylor addressed the one who answered his ring.   "I saw Bryan at Jimbo's and he talked me into going out to the lake. Oh, man, I forgot all about that stuff. Man, is she sore?" It was obvious to everyone in the room that Baylor was being yelled at. They kept quiet. "I will, I will. Is Harold there yet? Oh…. Does mom still need that stuff? All right. I'll be there in less than an hour. Sorry." He hung up. "Whew" he acted like he was wiping sweat off his brow. "He is hot." "What about your Mom?" Charlene asked. "He said she could go to the store herself. He doesn't treat her good." He got mad just thinking about how his father didn't even care that his mother would be inconvenienced. "What store does she go to?" Susan asked. "Stellars, over on Columbus".

Susan grabbed her purse. "Come on girls, Let's go shopping." Autie had put back on her clothes "We don't know what your Mom looks like Baylor." Baylor's heart was beating almost too fast for him to breathe. "She's really short and has brown hair. She pulls it back and it's kinda like wrapped in the back and pinned down. She wears a long skirt and a blouse. You won't miss her; she doesn't dress like most women. She carries a large purse that looks almost like a sack with a draw string.

Over at the Lackeys, Warren stormed in the kitchen "That son of yours is totally out of control" he yelled at Janice. She looked up surprised. "He went out to the lake with some kids. Said he forgot to go to the store." She pretended to be mad and held her hands up. "I needed that stuff." He looked at her a long time, thinking something didn't seem right, but couldn't put his finger on it. "Here" he pulled out some bills. "You'll have to go. He'll be back in less than an hour. Or so he says. He had better get here before Harold." He said in a manner that seemed like he blamed her for it all.

Janice put the bills in her skirt pocket, picked up her bag and headed for the back door. "Be back in a minute. Tell C.C. I'll bring her that special tea she asked about."

She started out the back door, then turned and took some keys off the wall. "I think I'll drive my car. I haven't had it out in a while." Waiting for Harold to come had Warren in a dither or he would have thought that was really strange that she were taking her car.

Janice sat at the end of the street wondering which way to go. Should she really go to the store? Why had Baylor called home? Was he really coming home? She felt fear well up inside her "Please ,no , Dear God, Please don't let him go back home. Let him keep going." But what if he did come home and she didn't. Then, he would really be in trouble. "I'll have to go back" she decided.

She headed north and was soon entering Stellars' parking lot. She almost ran as she went through the store picking up things that she had pretended to write on Baylor's list, to be safe. She picked up some herb tea for C.C. and a couple of candy bars that she knew Dallas had asked for. The line was long and Janice was getting anxious to get out and get home. She was afraid that C.C. would harm Baylor. In fact, she knew she would.

At last, she was through the line and going out the front of the store. She had to go down the sidewalk by the brick wall of the store to get to the parking area where she had put her car. She stopped as she felt dizzy. She put her hand against the wall. She felt like she was getting sick to her stomach. She saw the wall sway and move. She squinted at the wall. A lump of fear jumped up into her throat.

"Hello?' she asked the air, looking all around her. She felt stupid, but she sensed she was not alone. She kept that feeling all the way along the brick wall. Once she got to the end of the wall, she turned toward her car that was right by the wall. A hand came out of nowhere and grabbed her arm. A gurgled type of sound came out of her throat as fear enveloped her.

223

"Don't be scared" a voice was aimed at her head. "It's ok. We won't hurt you." She looked around, and saw nothing. She turned again toward her car. "Janice!" a sharp voice of a mother made her turn and stand still. A woman emerged from the wall. "I'm Charlene, and I have come here to save you. I've come to take you to Baylor." Janice felt her knees go weak but she stayed firm. "Who are you?" she asked. "I am what you call a Chameleon. I am no witch Janice."

Just then six more women emerged from the wall. "We are the Clade women" Connie announced. "Come with us Janice. Baylor is at our house." "What about my ca....?" she started to say. "Leave it" Susan urged "They'll think someone else took you." Janice let herself be put into a large SUV by women who were wearing only bikinis. Her chest felt like an elephant had sat on it. And, then it came over her, that she was free from Warren. She had dreamed of that, but then thought she would always feel guilty. But she didn't, she felt elated.

As the girls sped toward the ranch, they were putting on their clothes as Charlene told the dazed Janice the whole Clade story. When they got to the ranch and Baylor opened the door to find his mother, she had become calm and was allowing herself to take in a whole new world.

Back again at the Lackey's, C.C. came into the kitchen and then into Warren's Den "Where is your family?" she asked a little agitated. "Got me" he answered her, not wanting to talk about it. He was angry that Janice was taking so long. And that Baylor had not come back when he said he would. He didn't much appreciate this girl asking him questions like she were his boss or something. "Something's wrong." C.C. said arrogantly. "And I intend to find out before Harold gets here." She picked up her keys 'Where does Janice shop?" she ordered. "Stellars. It's just up the street, then turn right." Then she asked "And what lake was that son of yours at?"

"Lake Ming, I guess"

C.C. was fuming mad as she left. She didn't even take time to get Dallas to go with her and she was disgusted seeing him play computer games all the time. She just told Warren, "Come on, you're going with me." He followed and got in her car.

As she peeled rubber out of the driveway and headed down the street toward the grocery store she hissed "Jannnnniccce, you're a dead woman." Warren looked at her and saw a crazy person. He felt a chill go up his spine. "What did you say?" he asked angrily. "Your wife" C.C. screwed up her face at him "I think is a traitor." "She is not!" he screamed at her. "She doesn't do anything I don't tell her to do. She's not smart enough to think of doing something against us." He hit the dashboard with his fist. C.C. kept her eyes on the road ahead, her lips curled in a cruel smile "We will see Warren."

There in the parking lot at Stellars sat Janice's car. The car door was open and there was no one around it. Warren went into the store and asked the clerk if she saw his wife. "She was in here, alright" the chunky clerk smiled up at him, "But, it's been a long time ago." "Did you see her with anyone?" he asked. "Nope, alone as usual." She shook her head.

Outside, Warren looked over the parking lot. "I think I should call the police" he told C.C. "She couldn't put up a fight against anyone. She's too little." "The Police? Really Warren, Why not call attention to what we're doing." She snipped at him. "Come on, she'll show up, but if not, I don't think Harold would want the police involved with us right now." Warren, even though he was mean to Janice didn't want her to get hurt. He might want to hurt her, but she was his and he was seething at C.C.

for not wanting him to call the Police. He couldn't get the thought out of his mind that someone might molest her. He gradually got more agitated by the time they got back to the house.

When they entered the house Etienne was downstairs "Where did everyone go?" he asked. Just then Harold came through the front door without knocking. Warren was already unnerved and this made him even madder. After C.C. explained to Etienne and Harold what had happened, Harold put his hand on Warren's shoulder. "After we kill the Clade, Warren, you can call the Police and they can find Janice. Maybe, you had better try to call your son again. We really need to get this job done and get out of here. Etienne, I want you to go to this address, its Charlene's and check and see who is home there. Here is a name badge and some documentation that shows you to be a County worker, inspecting gas lines that go into a house. Call us when you know who and how many are in there." Etienne took the paper and left the house.

Dallas had come in off the porch. He did not want his father to find him playing computer games. "Dallas" he father ordered, "Here is the other address. Go and see who is home." He handed him a badge and paperwork like Etienne's. C.C. frowned at Harold's decision "I think I should go with Dallas" she spoke up. Harold cut her a sharp look then took a deep breath. "Ok, but don't do anything until we have made our plan. We can't afford to get caught. You two go and then get right back here and we will all decide what to do together. Understand?" he looked right into her eyes. They seemed illuminated. She hated to be told what to do, even by Harold. She headed toward the door. Dallas had to almost run to catch up.

At the ranch, the whole group had gathered in the kitchen. Susan and Connie had laid out leftovers, sandwich makings and a huge salad. As they stood around eating and talking, Susan said she needed to go back to their house and get her medicine. "That's not a good idea" Ron told her. "But I know you need your pills, so I will go over there and get them. You all need to stay here. I am sure they couldn't find out where this house is. "But they know where Grandma lives" Autie interjected. "If they could find that out, they might just know where we are"

"They don't." Janice spoke up. "They just know about Charlene and her daughter, I guess that's you" she looked at Susan, "and your kids. I know they don't know about the rest of you. I do think you might have time to go back to your house and get your medicine. If Harold has gotten to my house it must have just been now." She looked at the group. "Please be careful, they know what they are doing and they are so dangerous. They want to kill you and if they don't they will have to kill themselves or each other. I am sure C.C. has me and Baylor marked for death now." She looked down and sad "I think that Warren would kill us. He is so mentally entangled with this whole thing."

Baylor put his arm around his mother "Mom, I'm sorry I had bad feelings toward you." She hugged him "I know, but you were right, too" She leaned up and kissed his cheek "But now I'm free and back in my right mind" she smiled at him "And with the God of my childhood." His heart fairly swelled with joy at his mother's statement.

Autie came over to Janice. "I am so glad you are with us Mrs. Lackey." "Autie, call me Janice." She responded to the beautiful girl that seemed to be crazy about her son.

Ron took the van keys off the rack "I have an idea" his eyes twinkled. "Let's caravan over to the house, all of us, that is except Janice and Baylor. They can stay here with Charlene and Mike. We'll meet just around the corner of the house. You Chameleons can go in color while we, Blane and I, drive right up in the driveway and go in. Let's put your training to the test.

"Woo Hoo" RuDee jumped up and did a martial arts type kick. Bringing chuckles and laughs from the whole group. "Ok tiger" Richard put his hand on the top of her head "Let's kick some Adam's apples".

"Thanks Richard" Connie laughed   He gave her a questioning look. "For not saying the A word."   He blushed "Well" he responded "I wouldn't say it in front of my own mother and I won't in front of any of you."

Courtneay was the first to change into her bikini and swim robe. Soon they were all in cars headed to the Tanner house.

That evening in Oildale

Reed and Nicole were sitting outside with their feet in a child's blow up swimming pool. Reed was mulling over the fact that he had seen Autumn turn black. He had read and reread the letters from his box. He knew his history and what he was and now, he knew for sure there were more Chameleons. He had found out the he was an uncle of someone his own age. He also knew that there was a sign of a lizard in a hangman's noose and he remembered after he read that that C.C. had one under her upper arm. It had grossed him out. He needed to talk to Autie. But how? Nicole's kid sister Samantha had gone off to a Church teen retreat and wouldn't be back until he had gone home.

"Nicole" he turned to his girlfriend "I would like to go back by that house where we were last night. I would like to thank that family. Ok?" "Sure" Nicole stood up. "I'll change. Won't be a minute." Within five minutes they were in the car headed toward Autie and Jadin's house.

As Nicole's car turned on to Columbus which was just two blocks from Autie's house, Reed whispered loudly "Pull over." then louder, "Nicole, pull over right here." She quickly pulled over and stopped. "What's wrong" she had a lump in her throat. "Nicole" he looked at her "Do you trust me?"

"Yeah" she looked into his eyes trying to understand what he was saying. "Why?"

"I want you to go to that Coffee Shop up there and wait for me. I am getting out of the car now. Something is happening and I will tell you later. You have to believe me and trust me. I promise I will explain later." Nicole swallowed "Ok Reed, I will. I'll be right up there" she pointed to the coffee shop. "Drinking coffee and wondering what in the world you are doing. But" she continued "If you are gone over a half hour, I am calling the Police. OK?" she asked. He hugged her "OK." He slipped out of the car and she drove away.

He stood in the middle of the sidewalk and yelled loudly "Hey" then again "Hey. I know you're there. Show yourselves." Suddenly Courtneay appeared from the cement block wall that lined the sidewalk. "Reed?" She walked over to him her real color was back and there she was all of her accentuated by her camouflage bathing suit. "What are you doing here?"

"Me?" he yelled "What are you doing here? And who else is here? I saw the wall move and I knew. You are Chameleon aren't you?" She shook her head yes, "But you have to come over here." She pulled his arm and he followed her behind a huge oleander bush.

Suddenly there was a crowd of half naked people surrounding him. Richard spoke first "How do you know about us?" he asked in an angry voice. Reed slipped off his tee shirt and turned the colors of the oleander. "That's how." He said in an angry voice too. "What are you doing?" he asked again to the group. Quickly Courtneay told him they were under attack and that the enemy was there in Bakersfield to kill them. "Well, that means me too" he choked out. "So I am coming with you. I have Nicole up at that Coffee place waiting. She said she would call the police if I didn't show in 30 minutes. She has no idea what I am."   "Let her, that is if you don't get back, let her, maybe the police could be of some help." Dezza spoke up. "Come on" Jadin said. "Dad and Blane need us."

Reed stepped out of his jeans and they all disappeared into scenery.

At the Tanner house, Ron and Blane parked in the driveway and walked into the house. Ron found his wife's pills and then went through the house checking on everything he could think of. Samantha, their boxer was out at the ranch and the cat that thought it belonged to the family was outside the back sliding glass doors meowing for food. He poured some of the dog food out into a bowl and put out a large pan of water for the cat "This cat thinks we're its family" he told Blane.

Blane locked the back door and the two were walking toward the front door when the door bell rang. They both stopped in their tracks and looked at each other. Ron put his finger to his lips in a silent "shhh" gesture. Then they stood still. The door bell rang again. "Do you have a gun?" Blane asked. "No, I mean yes I do, but" he chuckled in a small whispery way. "I never bought any bullets for it."   Ron went to the door and looked out the peep hole. There was a red headed boy of about eighteen. He had a badge pinned on his shirt and was holding a notepad. "Yes?" Ron asked through the door. "CGE!" the boy announced. "We have a report of a gas main leak and want to check your gas line."

"You'll have to come back tomorrow" Ron yelled. "Can't sir" the boy yelled back. "There might be an explosion. I have to check it." Ron looked at Blane. Blane shook his head no. "It has to be one of them" he said. "Let's slip out the back and go over the fence." "What about the kids? They're out there somewhere."

Ron started to look out the back door. There was a girl, a beautiful girl standing at the back door. Just standing. "Who are you?" Ron yelled. She didn't answer, just kept staring in at them. "I can take her." Blane was mad now. He started to open the back door when he saw the gun. "She has a gun" he shouted as he threw himself away to the side of the door.

Ron ducked behind the couch. BAM! The sliding glass door shattered. "I'm coming in and you'd better put your hands in the air and come out. BAM! Another blast shattered the front door and Dallas stood inside the door with his gun aimed right at Ron. "Get up" he ordered. Ron and Blane got up and stood between C.C. and Dallas. "Who are you?" Ron asked with his hands still held up high. "Who do you want us to be?" C.C. laughed hysterically. "We are your worst nightmare" Dallas yelled. He had always wanted to say that and now was the perfect time. C.C. gave him an evil look. She thought he was so stupid.

"Tie their hands" she ordered him. With the gun in his hand Dallas felt big and indestructible "You." He threw back at her. She took her gun off Ron and Blane for a second and aimed it right into Dallas' face "I beg your pardon?" she said sarcastically. Dallas' face fell. "You " he pointed his gun back at the men. "Get on your stomachs with your hands behind you." Ron and Blane laid down. Dallas put his gun in his belt and stood over the men. "Give me your belts" he ordered. Ron and Blane were in the process of taking off their belts when Ron saw movement in his fireplace brick. He looked over at the window and saw it waver. C.C. was holding her gun at the men and watching the bumbling way Dallas was handling this simple capture. She wanted to take the belts and do the job herself. But she wouldn't give Dallas the satisfaction of her doing what she had told him to do. Standing by the wall, she waved the gun back and forth to show the men she could shoot either one or both of them.

Suddenly, a hand came from out of nowhere and grabbed the gun right out of C.C.'s hand. At the same time, a whole person came flying through the air and knocked Dallas to the floor, his gun went flying. Dallas' eyes followed the gun and saw it rise from the floor and seem to go up the wall. Then from the wall, a perfect looking girl stepped out holding the gun pointed at him. His whole body lurched backward at this eerie happening. "Don't move!" RuDee yelled.

C.C. stood staring at the person who took her gun. It couldn't be, but it was. There was Reed right in front of her holding her gun. She drew back in a state of shock as she saw one by one people come out of the wall, curtains and brick. All scantily clad but all real people. Her head was swimming. She was surrounded by the Clade. She looked around for an avenue of escape. Her eyes kept coming back to Reed. She choked out "You? You're a Chameleon?" He grinned at her "Looks like. And you C.C. what exactly are you?"

C.C. all of a sudden lurched toward the back door but was met by a flying Brie who tackled her and sent her sprawling. C.C. fought back but Brie was much stronger. She had C.C. down on the ground with her leg twisted back and up. Almost like bull dogging at a rodeo. C.C. was cussing and screaming to be let loose. She tried a maneuver like RuDee had taught Charlene and she squirmed right out from under Brie. Courtneay grabbed C.C.'s arm and slung her to the ground. C.C. scratched Courtneay's arm. "Ouch" she yelled as she grabbed C.C.s hair and pulled her back and down. Their heads touching as Courtneay held on to her with all her might. C.C. tried again

232

to poke her fingernail into Courtneay's arm and Courtneay grabbed her head tighter and bit her ear. C.C. screamed. "Ok, I'll stop." Courtneay held on tight still cutting her teeth into the flesh on C.C.'s ear. Blake came over and took C.C.'s hands and put them behind her back while Brie tied them to her ankle with the twine Autie had found for them. With Dallas and C.C. laying on the floor with their hands tied to their ankles, the group started talking about what to do with them.

Reed remembered Nicole. "Man, I have to go and see Nicole. She probably has already called the Police." "That's good" Ron spoke up. "We will call the Police and have these two arrested for home invasion. I know the Deputy Chief of Police." He went over to the phone and picked up the receiver and dialed 911. He told the police that he and his friend had captured a couple that had shot their way into the house and tried to shoot them. He asked for Deputy Chief Ganther to come to the scene. While they were waiting for the police, the Chameleons turned back into color and secretly left the house. "You know we will be out of jail in no time and we will be back for you." C.C. hissed at them. "Yes" Ron responded "I do know, but we will be ready for you and this time, we won't turn you over to police."

Minutes later Reed was walking up to the Coffee shop, clothed. He met a worried Nicole coming out. "I was about to call the cops." She said. She was furious. "What happened?' Suddenly, Jadin appeared and joined them "Hi, Nicole." He said cheerfully. Nicole just stared for a minute, then "Why are you almost naked?" "Naked?" he retorted "I have on a swimming suit." "Come on Nicole" Reed took her hand, "we're going somewhere." They got in her car and he told her to follow Jadin's vehicle. They headed for the ranch.

At the Lackey's, Warren and Harold sat waiting for the three to come back. It was getting late. Soon there was a knock on the front door and Etienne entered. "No luck" he said. "There was no one home and nothing in the house that I could find to show where they might be." He looked around "Where's C.C. and Dallas?" Harold shook his head. "Don't know yet." "What about Baylor or his mom?" he continued. This time Warren shook his head no. Etienne continued "Shall I go to the other address and see if I can find out what happened to them?" "No" Harold ordered. "You stay here. We will wait. I just hope C.C. didn't try to take them down. She is so hard headed."

Just then the phone rang. Warren jumped and took off for it. "Hello" he spoke rather loudly. "C.C.?" he raised his eyebrows "Where are you?" He handed the phone to Harold. Harold took the phone and walked into the kitchen. He came storming back into the room. "Those stupid kids got themselves caught" he grumped. "What?" Etienne looked concerned. "They are booked for home invasion and attempted murder." He informed Warren and Etienne.

"Now what?" Warren asked. "Well, I, for one, am out of here" Harold said coldly. "They are on their own. I'll call in tomorrow from San Francisco and act surprised my cousin and my son are in jail. I'll get them a local lawyer to get them out on bail. You" he looked directly at Warren "had better call the Police about your wife and son. Try to look like you are having a normal life. And you, Etienne, you had better lay low for a while. Go back to San Francisco and wait. I'll let you know what to do. Then we will come back and take these people out. C.C. said there seemed to be a dozen of them."

Etienne didn't wait to find out anything else. He really wanted out of there. He hated this whole thing and was secretly glad that C.C. and Dallas were behind bars. He personally thought they were crazy. He was in his car and on the freeway in the next fifteen minutes.

CHAPTER SEVENTEEN

Back at the ranch, they were buzzing about the happening. On the way out there, Reed told Nicole everything. She just looked at him in disbelief. Once inside the house, Nicole was brought very quickly to a believer. She sat quiet from then on just taking in this unreal atmosphere. Back in their clothes the group discussed ways to keep the enemy from hurting them.

Janice had found a new strength and Baylor was amazed at her boldness. He had never known her to be anything other than like a servant. She told them everything she knew about her husband's family and how and who they killed. She told them that she and Baylor should go far from there so that Warren could never find them. They all agreed, that is except Autie, She didn't want Baylor to leave. And Baylor thought they should too, but he didn't want to leave Autie. "Where will you go?" she asked Janice. Janice shook her head, "I don't know or even how we can do it. I don't have any money of my own and I can't get access to the money in the bank. He never let me have my name on anything." "Now that C.C. knows what I am," Reed spoke up, "my home is not the place for me to be either. I need to relocate somewhere myself."

Nicole finally found her voice. "No one knows me and Dad and I own a cabin in Northern Arizona. It's close to Flagstaff No one goes there and I can get you all a key. It's completely furnished and has two bedrooms and two baths. It's in a community built around a golf course. They couldn't possibly find you there. And I know they don't know about me, right?" she asked Reed. "Well, I told her your first name, but not your last. It'll take her a while to find us if at all. Great idea Nicole, can you do that for us?" he asked her. She shook her head yes. "We never go there, but always have it cleaned twice a year and Dad has someone who keeps the weeds down and

checks on it.   I'll get you the keys when I go home tonight."
She took Reed's hand "I have to tell my Dad."   He nodded.

"Do you have letters?" Connie asked Reed. "Yes ma'am" he
replied. I have all of them I think." He answered.   "Whose line
are you in?" She continued.   Everyone stopped talking and
listened to this conversation. "I'm from Victor Martinez. My
father was Bill Brown."   Richard sat up straight, "What?" he
asked "Bill Brown was my Grandfather." He repeated himself,
"Bill Brown was my grandfather and I never heard of another
child of his except my mother."   "Nevertheless" Reed
continued "I'm his child. I was adopted by my stepfather, but
the reality is that my mother and your grandfather had a
relationship and I am the product of it. I have letters and one
specifically from him. He thought it best that the two families
didn't know about each other."

 Richard made a face then came over and stuck out his hand.
"Welcome Uncle Reed." He grinned. "Thank you nephew, I
think." He shook his hand.   RuDee came up and pushed the
two together. "It is obvious that you two are related to Victor
Martinez, just look at your features. I knew you belonged
together the minute I saw Reed."   "I see it" Susan declared.
"Look at their teeth, they are practically identical. That smile
and demeanor. Ha. You two are like Connie and me." She
explained to Reed how she and Connie didn't know each other
until recently and then said "Look how we look alike."

Courtneay pulled out a paper she had in her bag. "Look" she
laid the paper on the table. "Here it is. Our genealogy. She
penciled in Reed. "It really doesn't matter how we got on this
chart. What matters is that we are on it and we are "family."
Richard couldn't keep his eyes off of Reed and Reed felt the
same. There was an instant connection, like twins finding each
other. "My mother doesn't know about this trait" Reed informed
them, but she is a great person. Do you think I should tell her?"
he threw out to the group.   "No" Susan said emphatically.

236

"Don't burden her. It will just scare her and if you find another place to live other than home, the enemy will only search you out. I'm sure, not your mother."   "I hope everyone is staying here tonight" Brie announced "Because Courtneay and I have made up some beds" "and I"   interrupted Blane "Suggest that we all use them. It has been a day I would like to forget." Reed made his good nights, shook Richard's hand again and left with Nicole. He felt a strange elation being a part of this Clade.

Warren sat in his quiet house, not knowing what to do. He hadn't called the Police yet, even though Harold told him too, he didn't know if he wanted too. He kept expecting one or both of them to come in the door any minute. He poured himself a large whiskey and sat in front of the TV; not watching or hearing what was on.

Harold was on his way back home still seething over C.C. messing up their quest. "I'll get them yet" he told himself. He knew that he would arrange to have C.C. and Dallas bailed out in the morning. His chuckling, over how he thought C.C. might be handling the solitude of jail, made his scar take on an under-worldly shape of maybe a devil as it turned purplish red.

He hoped that Warren would get his family in order. He had always distrusted Warren. Especially since he found out that he had not told Baylor about the Agreement until recently. His dislike for his cousin was growing. He thought of how C.C. would revel in taking Warren out. She had a killer's instinct and she enjoyed others feeling scared.

Harold had called his church's deaconess Nellie Shultz to meet him at his home. She would work out the details concerning C.C. and Dallas. She was happy he called as he had been very angry with her when she let the Tollison twins, Courtneay and Blake, get away and he hadn't called her until now. She was worried that she might have to die for her inefficiency. It had been a stressful stretch of time as she continually looked over her shoulders where ever she went expecting either Dallas or C.C. to be there to kill her. Relieved now that she was needed, Nellie started finding out how to get C.C. and Dallas released from jail not knowing that Harold was still planning her demise for a later date. She was needed right at the moment, but he thought her mistake inexcusable.

It was late when Reed and Nicole walked up to the door of her home. She was still in a sort of shocked state. She knew she loved Reed, but tonight finding out he was a Chameleon and then meeting the group, the Clade, she felt queasy. It was almost like finding out he was from outer space. And it was that big of deal as she knew she had to tell her father. Nicole Ramsey's dad was the Regional Director of the Federal Bureau of Investigation for the States of California, Nevada, Utah and Arizona. He was going to "flip" or so she thought. "Are you going to tell him tonight?" Reed asked as they walked into the living room. "I don't know" Nicole answered slowly "I think he ought to know. I mean, we are all in danger and I just think that the sooner we tell him the sooner I'll feel safe." Reed shook his head agreeing with her. "Sorry" he whispered into her ear. She put her arms around his neck, "Will you tell him with me?" she looked up into his face. He kissed her mouth lightly and held her tight "Yes, of course." Just then the light came on in the hallway "Nicole?" a booming voice beat the light into the darkened living room. "Yes Dad" she answered "It's me."

Dick Ramsey flipped on the living room light "It's a little late, don't you think?" he frowned at this daughter and this young man who had his arms around her. Reed quickly lowered his arms and stood away from Nicole. "Good evening, Sir" he said to Nicole's father. "Reed." he acknowledged the boy's address.

"Dad" Nicole came and stood very close to him. "Reed and I have something really important to tell you." Dick looked alarmed. "What?" he almost yelled, fearing something horrible had happened.

"Sit here" Nicole motioned her father over to his recliner. "Sit down and we'll tell you." Dick Ramsey's knees grew weak. He had been a single parent for ten years ever since Nicole was only 9. Sitting down, Nicole sensed his fear. "I'm ok Dad, Honest. I'm not dead, not in jail, don't need money. I'm not pregnant and we didn't go off and get married." Her dad chuckled thinking how well she knew him. Or had he expressed those things over enough times. So, for the next hour, Reed and Nicole told Dick what had happened. The reality of it didn't sink in until when they were through, Reed stood by the hallway wanes coating and wall. The top half of him that was not covered by a shirt and the bottom half not covered by his short pants were exactly the color and pattern of the wall and wanes coating. Dick suddenly realized his jaw had dropped open and stayed open. 'How many of you are there?" he asked. Reed filled him in on his story and as much as he knew about the rest, plus what he knew about the Agreement and Baylor's relatives.

Dick stood up. "It is too late to digest this now. I'm going out to the ranch in the morning and I need to meet these people. Ok?" he asked Reed. "Absolutely!" Reed answered. They said their good nights and Reed went to the guest bedroom. Dick held his daughter in his arms. "What in the world have you gotten yourself into little girl?" She looked up tears were streaming down her face. "I don't know. I don't know."

After spending the day with the Clade, going through the letters and hearing all the stories, Dick knew in his heart that these were good people. He witnessed their color changing and was impressed with the group of young people and these remaining parents. He agreed with Ron and Blane that C.C. and Dallas shouldn't be let out too quickly so they could make plans. He called his secretary and made arrangements to have the two stay incarcerated until such time as they felt it would be okay for the Clade. As he was going through the day learning about this strange group of people he remembered that he was supposed to meet with one of his staff on a stake out at an apartment complex, near the elementary school, where they were waiting to catch a drug dealer who had been selling to children under the age of ten. They had gotten tips that the man was a red head, but had never been able to spot him or be there when the deal was going down.

He was telling the group this as he was needing to leave when Courtneay asked him if they could help. "We could stand there and wait for it to happen. He won't see us." She told him. "It's too dangerous" Dick told her.   "Too dangerous?" RuDee interjected from the other side of the room.   "I think we are used to danger." He laughed "I guess you're right, but you would have to become like volunteers or employees or something.   It is a thought." he mulled this over in his head. Richard stood up and crossed over to him "Let us help. We are not victims anymore and we want to help anyone in trouble. We're going to get better, too. We are going to be ready when the Agreement people come back."

"I have to think about it tonight." Dick threw at them. He was still reeling in his brain with all this information that seemed hard to process. "Lizard people" he wished Nicole were eight again and not a part of this crowd, but there she was, evidently in love with a boy that could change colors. "I have to get permission to use you" He said "and I might have to bring you in so that I can show my superior that I am not lying." He dreaded that process. "It'll take some time."

When he left that evening, the "family" sat in the living room going over the possibilities of not only helping themselves stay alive, but being an asset to society. "We can help others" RuDee smiled.

Just then a phone range. Everyone looked around to see whose was ringing. It was Jadin's. "Hi Summer. No, I haven't seen Baylor" he lied as his eyes went straight to Baylor's scared look. "Why?" he asked the caller. "Oh. No, haven't. Ok, talk to you later. Bye." All eyes were on him "It was Summer Jennings. She said Baylor's dad called looking for him and his mother. She told him she would check around." Janice sat very still and silent. Baylor came over and put his arm around her shoulder. "It's ok Mom, he won't find us."

It was decided that Baylor and his mother would go to Arizona to Dick's cabin and stay there for awhile at least to find out what to do next.

Blane said that since the enemy knew they were there, there was no use to try to completely hide. "We will be ready to fight back when they come back." He told the group. "And, I think that we should start living again" he looked at Brianna. "Brie, since we seem to have some time, I think that you should go back and get Chieftain and bring him out here. Brie jumped up and did a victory type dance. "Brie get him. Brie get him" she chanted. The room rocked with laughter. Autie rolled on the floor pointing at Brie "You are few funny." Baylor pulled Autie up and onto his lap. "Look who's few." He laughed at her antics.

Blane continued when the room got quieter, "As for the rest of you" he looked around the room. "I think that we should all figure out where we want to live. You are all welcome to live with us here, get an apartment or stay at Ron's house. Think it over. We will get ready, but we are going to have lives. I am obligated to work this ranch for a year, and then I plan on moving my family back home, Lord willing."

"I'm going to settle the rest of my estate and see what happened to my Mom" Richard chimed in.

There was an air of happiness that went through the Clade. Like an army taking a quick RnR before the battle.

Richard suggested that he, RuDee and Brianna go through Flagstaff, take care of his business, than go up to Wyoming and get her horse and more of their personal belongings.

Dezza wanted to stay with Connie at the ranch and keep the kitchen.

Blake and Courtneay promised to help Blane on the ranch and Autumn and Jadin were going back to their normal lives at home. Except that Autie, was already planning to go with Baylor and his mother to Arizona to help them get settled in then she was going to ride the train back.

Reed was going back to the coast to figure out with his mom and step dad what they were going to do. Nicole was going with him and get back into her college there at San Luis Obispo.

After everyone shared their plans, Ron suggested that maybe they should help Dick catch that dope pusher before they all went separate ways. RuDee's eyes lit up. She was ready. Ron told them he would talk to Dick in the morning and see what they could do.

"Well then" RuDee took charge. "Tomorrow, we will practice"

"But tonight" Courtneay shouted "We're going out!" "Parteeee" shouted Jadin. Ron, Susan, Connie and Blane shook their heads grinning and left the room. "Where?" Brie asked   "Jericho's" Autie answered   "Let's go dance." Jericho's was a dance hall that was frequented by people from seventeen on up to about twenty two. It did not have a liquor license, however, the bands were hot and it was always packed and "rockin." It took only 20 minutes for them to get ready and the group headed out into the crisp winter air to the Central part of Bakersfield. A chance to be "normal, to be party animals, before their work began. The work of staying alive. The work of getting the enemy before it got them. "Self Preservation" Dezza called it.

Reed went to pick up Nicole. She had left with her father. When he got to their house, Dick was still up. He took Reed into his den while he waited for Nicole to change. Dick gave Reed the keys and directions to his cabin for Baylor and his mother. "Tell them to make themselves at home. I called the woman that cleans twice a year and she is going to stock the kitchen with all kinds of food for them. That's my gift to them. I also have called a friend that lives in the area and he will see that she gets a job and he gets into the local high school for now. Then, when Nicole came in, he showed them the sketch of the drug dealer and told them where they suspected he was selling to children. "I'll talk to my boss tomorrow and see how to go about using your Clade to help us out. Now, you to go out and be normal." he stood up "Good normal that is." He looked directly into his daughter's eyes.

The mattress was hard and lumpy and the sheet C.C. tried to stretch over her was coarse and itchy. She had asked for a better one, but the matron had quickly told her that they were all the same and to "deal with it." C.C. hissed at the woman envisioning choking her. "Where is Harold?" She thought. It was already the second day and no one had contacted her. Demanding her rights, she asked for another phone call. The first one she made was to Harold to tell him what had happened. They wouldn't give her another one until the following day. The minutes were hours long and the smells were almost unbearable.

She scolded herself for letting the Clade sneak up on her. There were so many of them. She couldn't remember exactly how many. And Reed, how in the world was he one of them. She was still in shock over that fact. There he was though, coming out of the wall like the rest. Her cold heart actually ached thinking that he wouldn't be a hunter with her. But now he was to be the hunted. "And I will hunt him" she thought wildly 'And I will cut his heart out and eat it" she threw that horrendous thought up in the air. She wondered which one of the girls was Moonshadow's daughter. She couldn't tell because of the light which one might look Oriental. She wondered why some were different races than others. It seemed to be a family trait. "Wasn't it?" she searched the recesses of her mind.

She had begged the nurse to give her a sleeping pill or a valium when she came in to put a bandage on her ear. Courtneay had bit it almost in half at the top and the swelling was painful and the laceration wouldn't close tightly, so the nurse put some butterfly bandages and did the best she could to get the two sides lined up. The bandages pulled her face up and to the left making her look even more evil. The nurse wouldn't give her anything. She told C.C. that she would just have to wait until she was really tired, then she would sleep. C.C. felt like hitting her, but didn't think at this time it would be beneficial for her to do that.

C.C. mulled over in her mind why Harold hadn't called or come by. Suddenly it dawned on her that he didn't want their work to come out in the open. "I have to cool down and wait" she told herself trying to get control of her feelings which at that point seemed to be bouncing off the wall eager to get out, eager to hunt and kill. "ooooouuuuu" she hissed at the ceiling "I am going to start with you Reed. You will be the first to die. Then your mother, then your sweet little girlfriend." Her thoughts then went to Etienne. "Maybe" she thought, "He'll get me out of here. Yes, he'll come for me. We'll hunt them together. They all must die."

In the opposite end of the Jail where the men were housed, there was an annoying noise of a man sobbing. In his cell, Dallas was crying pitifully into his pillow. He was scared and at the same time mad. "How dare they treat me like this?" He told them his father would be there in the morning. He begged for something to do, a TV, a play station, a computer, anything, but they ignored each request. He wanted his cell phone. He cried well into the night until sleep took him, and then he dreamed horrible scary dreams making him toss and turn and cry out in his sleep.

When Nellie had called an attorney in Bakersfield to get the two out of jail, the first attorney who agreed to take the case called back and told her that in no way would they take the case. They didn't give her a reason. The second told her that it would be another week before they could get out on bail, because something to do with the Feds being involved as it was a home invasion type situation. She relayed the information hesitantly to Harold who just shrugged his shoulders. He, himself, wasn't in any hurry to have the two of them back with him. "Let'em rot" he told himself as he planned to go out to a lavish restaurant to reward himself for the horrible time he had had. He planned to make C.C. and Dallas go up to his cabin in Washington State for a few months when they got out of jail and let things die down a little before they went on a death hunt again. He had told Etienne to go somewhere and just wait until he called him. He didn't bother to call Warren. He knew Warren would be in touch with the police over his wife's disappearance and his son missing. He thought that when they did go on the death hunt later, C.C. would be the one who would take out Warren. "Worthless Cleric" he thought toward Warren. Harold knew that starting tomorrow he would throw himself into his church work and endear himself to his flock.

At Jerico's, the party was in progress by the time Reed and Nicole caught up with the group. Autie had found a short red wig she had used in a play last year. It changed Baylor's appearance totally and with some of Jadin's clothes, they were all sure no one would know he was Baylor, except for the fact that he was dancing with Autumn. They decided to take the chance. A last fling with danger. The cousins never felt closer and at ease with each other. Their old lives had faded into a dream like memory. It seemed like they had always been together. Jadin told his Mom earlier that evening that he felt like his life had purpose at last. She laughed, smiling on the inside as he had shared with her that he definitely would be in college in the fall and taking police sciences. He wanted to work for the FBI or CIA or DEA or something like that. After that afternoon with Dick, all of the Clade turned their thoughts to using their gift for law enforcement of some type. That is except the two mothers and they just wanted to keep all of them alive.

After the club closed, they went to the Truck Haven and had breakfast. Reed showed them the sketch of the drug dealer and told them where he was supposed to be selling. "When do they think he sells?" Dezza asked "Daytime" Nicole answered her. "But when, they don't know. They keep missing him or he is some sort of Houdini." "We're driving to Arizona in a couple of days" Autie informed them. "We'd better do something tomorrow. Got any ideas?" Courtneay, mostly quiet, headed the discussion for what to do and they decided to end the evening.

Reed took Nicole home and headed for the ranch. He decided to take Blake's offer to share his room. The rest went to their respective homes and to bed. The night had been therapeutic and had brought them all closer than before. Life would never be the same for any of them again. For Dezza and RuDee it was a peaceful transition from the cultures they grew up in. They both felt that not only were they embraced as cousins, but their cultural differences were welcomed and included in the "Clade." Not once did they fell that their color was an issue. One of the games they played when they were practicing was changing their color to match the color of whoever they were near. Autie loved to sidle up and turn their color then she wanted them to turn so she could see what they looked like with the fair almost translucent skin she had.

Autie had packed a backpack with just a few clothes as she would be coming home on the train. Baylor and Janice had left all of their things to make a new life. Everyone came up with money from their bank accounts to set up a checking account in Flagstaff for the two. The girls fixed Janice up with clothes and Baylor got enough clothes from the men to get started. Susan and Connie convinced Janice to change her appearance. She allowed them to cut her long hair and give her a modern style. She looked at least ten years younger and when she donned a pair of Capri's and a v neck tee shirt she almost looked like she were in her twenties. Janice stared at herself in the mirror. She didn't feel any type of regret for what she was doing. She felt exhilarated. It made her stomach sick when she thought of Warren. "How dare he do that to me" she thought of the years of abuse and meanness. She slipped into some soft comfortable tennis shoes and wiggled her toes, the old lady type loafers that were stiff and unbendable were laying in the trash can. Brie had bought her a purse with black and white zebra stripes and lime green handles and bottom. Janice ran her fingers over the purse. It was the first time since she was a child that she had a pretty purse. She hugged Brie so tight, Brie had to catch her breath.

CHAPTER EIGHTEEN

Courtneay came into the living room in her camouflage bathing suit. "Let's go" she said with her hands up in the air in a questioning way. They all stared at her for a brief moment then they disappeared, returning in a few minutes dressed as scantily as Court was. Susan coughed. "Ahem. Wear something over those suits please. You might get arrested yourselves." They all went and slipped into tee shirts and jeans and crowded into Ron's SUV.

At the corner of Drexell and Marks, they parked the car behind some dumpsters, slipped off their outer clothing and slowly walked along the cement wall. Soon they had all changed colors and all any observer might see was maybe a slight wave in the wall as they walked toward the school ground. A laugh escaped Autie's lips as they left the wall and walked in amongst the bushes that surrounded the playground. She was always amazed at changing as if it were the first time and she had just slid into Samantha, her boxer. "Shhhhh" Jadin quietly scolded her, but still with a smile. He, too, was enjoying this immensely. They all were.

Courtneay took the lead position at the corner of the bushes where there was a chain link gate hooked onto a red brick school wall. She was part brick and part gate. Richard stood directly behind her admiring her skill to separate the colors and look just like each of the scenery parts. They waited quietly. It was seven a.m. and school didn't start until eight fifteen. Several small groups came through the gate, children from kindergarten to about third grade. After they had passed the group Dezza whispered "They must be coming for the breakfast the schools feed kids now days."

Then and almost like he appeared out of nowhere a man matching the man in the sketch was standing by the brick wall just about six feet from the gate. Two boys about seven years old walked up to him and each of them handed him something that looked like wadded up money. He in turn gave each of them a clear bag of something.

Blake made a gesture to the group in back of him toward the little boys. Autie, Dezza and Brie nodded yes. Richard touched RuDee's arm and pointed to Blake, Jadin and himself and to the man. RuDee stepped back behind the guys and next to Courtneay. As soon as the drug deal was done, the little boys turned and started walking away from the school, Autie and her group followed them. The guys started toward the man as he walked away along the brick wall. Then the man disappeared.

"There" RuDee shouted pointing at the brick wall right below a window. They saw the wall waver and all three jumped toward the slight movement. Richard hit the man smack on and they both fell away from the wall. The man turned his own color and Jadin and Blake were on him in a second; holding him to the ground. RuDee had a rope ready and she was tying his wrists while Courtneay sat on his feet.

RuDee grabbed the man's hair and jerked his head up. Looking into his face she screamed "You're a Chameleon." The man looked scared. Richard grabbed his shirt and lifted him up and pushed him against the wall. "Who are you?" he asked the man. The man stood silent but his eyes were on Courtneay who was standing by the brick wall and the exact same color of it. Then he looked at Jadin and the rest "I'm obviously not the only lizard" he grinned a sick sort of smile.

At that second, Autie, Brie and Dezza came back around the corner with the two boys by the arms. The boys were crying and yelling they wanted to go home. "We caught these two and look at what is in there sacks." Dezza held up the sacks.

RuDee took the sacks and opened one of them, pouring out the contents into her hands. There were small irregular pieces of something in a mixed variety of colors. "They look like pop rocks" She touched the tip of her tongue to one. "They are." She frowned at the man.

The man looked squeamish. "They think they're buying dope."

"You're selling pop rocks to babies and they think they are getting dope? Is that what you're saying?" Richard had the man by the throat and pushed against the wall. "Yeah" he answered, keeping his eyes down.

Just then sirens were screaming down the street and three police cars pulled up next to them. All the Clade but Richard, Reed and RuDee colored and became as the wall. Dick was the first out of the car. "I kind of suspected you guys would get this guy. RuDee held out her hand "This is what he was selling and there are two of his victims." The little boys were sitting on the curb with their heads in their hands as Dezza had told them to do. Dick took the "dope" and put it in a bag. Two of the officers untied the man's hands and put him in cuffs and then into the squad car and another officer put the little boys in his car.

Soon just Dick was with the Clade. "Thanks" he told them "Dick" Reed stopped him from going. "That guy is a chameleon. That's why you couldn't catch him. He was turning the color of his surroundings. We'd like to talk to him at some point and see if he is part of our family. I hope he isn't but this is too weird." "Ok" Dick responded "I'll call you later and let you know when." With that he was gone.

After relating the events to Ron and Blane, the Clade started disbursing into different directions. There were hugs and kisses and almost tearful goodbyes. Susan comforted them. We'll all be back together soon. Just stay safe. Connie and I will keep you all informed of what is happening. Autie headed for Arizona in the new car the Clade had bought for Baylor and Janice and right behind them in the ranch's pickup was Richard, RuDee and Brie. They would caravan with Autie's group until Flagstaff where they would then go separate ways. Blake, Courtneay and Dezza would be staying at the ranch and Jadin would go to his own home. The two vehicles pulled out of the driveway, Ron, Susan and Jadin got into the SUV and left. Dezza announced that she would have dinner on the table at six as Courtneay and Blake followed Blane out to the barn to begin chores. Connie watched until she saw the pickup Brianna was in go out of sight then went into the kitchen to be with Dezza.

"Why haven't you called?" C.C. screamed into the phone. "We have been here six days." Harold waited until she was through screaming and told her that Morgan Vance, the attorney would be down there to bail her and Dallas out and that they were to head straight for his Washington cabin and they were to stay put until he told them what to do. "No hunting until I say so C.C." he yelled back at her in a mean and demanding voice.

C.C. started to talk in a sensible voice after that even though in her thoughts she was choking him. "Ok Harold. But we'll need some money. What about Warren? What about his family?" Harold told her that Warren's family had not come home and he had called the police. "Can I kill him?" she whispered loudly with a hiss in her voice.

There was silence then "Yes. But not yet. I'll say when." Her almost smile turned upside down and she snarled. "Ok. I'll get Dallas as soon as we get out of here and we'll go to the cabin." "Good" Warren hung up without saying another word. "Creep" C.C. slung into the phone and slammed the receiver down.

It was three in the afternoon when the matron unlocked C.C.'s cell and told her bail was made and she was being released. C.C. shoved past the matron to get out of the jail. Once out of the facility, she spotted Dallas leaning against the wall of the jail. She walked past him without looking at him, stopped and threw back over her shoulder. "You coming?" Dallas started following her down the street. At the end of Mason Street, C.C. waved down a taxi and they climbed in. Soon they were getting out at C.C.'s car.

"Do you want to kill Warren with me?' she looked over at Dallas with her devilish grin and eyes lit like a Jack-o-lantern.

"Dad said we were supposed to go to the cabin."

"You are such a pantywaist" she sneered at him. "Great, we'll go to the cabin, but, I get to kill him" then she said in a little girl voice "When Daddy says I can."

She turned the car down Truxton and entered the freeway going north. "Do you have a Cigarette?" she asked Dallas who produced a pack and handed it to her. She took the pack and pulled one out and reached down to pull out the lighter. After lighting the Cigarette, she looked up and saw that the on ramp to Hwy 99 was, suddenly, right there. She swerved and the lighter flew out of her hands onto the seat. Hissing, she swerved again as she tried to pick up the lighter, the fleshy part of her finger went onto the hot coil. "Ouch!" she yelled "You put it up." she screamed at Dallas. Dallas reached over and put the lighter back into its hole. C.C. tossed the lit cigarette out the window and put her burned finger in her mouth trying to take away the pain. Then, she put both hands on the wheel as the traffic on the freeway was bumper to bumper and going over eighty. Dallas' eyes were straight ahead watching the traffic, totally in a panic over the swerving C.C. had been doing. C.C. kept a firm grip on the wheel as she wove in and out of the speeding cars and semi-trucks.

They were on their way, both oblivious that the inside of C.C.'s right hand had turned the same color as the steering wheel.

This story continues in

THE CLADE LETTERS, The Children of the Agreement

Elizabeth Stockton Norris

Nora Marie Norris aka Nora Lansing Coup

Jewell Norris Johnston

James Johnston

Hattie Johnston Bonne

Jaime Bonne DeBurge

Adrienne DeBurge Douglass

Mildred Douglass Jones

Charlene Jones Willis

Susan Willis Tanner

Autumn Tanner

Jadin Tanner

Viola Johnston Martinez

Mary Martinez Roll J

Beth Roll Darnell

Mercy Darnell Hart

Crystal Hart Jenkins

Connie Jenkins Benson

Brianna Benson

Judy Hart Weber

Windy Weber Tollison

Courtney Tollison

Blake Tollison

Sarah Martinez Barnes

New mom Madeline Straumberg

Willow Straumberg Ming

LuSong Ming

Eric Ming

Moonshaddow Ming

Dezza Ming

by Luz Mason

Martha Mason Radcliff

Rita Radcliff Tyrell

Shirley Swann

Bob Swann

RuDee Swann

Victor Martinez

Lilly Martinez Brown

Rudolph Brown

Bill Brown

Dawn Brown Bell

Richard Bell

By Sara

Reed Laudin

256

Joshua Wells

Barton Well

Wilson Wells
Winston Wells
Joel Wells
James Wells

Jonathon Wells

Patricia Wells Straman

Raymond Straman

Tonya Straman Knott

Robert Knott
Harold Knott
Dallas Knott

Bill straman
Jonas Straman
??
??

Phillip Wells
Joshua Wells
Brown Wells

Clarise Wells Lackey

Josh Lackey
Warren Lackey
Baylor Lackey

Medford Wells
Mary Wells Martell
Lars Martell
C. C. Martel

Joe Wells
Robin Wells Soliere
Etienne Soliere

6447711R0

Made in the USA
Charleston, SC
25 October 2010